MW00364434

SS
ASSASSINS

BY RONN MUNSTERMAN

FICTION

SGT. DUNN NOVELS

Hunting Sgt. Dunn
Lethal Ground
Raid on Hitler's Dam
Sword of Ice
Castle Breach
Rangers Betrayed
Capture
Saving Paris
Brutal Enemy
Behind German Lines
Operation Devil's Fire

NONFICTION

Chess Handbook for Parents and Coaches

SS
ASSASSINS

A SGT. DUNN NOVEL

RONN MUNSTERMAN

SS Assassins is a work of fiction. Names, characters, places, and incidents are the product of the author's imagination or are used fictitiously. Any resemblance to actual events, locales, or persons, living or dead is coincidental.

SS ASSASSINS – A SGT. DUNN NOVEL

Cover Design by

David M. Jones
www.triarete.com
and
Nathalie Beloeil-Jones
www.nathaliesworkshop.com

.

Printed in the United States of America
10 9 8 7 6 5 4 3 2 1

ISBN-13: 978-1-69-432679-9

BISAC: Fiction / War & Military

Acknowledgments

Hello readers! We've reached December 1944 in Dunn's story line, having taken twelve books to do it. Thank you for your support along the way.

The more I read and write about WWII, the more I realize how much I don't know. Filled with individual heroic stories to civilization changing events, a hundred writers could write WWII novels for a lifetime and never cover it all. By focusing on the exploits of our heroes Tom Dunn and Mac Saunders, we can enjoy stories in a small sector of the war.

As you know, I'm always reading something about WWII, partly for the knowledge and partly for finding possible stories. This time, the main story line comes from an online article my son, Nate, found and forwarded to me. It was about a Nazi SS attempt to assassinate FDR, Churchill, and Stalin in Tehran, Iran. That article led directly to this book. Saunders' first mission to Sweden is also based on a real Commando mission. More on these in the Author's Notes.

Thank you to my wife for her editing, which she only gets to do after I've done five edits myself. She really would run out of red ink if she got it any sooner.

As always, my FIRST READERS get me out of trouble either with grammar, story goofs, or fact errors. Here they are:

Steve Barltrop
Gordon Cotton
Dave Cross
Jackson Cross
David M. Jones (Jonesy)
Zander Jones (Jonesy II)
Nathan Munsterman
Robert (Bob) A. Schneider II
Charlie Shrem
John Skelton
Steven D. White

Thank you to the talented duo of David M. Jones and his wife, Nathalie, for the gorgeous cover. This is Jonesy's eleventh cover and Nathalie's fifth. Their websites are on the copyright page. Check them out.

Thank you to my dear friend Derek Williams for his years of friendship and support.

Thank you to the people who made all the D-Day 75th anniversary events possible. I hope you were able to participate or view online some of those marvelous gatherings.

Thank you to the Greatest Generation: the men and women who did whatever was asked of them to preserve freedom around the world. The enormity of what they accomplished is difficult to comprehend, but thanks to them, and to some wonderful historians like Stephen E. Ambrose (*Band of Brothers* and other books), we have ready access to the stories of heroism, of courage, of getting the job done.

For Deborah Ellen Elder Brown
A strong-willed warrior

SS
ASSASSINS

Chapter 1

White House Rose Garden
Washington, D.C.
7 December 1944, 1515 Hours

The Rose Garden no longer displayed any of its famous blooms due to winter settling in. The garden had been established in 1913 by Ellen Louise Axson Wilson, President Wilson's wife, and had become a fixture.

Light gray high clouds blanketed the city. A north wind blew, the leafless trees swaying, and it made the forty degrees Fahrenheit feel a bit worse for President Franklin D. Roosevelt, who wore a black knee-length coat, gloves, and a hat.

His personal aide, Charlie Bascomb, pushed him along the paved walkway in FDR's hand-crafted wooden wheelchair. Bascomb attended to the president's personal needs and helped him get around in the massive White House, the only exceptions being the residence and the Oval Office. In those locations FDR preferred his independence, rolling himself.

FDR lifted a long black cigarette holder with an unfiltered Camel in it to his lips. He drew the smoke in deep, savored it for a few seconds, and released it in a cloud immediately dispersed by the wind.

Bascomb pushed the chair off the walkway and into the grass, which was winter brown. The big wheels made it relatively easy for the mid-fifties, thin yet strong, black man to push. He'd been with the president for over five years and had traveled with him for the 1940 and 1944 election campaigns.

"How you doing, Mr. President?"

He guided the chair toward the far side of the garden.

"It's lovely out today, Charlie."

"Yes, sir."

They reached the other side and Bascomb turned the chair back around. "Stay or go, sir?"

Roosevelt pulled out his Audemars Frères gold pocket watch, which had been made in Switzerland in 1900. Eleanor had given it to him on their March 17, 1905 wedding day and he'd worn it daily since then. Its 18k gold hunter style had an ornate lid over the watch face. He snapped it open. Inside the lid was a picture of his wife.

He checked the time and said, "Five minutes, please."

"Yes, sir."

Bascomb took his hands off the wheelchair and stood quietly behind FDR.

Roosevelt swiveled his head to take in the winter beauty. He much preferred spring, though. Somewhere out of sight, a multi-engine aircraft flew by. He sighed deeply, remembering. Although he didn't need the sound of an airplane to remind him of what day's anniversary this was. When he'd awakened the first thought in his mind was of the 2,400 people who'd died at Pearl Harbor. The recollection of the pain he and the country went through when everyone realized war had been thrust upon them was still powerful.

"Charlie, it was almost this exact time of day three years ago when I was told about Pearl Harbor."

"Yes, sir, I remember. A difficult time."

"Yes."

"I loved your speech, sir."

The day after, on December 8th, Roosevelt had given what became known as the "Day of Infamy" speech to a joint session of Congress. He'd requested they vote to declare war on Japan, which they did in less than an hour; the Senate by a vote of 82-0 and the

House by 388-1. The lone dissenter was committed pacifist Jeanette Rankin of Montana, who'd also voted against the first war. Roosevelt signed the declaration just over three and a half hours after giving the speech.

"Thank you, Charlie. I guess we'd best get back in. I have that phone call."

"Right away, sir."

Bascomb took off at a good clip.

Soon they were racing down the columned portico. The pillars were decorated for Christmas with red and green bows. A Christmas tree was set up in the East Room. Bascomb wheeled FDR inside and through the curved door set in the Oval Office. He parked him behind the president's desk. FDR was using Herbert Hoover's desk. It had been a brand new gift in 1930 from the Grand Rapids Furniture Manufacturer's Association following a December 1929 fire that caused the White House staff to rebuild the Oval Office.

Bascomb stepped back and to the right of the president.

"Anything else, sir?"

"No, Charlie, take a well-earned coffee break. If I need you, I'll have Betty call you."

"Yes, Mr. President."

Bascomb left through the same door, leaving it open for Betty.

Betty Nichols, the president's faithful and efficient secretary, stepped through the door just a moment after Bascomb disappeared.

"Good afternoon, Mr. President." She carried a brown leather notebook held close to her left breast. She was a slender woman in her early sixties with silver hair and sparkling brown eyes. Known as a no-nonsense woman, people learned quickly, and sometimes the hard way, not to waste her time. The only thing one could possibly do that was worse was to waste the *president's* time.

"Hi, Betty. I'm ready for my call with Winston."

She took a seat to his left and opened her notebook, a pencil ready in her right hand. "All set, sir." She'd take verbatim notes that she would transcribe on her typewriter soon after the meeting was over. FDR would hold the phone so she could hear the British prime minister, who most definitely never needed a bullhorn.

His desk was cluttered with at least two dozen objects, including a picture frame containing four individual photos of his sons in their uniforms. Other items were his black phone—no dial—a pen and pencil holder, and of course a brass ashtray.

Picking up the phone, he waited a split second for the White House operator to come on the line. "Hi Gladys, let's get Mr. Churchill, shall we?"

"Right away, sir."

The two men used a phone line through the encryption machine SIGSALY. FDR's machine was located in the Pentagon with an extension line running into the Oval Office. Churchill's phone had been installed in a basement broom closet at 10 Downing Street connected to a machine 200 feet below Selfridge's Department Store on Oxford Street. FDR knew that on Churchill's end, there was a young woman by the name of Ruth Ive whose sole job was to prevent the prime minister from blurting out information that might jeopardize intelligence or operations, which he had the distressing habit of doing occasionally. When either of the men crossed the "line" she would warn them she'd have to report their indiscretion to a "higher authority." Who that was, no one knew, for neither had ever been contacted about a verbal carelessness.

The phone rang three times before Churchill answered. Roosevelt pictured his friend calmly lighting a cigar first.

"Hello, this is your Former Naval Person!" boomed Churchill.

The president laughed. Churchill loved to call himself that because of his service as the First Lord of the Admiralty, the political head of the Royal Navy.

"Hello, Winston."

"Franklin, we must discuss having a meeting somewhere, hopefully warmer than our home cities, at the earliest possible moment."

Roosevelt frowned. Another meeting? In the dead of winter? "You and I are already scheduled for Malta next month. Why another one? Have you already talked to Stalin?"

"Bloody hell. No, I haven't talked to him! He's why we need another meeting. A pre-meeting meeting if you will." He chuckled at his own joke.

Roosevelt, usually quite circumspect in front of staff, looked at Betty, and looked upward shaking his head. Her expression remained unchanged, but she understood full well he wondered if Churchill had lost the plot, as the British liked to say.

"I see. This meeting would include whom?"

"Why, you and me. And our staffs, of course."

"What are we discussing?"

"How we're going to beat him to Berlin, of course."

"Shouldn't we leave that for Eisenhower and his staff?"

"Oh, good heavens, no, Franklin. We need to provide guidance and maybe some needed motivation. You know, especially since Market Garden was a complete fiasco."

Roosevelt sighed. "Need I remind you whose idea that operation was?"

"Of course not! I know Monty buggered that one to high heaven. That's neither here nor there. What matters is what we come up with to make the push the rest of the way actually work."

"Would I be correct in believing you already have some ideas for this 'push'?"

"Very perceptive, Franklin."

"Where were you thinking of having this meeting? It does require some planning, you know."

"Well, I admit that's true. I first thought of Corsica, but I realized we'd probably have to invite that damnable Frenchman, since that's his territory."

Roosevelt smiled despite himself. "That Frenchman" was no other than Charles de Gaulle. Neither the president nor the prime minister cared much for the man. They both thought he was an insufferable monotonic sounding man who was incapable of seeing the "larger picture." Add to that his seemingly unerring inability to display or understand humor made him the kind of man everyone would rather not be around.

"Where?" Roosevelt pressed.

"Sardinia."

"The island south of Corsica?"

"Yes."

"When?"

"Starting December twelfth for a few days, maybe a week. The warm weather will do you some good, Franklin."

Roosevelt glanced at Betty, his expression a question mark.

She nodded. She'd be able to swing the travel details.

"Fine, Winston. I must say it will be nice to see your cherubic face again."

"Wonderful! It will be good to see you again, too. I'll have Simon set up a villa for us near Cagliari, which is at the southern tip of the island. Quite a beautiful place it is."

"I'm sure we'll talk again prior to departure. Is there anything you might like me to bring along? Perhaps some Cubans?"

"You are a prince, Franklin! I'm down to one box of those magnificent cigars."

"Take care of yourself, Winston."

"You, too, Franklin."

The two leaders ended the call.

The president looked at Betty.

She nodded. "Cagliari, Sardinia should be warmer than here at least." She rose, taking her notebook and pencil with her. "I'll get started on the arrangements, sir."

"Thank you."

After she left the office, FDR rolled over by the windows and sat there a long time, smoking and deep in thought.

Chapter 2

Headquarters of the *Reich* Main Security Office
Prinz-Albrecht-Straße
Berlin, Germany
8 December, 0703 Hours, Berlin time, the next day

Hauptsturmführer, SS Captain, Erhard Krause double-timed down the long hallway on the third floor of the *Reichssicherheitshauptamt* (RSHA) Headquarters building. He skidded slightly as he rounded a corner at the end, but stayed on his feet. He slid to a stop outside RSHA Chief Ernst Kaltenbrunner's office. He rapped hard on the closed door a couple of times, catching his breath as he waited for permission to enter. He'd run all the way up from the basement.

Thirty seconds passed and the young man began to wonder if the Chief had stepped out to an early meeting elsewhere in the building. But he heard through the thick door a gravelly voice, "Come in!"

With one hand clutching a small sheaf of papers, he opened the door with the other and stepped through. He'd been in the Chief's office a few times over the past two years and knew to close the door behind him, which he did with a heavy sound.

He marched to a spot right in front of Kaltenbrunner's desk and snapped off a Nazi salute. *"Heil* Hitler, *Obergruppenführer."*

General Kaltenbrunner returned the salute and said, *"Heil* Hitler."

The general was forty-one and had been born in Linz, Austria. He wore a black SS uniform, but worked without his jacket on. A big man just under two meters tall, he was imposing even when seated. His long face was scarred in several places, reportedly from fencing duels at school, although some thought they were from an automobile accident. His brown hair was parted on the right and combed back. Dark brown eyes seemed to smolder at Krause. Known for his quick temper, people learned to be oh so very careful around him.

In March 1938, he assisted with the *Anschluss* on orders direct from Hermann Göring. He was rewarded for his work by being named the State Secretary for Public Safety in Austria. He led the Austrian SS as part of his duties to control the Austrian population. Two years later, he was appointed to the position of Vienna's Police President, a job he held for a year. For almost two more years he worked in Austria in various SS roles and came to the attention of Heinrich Himmler because of the wide-ranging intelligence networks he'd built up. In January 1943, six months after Reinhard Heydrich was assassinated in Prague, Kaltenbrunner was named to replace him as head of the RHSA by none other than Himmler himself.

He gave the captain what passed for a smile: a slight upward tick of the outer corners of his mouth, which looked more like a smirk. He pointed at the chair in front of his desk and the captain sat.

"I have something you should see, sir." Krause held up the papers.

Kaltenbrunner waved a hand impatiently and the captain leaned forward to hand them to him.

Reading them thoroughly, he paused on page two and glanced up, frowning.

"You're sure of this? This is a message about the logistics of a top secret meeting. Roosevelt and Churchill use an encrypted system to talk to each other. We know about it but haven't cracked it. Where did this come from?"

Krause fought the urge to swallow under the man's dark gaze. "Yes, sir. I had the messages decoded by two independent analysts. The results were identical. The Americans still don't realize we've broken their naval codes. The people organizing the meeting used those codes to transmit."

"I see. Well done."

Krause nodded nervously, glad to have given a good answer.

Kaltenbrunner laid the papers down and rose, pushing his chair out of the way so he could walk to the wall behind his desk where a two-meter wide framed map of Europe hung from a pair of silver chains. He leaned close and stared at one spot for a time.

He returned to his desk and sat down.

"Find Skorzeny for me."

"Yes, sir."

The captain rose, and the men exchanged the Nazi salute once more.

Krause left the office making sure to close the door behind him. He ran back down the stairs to his basement office. He darted inside and around the tiny space to his desk. Sitting down and flipping open a black-covered phone book at the same time, he found the number quickly.

The call was short. He was so excited by the mission, he didn't have time to be nervous about talking to the most famous SS *Kommando* ever.

An hour later, *Obersturmbannführer*, Lieutenant Colonel, Otto Skorzeny entered Kaltenbrunner's office and shut the door. They exchanged the Nazi salute.

Kaltenbrunner smiled, got up, and went around his desk to shake hands with his old comrade.

"It's good to see you, Otto."

"Thank you, sir. You, too."

Kaltenbrunner waved at the chairs in front of his desk and the men sat down, somewhat facing each other. Kaltenbrunner saw a lot of himself in the man who was five years younger. They were the same height, and weight, about 115 kilograms. Both bore the "smile" marks from their university dueling days on the left cheek, but Kaltenbrunner had another one just above his left temple.

Skorzeny had fought on the Eastern Front and took a piece of shrapnel to the back of his head in late 1942. While recovering in Berlin in a staff position, he'd begun work on his unconventional commando techniques which included fighting deep behind enemy lines, wearing enemy uniforms while fighting, and conducting all kinds of sabotage. He'd wanted to create specialized units to carry out these attacks. His ideas attracted the right kind of attention and they came to fruition with remarkable successes.

Like Kaltenbrunner, he was also Austrian, born in Vienna. Skorzeny had returned to his native country for the *Anschluss*. On March 12, 1938, he'd saved Austrian President Wilhelm Miklas, who the Austrian Nazis wanted to execute by firing squad.

It had been Skorzeny who Kaltenbrunner had entrusted to rescue Benito Mussolini in late July 1943. Although the overall command of the top-secret mission had been carried by *Sturmbannführer*, Major, Otto-Harald Mors, Kaltenbrunner had given Skorzeny specific instructions on flying out with Mussolini in the same airplane. He was further instructed to make a public showing in Munich upon arrival to show the world the Germans had rescued the dictator. Skorzeny had done exactly that, although the terrified pilot of the small plane worried on takeoff whether Skorzeny's extra weight would crash the aircraft.

With his record of creativity and mission successes, it was an easy choice for Kaltenbrunner to assign the planning of this mission to his old friend.

"I have some interesting news that will give us another opportunity I think you'll be especially happy about," Kaltenbrunner began.

Skorzeny leaned forward, an eyebrow raised.

"Roosevelt and Churchill will be arriving on Sardinia for a secret meeting very soon!" Kaltenbrunner grinned, the skin around a scar puckering.

Skorzeny looked incredulous. "Another meeting? Right under our noses?"

"So they think. They're set to arrive on the twelfth."

"This will make up for missing them in Tehran."

Skorzeny had been given the mission to assassinate the Big Three, Roosevelt, Churchill, and Stalin in Tehran, Iran just over a year ago. Circumstances simply did not come together and a reluctant and frustrated Skorzeny had been forced to abort the mission.

"It will indeed." Kaltenbrunner glanced away briefly, and back at Skorzeny. "I know you're working on a new assignment that has the highest clearance and is direct from the *Führer*."

Skorzeny nodded. Of course Kaltenbrunner would know about Hitler's brilliant planned attack through the thick Ardennes. It would be a replay of May 10, 1940, when German armor shocked the French and British armies by charging through the forest that had been previously thought impenetrable by armor. Skorzeny would lead a couple of dozen American-English speaking Waffen-SS soldiers dressed as Americans. They would infiltrate the American lines with captured jeeps to disrupt communications and traffic, the latter by changing road signs.

"Are you concerned about the timeline?"

"No, sir. I have just the man to assign this to. I'll get him over here and we'll draw up the plans."

"Excellent! I knew I could count on you, Otto."

"Thank you, sir. I appreciate that."

"What can I do to help?"

"First thing that comes to mind is I need the name and contact information for an asset already in Sardinia."

"I'll get you the name and information within the hour."

"Do we know the precise location for the conference?"

"No. I'll direct that same contact to start working on that very soon. I'll be sure to inform you immediately when I find out."

"Thank you, sir. There will likely only be a few places in the area that would attract Roosevelt and Churchill. Of course, perhaps they'll simply tell us where in one of their navy messages."

Kaltenbrunner chuckled. "Perhaps they will."

"I'll summon Major Becker for our planning session. After that we'll meet with the men we'll have selected and start preparations. We should plan for the attack force to arrive before dawn on the fourteenth to have ample time to reconnoiter the location. With the general's permission, I'll ask Captain Krause to arrange transport with a U-Boat."

"Of course. Permission granted. Call me if you need any other support."

"Yes, sir!"

"I have a meeting with the *Führer* tomorrow. I'll advise him of the new mission."

"Very good, sir."

Both men rose and stared at each other, hope written on their faces. They nodded to each other and shook hands.

They exchanged the stiff-arm salute again and exuberantly cried, "*Heil* Hitler!" together.

When Skorzeny walked down the hallway he had a spring in his step. He was thinking one word: *redemption.*

Chapter 3

Camp Barton Stacey Hospital
60 miles southwest of London
8 December, 1130 Hours, London time

The patient wards had been decorated for Christmas by volunteers. In this particular ward, a ten-foot tree, fully decked out with multicolor lights, ornaments, silver tinsel, and an angel tree topper was right by the door. Wreaths hung on each wall. A record player playing at low level sound, filled the room with Christmas carols.

Earl Hardwicke, Master Sergeant Tom Dunn's father-in-law, lay in the hospital bed with several pillows behind his upper body so he could sit up. Sitting next to the English farmer were his wife, Florence, his daughter, Pamela, and Dunn.

Hardwicke had been shot in the stomach by a German SS killer who'd been after Dunn and his family on orders from Nazi Minister of Armaments Albert Speer himself. Dunn and Colonel Kenton, his boss, had agreed that when Dunn had come face to face, so to speak, with Speer on a recent mission, he'd become a target. Add in the factor that Dunn always seemed to disrupt Speer's deadly plans, probably added to the hatred that led to sending a team of two killers to wipe out Dunn and Pamela and her parents.

The attack had been five days ago when the family's Sunday lunch had been horribly interrupted. Dunn had gone on to confront and kill the male attacker with his bare hands. Mrs. Hardwicke, a surprising hero, had captured the man's female accomplice with the assistance of Pamela's two dogs. A memorable Sunday for sure.

Hardwicke was in good shape considering. He felt better and was getting fidgety lying in bed all day. What farmer wouldn't?

"Earl, it's just one more day," Mrs. Hardwicke told him for the tenth time. Florence had been with him in the hospital most of every day, going home only to sleep. Neighbors were coming over to handle the daily chores.

Hardwicke looked at his wife, then at Dunn and Pamela. Seeing no help there, he said, "I'm bored, Florence."

She leaned over and took his hand. "I know. Want me to read to you? I brought this week's Andover paper."

Hardwicke sighed the sigh of the put upon, but relented. "Right. Okay."

Pamela rose to her feet and leaned over to kiss Hardwicke on the forehead. "Love you, Daddy. Glad you're getting better."

Hardwicke patted her cheek. "Thank you. Can't wait to get home."

Dunn got up and offered his hand, which his father-in-law shook with a smile.

Tom Dunn, a Cedar Rapids, Iowa native, stood six-two and weighed 180 pounds. He had brown hair, parted on the left like most right handers. His dark brown eyes, which could flash black in anger, peered out over a slim nose.

He and several of his college friends had signed up the day after Pearl Harbor, dropping out with only one semester to go. His introduction to combat came in North Africa, at the Battle of Kasserine Pass, the place where the American army got its nose severely bloodied by the much more experienced German troops. Dunn had managed to earn the Bronze Star when he'd taken over for his fatally shot squad leader and led the squad in destroying a machinegun nest that had been mowing down other Americans.

That event and his calm demeanor throughout when everyone else was losing their head brought his name in front of the battalion commander. That man, willing to do what was best for the army, not just for his unit, put Dunn's name in front of the Commando / Ranger School at Achnacarry House, Scotland. Dunn became a Ranger and after continually proving himself, he'd been selected to lead a squad of Rangers, based at Camp Barton Stacey, on top secret missions.

He'd met Pamela in the camp hospital. He'd been accidentally shot during a live-fire training exercise at Achnacarry House, when a recruit had inexplicably stood up. Dunn tackled the young man, taking a bullet in the shoulder for him.

Pamela had been the primary nurse who took care of him on a daily basis. Unknown to Dunn, she'd told the other nurses that she would take personal care of this particular soldier. He'd noticed her extraordinary beauty the first time they met, he lying on his back and she taking his temperature to check for infection. He'd been immediately taken by her but assumed someone so beautiful already had a boyfriend.

Pamela, for her part, was enamored by Dunn's dark good looks and calm outlook on life. He never complained, even when she knew she was hurting him when changing the bandage during the first few days. When after several days, he seemed unwilling or unable to ask her out, she'd started giving hints that she was indeed available, suggesting various fun events coming up in and around Andover. His failure to pick up at all on her hints drove her to distraction. He was like a none too bright mule who needed to be hit in the forehead with a two-by-four.

Finally, one day after she'd mentioned a good place for dinner for the fourth time, Dunn seemed to realize what was happening. However, he'd asked her out in a particularly stupid way: "You wouldn't want to go out with me, would you?"

Completely exasperated by him, she'd somehow remained calm. Instead of shouting, "Yes! Yes! You big lunk!" she'd said, "Why, I would just love to, Thomas." Back then she always called him Thomas. Now it was Tom, unless of course he was in trouble.

Dunn waited for Pamela to slip her hand through his arm, and after saying a final goodbye to her parents they left the ward and walked down the hall toward another ward.

"Your dad's looking a lot better."

"He is. I talked to his nurse and she said the wound seems to be on the way to healing properly. He doesn't appear to have an internal infection, which is always the biggest concern, so that's very good news."

"I'm so relieved. You know how guilty I'm feeling about this."

"I know you do, and I wish I could convince you that none of us blame you for it. This *is* war, after all. Remember a lot of Brits suffered and died during the Blitz. Sometimes the war does come home to us."

Dunn shook his head. He was amazed by how the British people had come through the bombings. He'd often thought about how Americans in the 48 states had never suffered that particular fate. Yes, they were losing fathers, sons, husbands and brothers to combat, but no bombs had fallen on continental American cities. He recalled the horror of hearing about Pearl Harbor, though, and how it had affected the entire nation. The day before had been the third anniversary of that attack and he'd taken time to say a prayer early in the morning.

"Thanks, Pamela. I think it's gonna take some time to adjust to it."

She stopped walking and Dunn turned to face her.

She raised her face to his and he marveled, not for the first time, at her absolutely stunning beauty. She had long blond hair. Today, she had it tied in a bun the way she usually did when she worked or, lately, volunteered at the hospital. Her Arctic-ice-blue eyes were dazzling. Her fair skin was smooth, and her nose was slim like Dunn's, and she had full lips. He always had to lean down for a kiss, which he did happily. It was a brief one since they were standing in the hallway outside another ward, but it felt wondrous to Dunn, as it always did.

Pamela wore a light blue dress that accented her eye color. The dress was a looser fit than she normally preferred due to her being four-months pregnant. She was starting to show and felt she should wear the looser fit for a while, before switching to dresses made for pregnancy. Perhaps another few weeks or a month.

They'd already settled on a name if it was a boy, Thomas Percy Dunn, Junior. It might have been a technically improper use of junior because Percy wasn't Dunn's middle name. Instead it belonged to Pamela's late older brother. He'd died over four years ago at Dunkirk fighting a rear-guard action that helped the over

300,000 British and French soldiers escape the clutches of the German army.

Pamela had taken the job at the camp hospital to be closer than London to her parents. They had been doing poorly after losing Percy. Her presence had a calming and stabilizing effect on both parents. When she'd announced she was going to marry Dunn, they had been completely supportive and thrilled to have such a good man join the family. While he could, of course, never replace Percy, they did consider him a son and had told him so recently. It had meant so much to Dunn that it made him cry, not something a tough Ranger did often.

"Do you want to go with me to see Stan?"

"I'll stay just long enough to say 'hello.' That way you can just catch up with him on your own. I'll go check on some of my patients."

Following a scare with her pregnancy while serving as a nurse in France, she'd been sent home and restricted from nursing duty. Sill wanting to contribute, she volunteered to read to the patients, everything from letters to newspapers to books. Westerns were the favored, especially Zane Grey's novels. Even though she wasn't on "duty," she couldn't come into the hospital without visiting the men.

"Okay, swell. He'll be happy to see you."

Dunn led the way into the ward. He spotted his man, Sergeant Stanley Wickham, across the large ward. He was situated between two other patients, one of whom had his left leg in a full-leg cast that was supported by some kind of contraption with ropes and pulleys. It made Dunn wince.

"Hey, Stan."

Wickham looked up from his newspaper, the latest from Andover, the same issue Florence was reading to Earl.

Wickham's broad, handsome face lit up. "Hey-ya, Sarge!" He laid down the paper. His eyes shifted to Pamela. He started to get up for her, but she placed a hand on his shoulder.

"Don't you even think about it, buster."

He gave her an aw-shucks grin and settled back in the bed.

She leaned over and kissed his cheek. He blushed.

"Hi, Mrs. Dunn."

"Pamela," she said automatically. "I just wanted to say 'hi.' I have some things to do. I hope you're feeling better."

"Yes, ma'am, I am."

"You take care, Stanley."

"Yes, ma'am."

Pamela bussed Dunn a quick one and said, "See you later, yeah?"

"I'll come find you."

"Right."

Dunn grabbed a chair from nearby and set it next to Wickham's bed.

Wickham was sitting up. At the neck of his pajama-style clothing Dunn could see the edge of a pretty big bandage on his friend's right trapezius muscle. That's what happened when a German 20mm cannon round burned its way across your muscle. It hadn't penetrated, being a nasty "graze" instead. It looked like someone had pressed a red-hot poker against the skin and held it there, like branding. It was the result of a boat battle the squad had fought against a couple of German E-boats on the Elbe River near Hamburg. Wickham and Hugh Kelly had been manning one of the 20mm cannons aboard their own stolen E-boat. In the same enemy burst Wickham had received his wound, Hugh Kelly had been instantly killed.

Wickham was an East Texas boy, growing up in Longview a hundred twenty miles east of Dallas. He'd been a star high school football fullback, breaking most rushing records. This performance stirred college interest and he would have gone to the University of Texas, but he chose to enlist right after graduating from high school in June 1942. He'd eventually found his way to Scotland and Ranger School where he was assigned to a new squad leader named Dunn. They'd become friends quickly. They were still together, although the two of them, plus Dave Cross, were the only survivors of the original squad.

He had a square jaw with a Kirk Douglas dimple. His size was daunting, even lying in the hospital bed, which looked two sizes too small. Standing, he would be six-three, and he weighed two-twenty.

"How are you doing today?"

Wickham lifted his right arm straight up and flexed it. "Lot's better. Doc says it's healing well."

"How soon can you come back?"

Wickham grinned. "I get out tomorrow."

"You sure you'll be ready?"

"Yeah."

Dunn noted that Wickham's peculiar blend of a Brit-Tex accent was nowhere to be heard. This typically happened when Wickham was stressed or focused on a task. The fact that there were no women around, who inevitably loved it, surely had nothing to do with its disappearance.

Feeling a little doubtful, Dunn decided to test things. "Raise your arms like you're holding a weapon."

Wickham raised an eyebrow but did as he was asked.

Dunn watched Wickham's face intently, not the arms. There were no signs of distress, winces or cringes.

Dunn held out his right hand. "Squeeze it."

Wickham complied. Dunn smiled at the vice-like grip.

"Okay. I'll let the colonel know you'll be back."

Wickham grinned.

Dunn held up a hand. "However, you're gonna have to run the obstacle course in full gear. I have to make sure you can handle it and your wound doesn't pop open."

Wickham lost the grin, but said, "Whatever you need, Sarge."

Dunn had expected nothing less from the dependable Texan.

Dunn nodded. "Okay."

Wickham glanced around quickly, and lowered his voice. "Any news on the next one?"

"Meeting with Kenton tomorrow morning. I'll fill you in when I can."

"Okie Dokie."

Dunn grinned. "Really? Okie Dokie?"

Wickham shrugged and switched on his Brit-Tex accent. "Yes, indeed, my dear sergeant. That's how those low-brow people from you know where, Texas, actually talk, don't you know?"

Dunn shook his head at Wickham's goofiness, but he was glad to see him in such good spirits.

The men chatted for a few more minutes and Dunn got up and left telling the big Texan he'd see him soon.

RONN MUNSTERMAN

Chapter 4

Colonel Rupert Jenkins' Office
Camp Barton Stacey
8 December, 1145 Hours

Sergeant Major Malcolm Saunders, a five-year veteran of the British Army and a top-notch Commando, eyed his commander, Colonel Rupert Jenkins. Saunders and his second in command, Sergeant Steve Barltrop, had been called to the colonel's office with an "urgent" attached.

Saunders, a twenty-six-year-old Cockney from London's East End, was a six-foot, wide shouldered man with bright red hair and a matching handlebar mustache. In contrast, Barltrop was a slim man just under six-feet tall with light brown hair and brilliant blue eyes. The two men had followed General Bernard Montgomery all over North Africa. From there, they were both sent to Commando School at Achnacarry House, where they'd met Colonel Jenkins, who was the school commandant.

Their squad of dangerous Commandos were members of an elite unit specializing in top secret missions. Some of their past missions included helping steal a German jet bomber, destroying a bioweapon facility, and breaching an Austrian castle. They'd once rescued an entire British Army company in Holland, and saved the Pope from an SS squad.

Today, they were about to receive their next mission.

Also joining the group was Jenkins' aide, Lieutenant Carleton Mallory.

As was his custom, Jenkins got right to the point. Over the past six months he'd become more personable, particularly with Saunders, who he viewed as his best squad leader, and by far the best Commando under his command. He completely trusted Saunders and despite himself had grown closer to him than any other soldier in his long career. Typically gruff and plain spoken, Jenkins could be said to have mellowed with regard to the big redhead. Whether this was due to his beginning to view Saunders as the son that never was, no one knew, but Saunders and Barltrop had both noticed the change over time.

"Have a rather unusual one for you, Saunders."

Saunders smiled. "Aren't they all, sir?"

Jenkins harrumphed, but a corner of his lip twitched almost into a smile. Only Saunders could cause that.

"The Royal Navy has confirmed that the German Navy is using cargo ships flying neutral Sweden's flags to refuel and otherwise assist the U-boats working in the North Atlantic. Two of the ships are currently docked in Gothenburg, Sweden, a deep-water harbor."

"You'll leave at twenty-three hundred from London by sub. The sub will run submerged in daylight and on the surface at night. It should take about fifty-three or four hours to get there. You should arrive the eleventh around oh three hundred hours. You'll make your way to the two ships. A contact we have there will invite the crews to a party to get the majority of them off the ships. You'll take out any sentries, set charges, and get back to the sub. Lieutenant Mallory has the names and some photos of the two ships for you. Any questions?"

Saunders glanced at Barltrop, who whispered, "Chadwick."

Timothy Chadwick had been severely wounded in a firefight with Germans in Bremerhaven. Only quick thinking by Saunders when he patched up a sucking wound in Chadwick's chest by using duct tape to seal it, saved Chadwick. He would be in the camp hospital for the foreseeable future as the doctors continued to watch and worry about internal infection, and out of action for a lengthy period to recover.

"Yes, sir. We'll need a replacement for Chadwick. We need someone who knows what he's doing since we don't have time for training. I was thinking Sergeant Major Kirby would be our best bet. I believe his squad is on the base."

Harry Kirby was a squad leader who Saunders knew well, and who had a terrific reputation, as did his men.

"Done." To Mallory, Jenkins said, "Make the arrangements, won't you?"

"Right away, sir." He wrote a note down and looked at Saunders. "I'll have him report to you ASAP." He held out a folder for Saunders, who took it. "The ship names and photos."

"Thank you, Lieutenant. Anything else, Colonel?"

Jenkins shook his head. He stood and offered his hand, which the two Commandos shook, rising to their feet, too. "Best of luck. Be careful, won't you?"

"Thank you. Indeed we will, sir."

By the time the two Commandos made it back to the barracks, having walked through the cold December weather, they'd hashed out an overall plan and would work on the details after they boarded the submarine.

The squad members were lounging around on their barracks clad in uniform pants and shirts to help stave off the cold. They jumped to their feet when Saunders and Barltrop entered. They knew their bosses had been off to see the colonel and were expecting a new mission.

"Where to, Sarge?" Christopher Dickinson asked.

"Sweden."

Most of the men raised an eyebrow or two. A neutral country?

Saunders grinned at his men. "Aye. Sweden. Gather around," he said in his gravelly voice.

He sat down on the end of Chadwick's empty bunk while the men formed a semicircle in front of him. With Chadwick in the hospital, he had eight men including Barltrop. He wanted to give the men a quick overview because they had such a short timeline; a matter of hours to get prepped and on the road to London.

Sergeant Major Harry Kirby would likely arrive at the barracks within the hour. He planned to give him the overview one-on-one.

The only boy in a family with four children, and the youngest at that, Saunders had grown up in a loving household. Although his dad worked for the railroad as a train engineer, Saunders wasn't interested in going up and down a rigid path every day. A disinterested student on a good day, he quit school at sixteen and had found work in carpentry. He immediately fell in love with using his own hands to build beautiful, functional things that would outlive him. After a mission to Rome concluded successfully, he spent an evening taking pictures of many of the sights there, including the Colosseum. His post war plans were to start his own construction business in and around London.

His other love was Sadie, his wife of just over two months. He'd met her at a dance hall in Cheshunt, her hometown only fifteen miles north-northeast of London's city center. He'd travelled there with Barltrop, for whom Cheshunt was also hometown, to stay with Barltrop's family while on leave.

Barltrop was a year younger than his redheaded best friend. Unlike Saunders, he'd been an excellent student, particularly in math and science. His father owned the garage in Cheshunt, and from a young age Barltrop had shown an unusual aptitude with mechanical things. At the age of six, he'd taken apart a toaster. His father had walked into the kitchen and discovered the safely unplugged toaster's guts laid out in precise order on the table. He'd simply asked the boy if he could put it back together. Barltrop's reply had been to do it in front of his smiling dad. He graduated to fixing bicycles for the kids in town, and a few adults. By age ten, he was helping his dad rebuild automobile engines. His dream was to work in the pits for the British Grand Prix team.

He'd met his girlfriend, Kathy Rosemond, at Saunders' wedding in September. She was Sadie's cousin. Whether they were going to get married anytime soon was unclear to them and everyone who knew them.

Sergeant Christopher Dickinson, a lanky twenty-one-year-old with brown hair parted on the left and hazel eyes, grew up in northwest England's Manchester. A Man United fan like everyone else in the city, as a teen he'd accidentally used his nose for a header shot, which resulted in a broken beak and a hysterical winning goal. Following in his older brother's footsteps, he'd joined the army at eighteen. The brother was in Italy fighting the Germans along the Gothic Line in an artillery unit. Dickinson was a gifted amateur magician and loved entertaining the men, and the kids of Andover. Chadwick's best friend, he was feeling pretty low at the moment, even though he knew his friend would eventually recover.

Twenty-four-year-old Lance Corporal Martin Alders had been an accomplished chef at London's Savoy hotel before signing up. He'd had to do some fast talking to prevent the army from throwing him into the mess hall as a cook. A London West End kid, his father was a banker, a business that bored Alders to death. He was a thin man of five-nine, but possessed wiry strength and excellent reflexes. A thorough and precise man, he was third best in the squad with explosives behind Chadwick and Dickinson.

Corporal Ted Bentley was the squad's newest member, having joined in early November. Tall and skinny, he was a natural runner who could run everyone else into the ground. Raised on a horse training facility in Bristol, he could also ride any horse. With an angular face, his brilliant smile seemed to take up all the room.

Corporal Cyril Talbot was the exact opposite of Bentley, standing a mere five-seven, but with a wide body. In hand-to-hand combat exercises the men had learned it was practically impossible to knock him off his feet. As a boy, his train engineer uncle had taken him on rides in the locomotive's cab and he'd naturally fallen in love with trains. He'd planned to go to work for the railroad, but the war came. He still planned on doing that after the war and work his way up to engineer.

Corporal Albert Holmes was from Plymouth on England's southwest coast. He'd spent most of his childhood in Cairo, Egypt where his father was in the Diplomatic Corps. Whenever he and his family had gone out in public, especially to the *souks*, the street bazaars, the Egyptians loved to tousle his bright red hair for good luck. He spoke Egyptian Arabic fluently, which had been useful on a previous mission when the squad traveled there to help protect the Suez Canal from rebels. He had a big toothy grin, which combined with his freckles, drew people to him.

According to his Southampton neighbors, Corporal Billy Forster should have joined the Royal Navy since he'd grown up in a port city. He'd chosen the army instead to honor his father, who had served as an infantryman in the Great War. He was good looking with green eyes and light brown hair.

Corporal Ira Myers, a farm boy from near Sheffield, had grown up with rifles and shotguns. He was the squad's sniper, using a scoped .303 Lee-Enfield whenever Saunders required it. He and Jonesy, Dunn's sniper, had an ongoing rivalry. In their first head-to-head competition, Jonesy had won in a moving target shoot-off by one point. A rematch was in the works. Myers had a self-effacing manner similar to Dunn's Stan Wickham; a sort of aw-shucks attitude that completely disappeared during missions when it was all business.

Saunders laid out the mission's details for the men in a clear concise manner. A few questions cropped up including one from Holmes about how long the submarine trip would be. Used to wide-open spaces, Holmes, like Barltrop, dreaded any amount of time spent inside a metal tube under water. Airplanes were tolerable because you could at least look out the window, even at night.

Saunders wrapped things up by saying, "Since our lad, Timothy, can't join us, we're borrowing Sergeant Major Harry Kirby. I think you lads know him."

The men nodded.

When he asked if there were any more questions, no one said anything.

"Let's get to packing. We don't have much time."

The men scattered and got busy.

Saunders pulled Barltrop aside.

"Nothing changes. *You* are still second in command here."

Barltrop smiled. He appreciated that Saunders didn't relegate him to third place with the arrival of another Sergeant Major, who outranked him.

"Thanks, Mac."

Saunders nodded. "You've proven yourself time and again. You deserve it." He patted his friend on the shoulder and they both joined the men in mission prep.

Chapter 5

The men packed up their weapons and gear, and formed a line facing their sergeant, Tom Dunn. They'd taken practice with their close in weapons, the 9mm Sten gun with the integrated suppressor, the Thompson .45 caliber submachine gun, and the M1911 Colt .45. Every single one of the men was rated an expert with all the weapons they used. They'd better be, they were Rangers after all. They were extremely competitive, as you might expect from a group of elite men. One round of beer and a sandwich later that night would be paid for by the lowest total score of the day. It was an unenviable position to be in due to the inevitable razzing. Consequently, the men worked hard to get off the bottom rung of the ladder.

Dunn examined his men's faces as they waited for him to speak. These men had been through some rough times, seen some awful things, fought hard and well, and successfully completed every mission thrown their way. With Stanley Wickham still in the hospital, and the death of Hugh Kelly in Hamburg, they were down two men. Dunn and Cross had debated several times over whether to recruit temporary replacements, but had come to no conclusion yet. It might come down to timing since Wickham had just told Dunn yesterday he thought the docs would let him out today. He'd said he was feeling good, and proved to Dunn he could lift his right arm as though firing a weapon. If they could get Wickham back, even at 80 or 90 percent, they would have an experienced, smart, and tough man rejoining the squad.

Today's low score fell to Corporal Chuck Higgins. He earned the spot by only one point, and the total difference from first to last was a mere eight points, showing just how close the men were to each other.

Higgins was the son of an archeologist, who was also a professor at Nebraska University in Lincoln, where the family lived during the school year. In the summers, Higgins and his dad had gone on digs for at least a couple of months. His mom was proud of her son following in his dad's footsteps, but drew the line at living . . . outdoors. A locally famous swing singer, she'd once performed with Benny Goodman. While husband and son were away, she sang and danced her way across the Midwest going from one state fair to another as well as many county fairs.

He was a redhaired dynamo with energy to burn. He was so outgoing that people grew to like him on the spot. At five-eight, and a hundred forty pounds, he was both lithe and strong. On a recent mission to the Arctic, his archeology knowledge had proved valuable when the squad had rescued millions of dollars' worth of treasure from an SS unit, specially selected by Himmler no less.

Staff Sergeant David M. Jones, known as Jonesy, was twenty-three. He was a quiet, lean, six-footer with longish dark brown hair and a widow's peak. The sharpness of his blue eyes helped him as the squad's sniper, using an M1903 Springfield bolt-action rifle with a Unertl scope. His father was a renowned architect in Chicago, having designed many buildings in the downtown area. Jonesy, having not fallen far from the tree, had been a student at the School of the Art Institute of Chicago until the war came along. He'd grown up in the Southside and was naturally a White Sox fan. He'd lost the season bantering with Dunn, who loved the Cubs, because the National League team had finished fourth, three higher than the American League Sox. They'd also won four more games.

Now that the season was over, he just told Dunn, "wait until next year!"

Jonesy's route to Dunn's squad began in Sicily where he became well-known in his company as the best shooter anyone had ever seen. His platoon sergeant noticed pretty quickly that Jonesy was routinely picking off Germans at over 400 yards *with an M1*, near the maximum effective range of the Garand rifle. When Jonesy heard the army was looking for Ranger recruits, he'd talked with his sergeant and the man had completed the sale of the idea to the platoon leader and the company commander. A training tour through Achnacarry House in Scotland prepared him for being selected for Dunn's squad. He'd arrived in late June.

Corporal Eugene Lindstrom served as Jonesy's spotter. They'd arrived together and after Jonesy was assigned as the sniper, Lindstrom had been tasked with protecting and helping the sniper. The two had grown into a terrific team. He'd been born and raised in Eugene, Oregon, which had led to a lot of unmerciful teasing as a kid. As a defense, he'd developed a quick wit and powerful sense of humor. He was the same height as Jonesy, but stockier. He wore his light brown hair in a buzz cut and peered out at the world with green eyes that typically were filled with amusement.

After joining the army at eighteen following high school graduation, he'd gone to North Africa long after *Operation Torch*. He'd eventually been reassigned to an infantry battalion in the Fifth Army commanded by General Mark Clark. Lindstrom had landed at Salerno in September 1943. After several months there he'd volunteered for the Rangers. When the squad went on a mission to an Arctic location, he'd come face-to-face with a polar bear. He'd scared off the beast and saved the rest of the squad, who were resting in their tents, from becoming meals. Later on the same mission, he'd been shot in the thigh and missed several missions. He'd taken to explaining his wound by saying he didn't *think* it had been a polar bear . . .

Staff Sergeant Rob Goerdt was a blond-haired blue-eyed man of twenty-two. He'd been born and raised near Dyersville, about forty-five miles northeast of Dunn's hometown of Cedar Rapids. The two men had attended the University of Iowa, but never crossed paths on campus. Like Dunn, he'd left college when the war started. Goerdt had joined the squad in early August following the terrible loss of three men who died and a fourth who'd lost his lower leg, all on a mission in Italy.

He'd distinguished himself and earned a Silver Star for destroying seven tanks with a bazooka and capturing three intact crews. Like Lindstrom, he'd come to Dunn by way of Italy and the Fifth Army. The previous spring, during the Battle of Cassino, he'd also earned a Purple Heart for the piece of German potato masher shrapnel in his right hip. Thanks to that wound, he sometimes had a hitch in his giddy-up as well as being able to tell you when it was going to storm. Goerdt came from a large farming family and was the youngest of ten children. Of German heritage, and having spoken the language at home and church, he acted as an interpreter whenever needed.

Staff Sergeant Alphonso (Al) Martelli, a handsome man with black swept-back hair, a black mustache, and brown eyes, was a through and through Italian Bronx boy. He pretty much carried his Bronx accent like a badge and was tough enough to defend it with his ropy, wiry strength. His parents owned a grocery store and the family lived in the apartment above. The second oldest of seven kids, he had five sisters, and one older brother who piloted a B-29 in the Pacific. His parents had immigrated in 1919. When Dunn had needed an Italian translator for the same mission to Italy that cost the squad four men, Martelli had been borrowed from another squad. He'd impressed Dunn so much that the squad leader requested the borrow become a permanent transfer.

At the end of the mission, Martelli had met a beautiful older Italian woman, who'd made it clear that if he knew what was good for him, he would come back for a visit after the war. The kiss she'd planted on his lips convinced him and he planned to do exactly as she had instructed.

Technical Sergeant Dave Cross, Dunn's second in command and best friend, came from Winter Harbor, Maine, about forty-five miles south of Bangor. He was a smart, and strong man of six-two and weighed just under 200 pounds. He had sandy colored hair and bright blue eyes. The son of a fisherman, he could pilot any watercraft. This skill had been instrumental in saving the squad from two German E-boats on a recent mission to Hamburg. In a three-boat battle on the Elbe River, his piloting skills had led directly to the sinking of one of the 100 foot-plus long torpedo boats. With Dunn's quick thinking they had set up the second boat so their own British submarine, submerged in the river, could fire its own torpedoes at the German boat, blowing it up.

He'd left home at eighteen, having grown tired of the fisherman's life, and moved to New York City to work at the Brooklyn Army Terminal as a warehouseman. Like many men his age, he'd enlisted in the army the day after Pearl Harbor. Having been in the army just over three years and experiencing combat so many times, he longed for the fisherman's life, to go out on the Atlantic Ocean again with his dad. He'd even recently written to a girl he'd known in high school. She was unmarried and though they hadn't dated, it turned out they'd been interested in each other. To his surprise, she'd agreed to continue to write to him and they'd see "where things went" when he got home.

A year younger than Dunn, they'd met at Ranger School, where the friendship began immediately. He viewed his job as giving Dunn advice whether solicited or not. He'd been Dunn's best man back in July, and thought the world of Pamela. When Dunn, and Pamela and her family, had been targeted recently by Nazi killers, Cross had led the squad out to the Hardwicke farm and helped his best friend regain his composure after Dunn killed the attacker with his bare hands. He'd personally taken the surviving attacker, a woman, to the Camp Barton Stacey MPs.

Sergeant Robert (Bob) Schneider II, whose dad, a Brigadier General working in the relatively new Pentagon building, had lived all over the United States, the last being Fort Riley in Kansas. Even though he'd been born in Texas, he had no particular accent because of all the transfers. He was the biggest man in the squad at six-four and two-forty. He had a rugged face with unruly black hair, and brown eyes. While he was the squad's radioman, he had other skills that Dunn relied on from time to time. First of note was his fluency in German and French. This was due to his mother starting him on the languages at the age of four. Apparently gifted with a knack for it, he was speaking both within a few years and began writing them at the same time he was learning to scribble English.

He'd become the unofficial medic for the squad as the men began to see he was also talented in treating patients. His quick thinking, along with Cross's help, had saved Dunn's life during a mission to destroy a German dam. Dunn had been accidentally knocked into the reservoir's black, cold water from the top of the dam's walkway. Cross had dived in and retrieved his unbreathing, heart stopped best friend. Schneider remembered something his dad had told him years ago and did chest compressions. Dunn soon revived and the event practically launched Schneider's reputation among the company as the best medic around. It had caused him to begin thinking about attending medical school after the war, hopefully at the top school of Johns Hopkins in Baltimore.

"Good job, men. When we get back to the barracks, take care of your weapons, and you can have the rest of the day off. Remember to meet at the White Hart Pub at eighteen hundred hours for Corporal Higgins's treats. Sergeant Cross and I are meeting with the colonel at ten hundred hours about our next assignment."

Higgins started to raise his hand, but Dunn stopped him by shaking his head.

"No idea what the mission is."

Higgins nodded.

Dunn gave a couple of commands and soon the squad was double-timing back to the barracks with him counting a sing-song cadence. He had a decent voice.

Colonel Mark Kenton's office
1001 hours

"Good to see you, gentlemen," Colonel Mark Kenton said to Dunn and Cross. Kenton was a full colonel, a graduate of West Point. He commanded a company of special mission Rangers who went behind enemy lines on a regular basis and created havoc and destroyed things the Germans needed.

A forty-one-year-old man, his dark hair was streaked with gray along the temples, something he loved to call his sergeant stripes because his sergeants had caused them. At five-nine, he was fit and strong. He had commanded a battalion during the Anzio debacle, making the best out of a bad situation. It was there he met Dunn and they'd grown to trust each other implicitly. Kenton came up with innovative methods and Dunn carried them out successfully. Kenton had been pulled out of Anzio to take over the Ranger Company at Barton Stacey. He had quickly requested Dunn's transfer to the unit.

A native of Kansas City, Missouri, he'd attended Westport High School on East 39th street. When he'd received the letter saying he'd been appointed to West Point, he'd smiled at the thought of attending two schools with West in the name. He'd married a girl from New York, Mary, who'd attended Columbia, right after graduating from the academy. Their son, Bobby, was attending West Point as a freshman.

Kenton had survived a deadly plane crash in late October that killed two other passengers on the C-47 departing for France. He'd broken his arm and suffered a concussion. While in the hospital, he'd had to suffer the indignity of his temporary replacement's self-serving and unethical behavior. The man had been summarily removed from command after all his misbehaviors came to the attention of General Hopkins, Kenton's boss. The men had been ecstatic to get Colonel Kenton back after his recovery.

"You, too, sir," Dunn replied.

Cross nodded at the colonel from his seat on Dunn's left, next to Kenton's relatively new aide, Lieutenant Fred Tanner.

Kenton's desk was sparse having only his black phone and a manila file folder on its surface. His nod to the Christmas season was a miniature tree with tiny wooden ornaments hanging on it.

He tapped the folder.

"I hope you guys remember your Arctic training."

Cross sucked a breath. Their adventure to the Arctic had been fraught with peril.

"What do you have there, sir?" Dunn asked instead of answering the implied question.

"The Alps in Northern Italy. Right on the Austrian border. Ever hear of the Brenner Pass?"

Both Rangers shook their heads.

"I've heard of the Donner Pass," Cross muttered helpfully.

Kenton gave him a small smile. "Brenner Pass is the route the Germans use for logistics through the Alps to their front line in Italy. Lately, we've been bombing the living hell out of it, but there are so many flak guns in the area—something like four hundred plus—that headquarters is beginning to doubt the wisdom of the raids. Losses are mounting.

"In addition to this problem, intelligence reports that the Germans have built a massive new radar station just west of the pass, facing Italy. Have you guys heard of radar-controlled flak guns?"

"Yes, sir," Dunn said. "In our travels, some of our pilots have talked about it with Dave and me."

Kenton nodded. "This new station will be used for two things: advance warning of our planes headed toward Germany, and to control the flak guns located around Brenner Pass. Headquarters is extremely worried that losses will get much worse. Even if they redirect around the Brenner Pass, which they'll have to do, it'll add lots of miles and time to the flights. That means increased risk over Germany from the Luftwaffe fighters who'll have plenty of warning to get ready and in the air."

Dunn glanced at Cross, who tipped his head.

"What's the weather like over there, sir?" Cross asked.

"Currently, an unusually clear area. No snowstorms or heavy cloud cover."

"How deep is the snow?"

Lieutenant Tanner answered this question. "Reports are that it's about two feet deep."

Cross whistled. "Oh, man. Okay. That's pretty deep to be parachuting in."

Dunn looked over Kenton's head at the wall, thinking. No one said anything.

After a minute or so, he lowered his gaze. "There must be some captured German transport aircraft in Italy."

"I'm sure there are," Kenton said.

"I can go find out for sure," Tanner offered.

"Do that," Kenton said.

Tanner rose and left.

"If we fly to an airfield the Germans have in use, with our white winter gear, when we get off, the Germans might not bother us. Especially if we can do it at night under moonlight. I think we're at about a quarter moon right now. Anyway, we fly in, steal a truck from the airfield and drive our way to the radar station. Blow it up and fly out."

Kenton looked skeptical. "A lot of things have to go right for that to work, Tom."

"Absolutely, sir, but I think it's the only way. Like Dave said, jumping in, with that much snow, and in the mountains, we could all be separated by way too much distance. Alone and surrounded doesn't seem like the way to start a mission to me."

"Still, what if the Germans raise the alarm on your arrival? Or you can't get a truck?"

Dunn shrugged. "We'll adjust as needed, sir."

They discussed the plan for a few more minutes and Tanner returned, smiling.

"Found several Junkers Ju-52s that are available. They still have the German markings, too." He handed the colonel a sheet of paper. "Those are the locations that are within to and from range of the pass. I also got the name and location of a German airfield near Brenner Pass. It's near a village called Obernberg am Brenner. It's situated in a half-mile wide valley almost five miles long."

Kenton smiled. Tanner had anticipated their needs very well. Kenton rose and walked over to the pinewood map table set against the wall to his right. Everyone else got up and found a place to view the three by three-foot topographic map of northern Italy. As usual, the map's edges were held down by glass ashtrays, some clear, some amber in color. An overhead light helped brighten things.

Kenton handed the paper from Tanner to Dunn, who read the first airfield's name. He leaned over the map and found it after a short search.

"Ramatelli looks like a good candidate," he said. "Anyone know the range on the Junkers?"

"Five hundred and ninety miles, Sergeant," Tanner said after looking at another note in his hand. "Ramatelli is too far, at about four hundred miles one way. I found another airfield a hundred and ninety-four miles closer up the coast at Rimini. It's only two hundred and twenty miles from the Alps target airfield. You could pick up the Junkers that's at Ramatelli, fly it to Rimini and refuel. From there you can go up and back without refueling."

Dunn checked the map and said, "Okay, I see Rimini." Dunn looked up. "Excellent work, Lieutenant."

Tanner smiled and nodded.

Cross edged closer to Dunn and leaned over the map. His gaze traveled north until he found the Brenner Pass, which was marked by a penciled-in circle. He touched the map with a finger.

Another circle and notation indicated the radar station. He tapped it.

Dunn leaned even closer to peer at the radar station's location. The map showed clearly that it was on the southern peak of a range running southwest to northeast.

"Hm, there's a draw running from the airfield's valley almost to the top of the peak. Hopefully that's been turned into a road and we can drive up there." He used a forefinger and thumb to measure the distance and placed them against the scale. "About three miles as the crow flies."

Dunn glanced over at Kenton. "Mind if we take this map along?"

Kenton shook his head. "By all means. Can you be ready to leave tomorrow?"

"Yes, sir, we sure can. Like Lieutenant Tanner said, we'll fly to Ramatelli, pick up that Junkers and head to Rimini. We'll plan on flying out from there to arrive on target around two or three in the morning of Sunday night-Monday morning."

"Very good, Tom. Lieutenant Tanner will make the arrangements for the aircraft and the pilots in my name so there won't be any problems."

"Appreciate that, sir."

Dunn pulled the map out from underneath the ashtrays and folded it into a neat rectangle.

"Contact us when you arrive at Rimini and when you return from the mission."

"Will do, sir."

Dunn and Cross departed, closing the office door behind them.

Kenton sat down behind his desk and Tanner took a seat in front of him.

New to his role, Tanner was still getting used to the extraordinary things Kenton's men could accomplish. Reluctant to ask, he was thinking about whether Dunn would be successful.

"Wondering if they can pull it off?"

Tanner nearly jumped out of his chair at the question. His expression changed to sheepish. "That obvious, sir?"

"Just a normal reaction when someone's not quite used to these things. Best way for me to put it is this: we specialize in the impossible. All of our squads do the unthinkable. And Dunn and his men are at the top of the company in success. No one is more attentive to detail or more able to think outside the box. Have you read his after-action reports?"

"Just the last one for Hamburg."

"Okay. I suggest you read them all, going back to Operation Devil's Fire." He paused. "Actually, start with the one just prior to that, when they went to Calais just before D-Day to blow up a German ammo dump. Its purpose was to help convince the Germans the invasion was headed that way. See what happened there, and when you read Devil's Fire, you'll see how he adjusted and recovered from a complete mission failure. At least in terms of blowing things up, which didn't happen. That was because they were betrayed by a French Resistance traitor who sabotaged the explosives' detonators. They were still successful because they did get the Germans to continue focusing on the wrong place."

"All right, sir. I'll do that. Thank you."

"Good. You know all the files are here in my desk?"

"Yes, sir."

Kenton got up. "I'll leave you to it. I think I'm going to go get an early lunch. Grab the files and read in your office."

"Yes, sir."

An hour later, Tanner sat back in his chair, rubbing his face with his hands. He'd just finished reading the detailed narrative by Dunn about his squad's first few top secret missions: blowing up the Nazis' atomic bomb laboratory, preventing a terrifying electromagnetic pulse weapon from being unleashed upon the Allied soldiers on the front line, wiping out an entire SS platoon in Italy after rescuing a downed intelligence officer, while also saving a village from massacre and destruction intended by the same SS platoon.

"Holy shit," he muttered as he reached for the next folder, his eyebrows climbing up his forehead.

RONN MUNSTERMAN

Chapter 6

The Farm, Area B-2, Catoctin Mountain Park
In Maryland, 70 miles northwest of Washington, D.C.
9 December, 1005 Hours, U.S. Eastern Standard Time

The cold December wind blew across the field from the north. The surrounding trees were all naked, their spindly branches swaying and snapping in the wind. It was overcast for the third day in a row and Gertrude Dunn was missing the warmth and sunshine of Bermuda.

Gertrude was tall with a lithe, powerful form. She had a quick wit and, especially for stupid or rude people, a scathing tongue. Wavy light brown hair framed her oval face and she had brown eyes. She had an elder sister at home, Hazel, whose husband commanded a submarine in the Pacific. Her brother, Tom, who was between them in age, was a U.S. Army Ranger based in England.

When she'd worked at the Rock Island Arsenal near Davenport, Iowa, Gertrude attracted the attention of the Office of Strategic Services. Two OSS recruiting officers had travelled to the Dunn family home in Cedar Rapids to give her a written test. She scored so high the officers had no choice but to offer her a job on the spot. Her initial training took place in St. Louis, and she managed to catch the attention of a higher-up woman who suggested she be sent to Bermuda.

She'd worked for Bermuda Station as an analyst, reading mail and telegrams going between America and Europe. She was looking for anything suspicious: information that could lead to the capture of a spy ring working in the States. And she had been successful.

An unexpected event had once again thrust her into the limelight as far as her superiors were concerned. She and two friends were walking on a dock late at night in Bermuda. A man tried to rob them, holding one of them at knife point. To put it simply, Gertrude, using training her brother Tom had given her while home on leave, had disarmed and pinned the man to the dock. When the police had arrived, they were shocked. And laughing.

The day after, she was interviewed by a man with the OSS. He'd tried to test her fighting skills with a fake knife in her supervisor's office. It didn't go well for him either and after picking himself up off the floor, he offered her the chance to become an OSS field agent. Which brought her to The Farm in Maryland. In winter.

Gertrude stood in a line of nine other women, all OSS trainees at The Farm located northwest of Washington D.C. She was the youngest one there at nineteen. A tall woman at five-eight, she could hold her own in the physical trials they had all experienced. She'd arrived just ten nights ago. Her first training exercise hadn't been announced as such. Instead, as soon as she got out of the car by the farmhouse, a woman wearing a nighty ran past screaming bloody murder. Gertrude spotted a pursuer carrying a gun, so she did what seemed right; she knocked the pursuer to the ground and took the weapon away from her. At that moment, the man in charge of The Farm showed up and announced the exercise was over. The pursuer, one of the instructors, had glared at Gertrude, and every time they crossed paths Gertrude got another angry stare. Gertrude didn't care the first night or any of the other times. She had done what she thought was right.

Rick, their instructor for most activities from physical training to the firing range stood in front of the women. He was in his early forties with black hair and a matching Errol Flynn mustache. A beanpole with hidden strength, when the women ran their early morning three miles, he was right at their side shouting to pick up their pace. Compliments were not forthcoming.

Next to Rick was the woman who always showed Gertrude anger, Mildred.

The women waited for him to speak.

He eyed them. They wore long khaki pants, boots, white shirts, and waist length brown leather jackets. On their hands were tight fitting tan leather gloves. Everyone wore a black or dark blue watch cap, scrunching their hair into impossible shapes.

"Count off!" Rick commanded.

The women at the far left of the line started and everyone called out their numbers.

"Pair up!" He called out the pairings numbers.

Gertrude happened to be number six and she was paired with number one, who went by the name Edna.

None of the people at The Farm used their real names. Gertrude's work name was Peggy. Everyone's past was kept secret. No one was allowed to discuss it. Doing so led to immediate dismissal from The Farm. Gertrude played a mental game of guessing where the other women were from by the way they spoke. The New Yorker talked so fast you could catch one word out of three. The Bostonian couldn't pronounce an R if her life depended on it, instead coming out as *ah*. The Midwesterners had their own drawl, but not quite as strong as the woman from the Deep South. The two West Coasters were laid back and slow talkers, which drove the East Coasters crazy. As for herself, she had grown up smack dab in the center of the Midwest.

The pairs of women had arranged themselves about two yards apart and stood facing Rick.

"Today you are going to learn some Judo that you can use against an attacker. Judo's primary goal is to help you get your attacker on the ground where you can immobilize him. What to do once he's on the ground is something we'll cover once you've all perfected the throws and takedowns. We'll begin with unarmed attackers. Mildred and I will demonstrate the first throw a few times, first at normal speed, then step by step."

Rick tucked his ever-present silver whistle on a lanyard inside his jacket and zipped it up. Facing Mildred, who was a good six inches shorter and fifty pounds lighter, he nodded. She walked away, toward the north and turned around when she was about ten feet from him. She began walking back to the south and ignored him, pretending not to see him. Just before she reached the point directly in front of him, Rick jumped out in front of her and grabbed her jacket by the lapels, pulling her close like a mugger might.

Her response was to grip the right side of his jacket with her left hand, and the other side above his shoulder with her right.

She first yanked backward with her left.

In a violent simultaneous movement, she snapped downward with her right hand and pushed up and forward with her left.

As his body twisted backwards to the right, she switched directions, rotating to her left pushing him off balance to her left.

She switched directions again, pulling him hard toward herself and to the right.

She swept her left leg backwards across his ankles.

He flipped over her left hip slamming into the frozen ground, landing on his right hip, facing away from her. As soon as he was on the way down, she let go and stepped back to be behind him.

Rick jumped to his feet, evidently none the worse for wear. He turned to the students.

"Now in slow motion as Mildred explains each movement."

He and Mildred went through the hip throw five times with Mildred stating what she was doing and why it worked. It was all based on the principle of leverage and powerful motion.

Rick told the women to face each other and take up positions, odd numbers being the attackers.

With Rick calling out each step, Gertrude successfully threw the smaller Edna a total of four times.

"Switch roles," Rick said.

He continued calling out the steps.

Edna had trouble getting the much bigger Gertrude to flip over her hip. Instead, Gertrude's weight forced Edna backwards and she fell onto her back with her partner crashing down on top of her.

"Oof."

Gertrude rolled off and got up. Reaching down, she helped Edna up.

"That didn't work," Edna muttered. Her face was pink.

Gertrude leaned close and whispered, "When you pull with your left hand to start things, really yank it hard like you're trying to open a stuck door. Slam me backwards as you spin right. That'll get the momentum started you need."

Rick paused long enough for all the women to get back to the starting point.

When he called out the steps the next time, Edna followed Gertrude's tip and everything worked right.

After a couple of more throws, Edna was breathing hard, but gave Gertrude a grim smile.

"Thanks," she said.

Gertrude nodded.

"Switch roles and alternate," Rick said again. "Each time the attacker starts everything and you both go at full speed."

As the women began, Rick and Mildred walked amongst them watching closely for form and mechanical errors. They both stopped different pairs and worked with them to get the throw down correctly.

After five minutes of work, all the women were huffing and red faced from the exertion.

Mildred walked over by Edna and Gertrude and watched them silently, hands behind her back. A smirk appeared when Edna got Gertrude a particularly good one, with the taller woman slamming hard into the ground.

Mildred walked away still smirking.

Edna had noticed it. She helped Gertrude up. She waited until Mildred was out of earshot.

"What's the deal with you and Mildred?"

Gertrude avoided turning around to look at the antagonistic instructor.

"It's nothing."

"It's not nothing."

"I'll tell you about it later. Come on. Back to fighting."

For another five minutes the ten women threw and fell and threw and fell.

Rick retrieved his silver whistle from inside his jacket and gave a long blast.

The women gratefully stopped what they were doing.

"Line up in your original order."

As the women organized themselves and faced Rick, Mildred jogged to the north and stopped fifty yards away, turning around smoothly.

"Wind sprints, ladies!" Rick shouted.

A groan went up from the women, who were worn out already. Typical Rick, pushing them and pushing them. Everyone knew it was for their own good, but that didn't make it any easier.

Rick blew his whistle and the women darted forward. When each woman crossed the imaginary line extending to Mildred's right and left, she stopped and returned to the start line, waiting. When all were ready, Rick blew his whistle.

On the fifth "back" of five down-and-backs, the women were gasping and struggling to run. When they finally all stumbled past Rick he called out, "That's enough. Edna, lead us back for lunch."

Edna and the others turned right. She started marching, setting a pretty fast pace, considering. The distance to the mess hall was only a quarter mile. The women trooped inside and made their way to the bathrooms to wash up and whatnot.

Soon, the women were seated around two big round tables, five each, and chowing down on some sort of mystery-meat sandwich and potato chips with water or tea to drink.

Standing by the windows, a blue spruce, cut from the nearby forest, provided a beautiful Christmas tree. The trainees had decorated it.

Gertrude sat with Edna and Ruby, who had finished just ahead of Gertrude in their first two-and-a-half-mile run. Edna had finished third. Where Edna was short, Ruby was tall, even a couple of inches taller than Gertrude. Also at the table was the woman with the Deep South accent, Pearl, and the New Yorker, Marjorie, who to Gertrude's surprise, was actually a nice person despite her origins. Both Pearl and Marjorie were brunettes and about five-four.

Edna leaned close to Gertrude. "What's the story with Mildred?"

"When I arrived at The Farm, they conducted a role-playing exercise with me the unknowing participant. It looked like a woman, who I later found out was Mildred, carrying a gun, was chasing another woman around the main house. I knocked her down and disarmed her. She took exception to it."

"Wow. So she's holding a grudge?"

"A big one."

"I'll keep an eye on her, too."

"Smart idea."

The women were so hungry, no one talked anymore. About the time they'd eaten enough to consider talking to one another again, The Farm's leader, David Walker, entered the large room. Walker was an imposing six-four with blond hair and blue eyes. He stood near the two tables.

The other table of five, whose women had started a low murmur of conversation, stopped talking.

"Good morning."

He received a chorus of good mornings from the group.

"You'll start your language training today. After lunch, please go to your huts and clean up. Make your way over to the classroom building. Each language instructor will be in a separate room. You already know the classrooms are numbered. Please enter the room with the number you were assigned yesterday. You'll be the only student working with your instructor. Whichever language you were assigned yesterday, remember, you have only two days to prove your aptitude in learning your new language. Failure means you'll be assigned only one more language. A second failure washes you out of The Farm."

The last was enough to make a couple of women swallow hard and look worried. Gertrude was not among them.

"A reminder that you are not to disclose to anyone what language you're learning."

With that comment, Walker left the room.

Forty-five minutes later, Gertrude entered the classroom building and walked down the hallway to her room. She knocked on the door, smiling.

A muffled voice said, "Come in."

She opened the door and entered.

A Filipino, perhaps in his mid-forties, greeted her from behind a table, "Hello, Peggy. Welcome." He stood and offered his hand, which she shook. "Please, sit."

She did.

"My name is Danilo Bondoc."

"I'm pleased to meet you, sir."

Nodding, he examined her face closely for a while, her light brown hair that was tied in a bun, her brown eyes which seem to reflect every beam of light in the room, her lips which were full and held a welcoming smile.

Not known for her patience, she endured the examination for as long as she could possibly stand it.

"Sir, tell me about the Philippines, please."

His eyes scrunched up as he gave her a light smile. "Have you ever visited the Philippines?"

"No, sir, but I really want to go help."

He nodded slowly, smile fading, his face a mix of emotions. He seemed surprised and deeply moved by her simple declaration.

Recovering, he cleared his throat. "Wonderful. My home is Dagupan, a coastal city about a hundred miles north of Manila. Let's begin. The primary language is called Tagalog . . ."

Chapter 7

Cagliari, Sardinia
410 kilometers southwest of Rome
10 December, 1532 Hours, Rome time

The Mediterranean island of Sardinia, long a part of the Kingdom of Italy going back to the early 1700s, was one of three large islands bordering the Tyrrhenian Sea, which was on the west coast of Italy. The other two islands were French owned Corsica just north of Sardinia, and Sicily resting on Italy's boot toe.

The island measured roughly 260 kilometers north-south by 110 east-west. Cagliari, the capital, was situated at the southern end of the island along the northwest coast of a thirty kilometers-wide bay. The island was mountainous along the eastern coast with the highest point being Punta La Marmora at just over 1,800 meters elevation. It was located about eighty kilometers just east of north of the capital.

Heinz Schulz, a German spy left behind when the Germans departed over a year ago following Italy's surrender, walked down the street in Pirri, an old centrally located area in Cagliari. He passed by the *Parrocchia di San Pietro Apostolo*, The Parish of St. Peter the Apostle. The catholic church dated back to a portion that was built upon a Roman building in the early 200s. Amazingly, this area of the city had not been bombed to rubble by the Allies the year prior and the church remained as it had been for centuries.

The sky was a deep blue and cloudless, leading already to a warm December day of around fifteen degrees Celsius. A pleasant breeze from the south and across the bay wound its way along the narrow streets, which formed wind tunnels.

An average looking man, quite the helpful trait for a spy, he had brown hair under his white Panama hat, and his face was craggy and tanned. In his late thirties, he could easily pass for someone much older, if need be, with the proper application of disguise implements and makeup. He wore gold-framed glasses he didn't need and carried a gold handled black cane to accommodate his limping walk. The limp was real, not feigned, due to a boisterous mistake in his early twenties. He and his friends in Frankfurt had taken to climbing on buildings and making their way across several blocks by rooftops after an evening in their favorite *bierhalle*. On the way back down one night, or early morning to be precise, a simple slip of the shoe was all it took to fall four meters and land on one foot. The left ankle had snapped into a dozen pieces that never healed properly. He chalked up the experience to having one too many steins of beer. He reduced his intake thereafter to the number minus one and it seemed to have worked.

His father, who had been a manager for the Mercedes production plant in Frankfurt, often traveled to France, England, and Italy to meet with other production managers, sometimes taking his eldest son along for the experience. The family of four, one younger brother, who died in 1926, ironically in a car accident, often vacationed in either Rome or Naples. Heinz had learned Italian just for the fun of it. As it turned out, languages were easy for him, and he'd added English and French to his list.

He'd moved to Berlin after graduating from Heidelberg College with a degree in business. He got a job with Bayerische Flugzeugwerke, which went on a few years later to manufacture the deadly Messerschmitt Bf 109 fighters. In the summer of 1938, when things were getting interesting for Germany, thanks to Hitler's inherent ability to outsmart and out bluff the gullible British and French, he'd applied for and was accepted by the *Abwehr*, German Military Intelligence. After starting out as a courier to places like Rome, he'd learned a great deal about spy tradecraft. A year later he was stationed in Rome, which was like going home to his old stomping grounds. Not long after, he was periodically sent to Cagliari for various reasons.

And so here he was. Still. Walking the streets of a city he'd grown to love. He often thought about settling here after the war. Maybe find the right girl . . .

Today, he had one job: discover where Roosevelt and Churchill were holding their "top secret" meeting. He chuckled to himself at the thought that top secret rarely was. This assignment had come in its usual way, a coded message hand delivered by a young courier just an hour earlier. The message had been noted as countersigned by none other than Ernst Kaltenbrunner, the Chief of the *Reich* Main Security Office. This was not necessarily a surprise, but it was rare for the SS to take an interest. It meant extreme caution and mission success were paramount to his career, perhaps life.

Naturally, he had numerous contacts in the city, but on the surface it seemed like an impossible mission. The Americans seemed to be everywhere. Between them and the traitorous Italians, it would likely prove to be an extremely difficult task.

At the moment he was walking downhill, which was harder on his ankle, which still hurt some days. Although to be fair, in Cagliari you almost always were going either uphill or down. Not many flat areas.

Before setting out from his apartment, he'd made a list of possible locations. There were a baker's dozen of them. Some were hotels, and some were villas that had plenty of open space around them, great for security. One was a former palace. He'd had absolutely no success. After driving all over Cagliari, he'd gone back to his apartment and parked his little Fiat on the street in front of the building. Feeling frustrated at the long day of no luck, he headed toward his next to last stop. It was within walking distance of his apartment.

The Savelli Hotel was a three-story affair built in 1899. Before the war it had been popular with the wealthy, and movie celebrities from many countries. As he stood for a moment in front of the hotel, he belatedly realized it seemed just the kind of place Churchill would choose because it was similar to his favorite hotel in Egypt, The Old Cataract Hotel in Aswan.

He'd briefly considered waiting until the airplanes—undoubtedly the two leaders would arrive separately—landed and simply follow the men to their destination. However, because the message was insistent upon a twenty-four-hour result, he thought that perhaps whoever was interested in their arrival might want to have some advance notice.

He entered the ornate lobby and crossed the marble floor toward the concierge desk. The man spotted him and stepped out from behind the chest-high desk with a grin.

"*Signore* Santoro! How wonderful to see you, *amico mio*." He held out his hand.

Schulz, whose name chosen for his role in Sardinia was Enzo Santoro, shook hands. "How are you, Antonio?"

"I am well. And you?"

Schulz nodded. "Doing well."

He draped a friendly arm around Antonio's shoulders and guided the man over by a two-foot diameter pillar, one of a dozen in the spacious lobby.

"As always, Antonio, I'm looking for a little . . . discreet help on a . . . minor matter."

"Of course." Antonio grinned. Schulz's help requests always came with a little money.

Schulz glanced quickly around to ensure they had privacy in a public place. He pulled a small roll of money from his pocket and made sure Antonio could see the size of it. "Have you heard any news on a . . . wealthy American arriving soon?"

Antonio raised an eyebrow. He cleared his throat nervously. "I'm not sure about this, *Signore*."

"Understandable." Schulz pulled another roll of money out.

"You remember my cousin is chef at the *Villa Bellavista*."

"Yes, I remember," Schulz said calmly. He gave no outward sign, but inside he grew excited instantaneously. That villa, a dozen or so kilometers outside the city, was the last place on his list.

"Go on," he said calmly.

"He received instructions to be ready to prepare some unusual meals for an American like grilled cheese sandwiches and, er, hot dogs, and fish chowder." His nose wrinkled at the mention of hot dogs.

"Hot dogs?"

"*Si*. Like sausages." Antonio shrugged as if saying there's no explaining Americans.

"Yes, I know hot dogs." Schulz deftly palmed the two rolls of money into Antonio's hand.

"That sounds like the businessman I've been trying to contact." He leaned closer. "I'm thinking of expanding my export business there after the war. I may be looking for someone to travel there as my representative."

"No, *Signore*! And you think I could do such a thing?"

Schulz nodded gravely. "I have the utmost faith in you. But of course, we must keep this quiet."

"*Mille grazie,*" Antonio whispered.

"*Prego*, my friend." He patted the man on the arm and said, "*Arrivederci.*"

"*Arrivederci.*"

Schulz left the lobby and walked back to his apartment. Uphill of course. Once inside his small unit, he opened a bottle of red wine to celebrate. All that was needed was to confirm the information with Antonio's cousin, whom he also knew well. He would do that by posing a different question about food: does he have instructions to prepare some special *English* foods?

At one a.m., after Antonio's cousin got home from work at the *Villa Bellavista*, Schulz confirmed with him the impending arrival of a wealthy English guest, name unknown. He returned home and, using his hidden radio, sent a coded message with the name of the location and the likely day of arrival, Tuesday, December 12th.

Satisfied and proud that he'd done his job long before the twenty-four-hour deadline, he got into bed and fell asleep immediately.

RONN MUNSTERMAN

Chapter 8

In flight over northern Italy
11 December, 0248 Hours, Rome time

The squad's transfer to the captured German-marked Junkers Ju-52 at Ramatelli airbase had gone smoothly. After landing at about 1700 hours Sunday night, they'd connected with their Ju-52 pilot and copilot. The flight to the more northern Rimini airbase was uneventful and shortly after landing, the aircraft was in the process of being refueled. The squad had eaten a hot meal at Rimini's mess hall. Dunn had arranged for bunks for the men and they slept or rested until midnight. They scarfed down some coffee and some sandwiches in the mess hall and prepared for their 0100 hours departure.

The Ju-52 was the German workhorse aircraft roughly equivalent to the American C-47. This one had room for seventeen passengers, a pilot, and a copilot. Its cruise speed was much slower than a C-47, so the flight time for the last leg would be just over an hour and a half. After they'd flown beyond the Allies' front line, Dunn breathed a lot easier. Getting shot down by an alert Allied night fighter pilot was not something he wanted to experience.

Each Ranger carried a suppressed 9mm Sten, the always loud and last resort 1911 Colt .45, a combat knife, fifty pounds of plastic explosives plus the timers and detonators, food for three days, and a full canteen. Everyone wore two pairs of socks with another pair stuffed into their packs. Wearing their Arctic snow gear, they also wore Long Johns underneath everything. Their helmets were white as were the gloves. Snowshoes were tied onto their packs.

The squad was back to full strength. Wickham had managed the obstacle course in good time, with no trouble, and his wound still looked okay, with the scab and stitches intact under a fresh bandage applied by the squad medic, Schneider. Dunn and Cross had finally decided to bring someone new along.

The new man, Corporal Sid Brooks, was sitting next to Dunn and would follow Cross out the door. He was a good looking man, rivaling Wickham for movie star status, which was made more interesting because Brooks' father was a bigtime movie producer in Los Angeles. It was ironic, too, because despite his looks, he had absolutely no interest in going into "the business." He was far more fascinated by civil engineering, specifically bridges. Long ones. Really long ones. At five-nine and 155 pounds, he was one of the smaller men in the squad, just a hair taller than red-headed Higgins. He had pale blue eyes and blond hair that was closer to white. At twenty-one, he was near the average age of the squad members. He'd done well in boot camp and had volunteered for Ranger School even before leaving the States. He'd graduated from Achnacarry House just a couple of weeks ago and this was his first post. Brooks seemed quiet and introspective, so Dunn had been forced to draw out the young man to learn those little bits about his past when he'd first talked with him.

Dunn got to his feet, walked a few steps and entered the cockpit. He stood behind the pilot and copilot.

"How we doing?" he asked, putting a hand on the back of the copilot's seat to steady himself as the plane bore through the bumpy cold air.

The copilot checked his watch. "About four minutes."

"Excellent," Dunn said. He peered through the windshield, and out the window by the copilot.

The landing had only been possible because the moon's phase was at a quarter. In four more days, it would darken in the new moon phase. Below him, Dunn was treated to a stunningly beautiful landscape covered in white, with crisp shadows indicating sharp ridges.

"Here we are," the copilot said.

The plane was flying as low as possible to avoid being spotted by the radar station Dunn was planning to destroy. While that was inherently dangerous in mountainous regions, the sky was clear.

They zoomed over a peak and the relatively large expanse of the half-mile wide valley where the airfield was located appeared, running southwest to northeast. It was pure white, dotted by a few black buildings at the airfield, several rectangular blocks, which Dunn took to be trucks, and a couple of planes that could have been sister Ju-52s.

The plan was to do a flyover to get a feel for activity around the airfield. Nothing was moving and there were no lights anywhere. Dunn was surprised, knowing what he did about the Germans and their flak cannons located in the valley just to the east and all the men those guns would require to fire, maintain, and repair.

"Do either of you see anything?" he asked the officers.

The plane was nearing the far end of the valley.

The pilot turned the yoke for a sweeping left turn. Dunn tightened his grip on the seat back as the plane banked.

"Nothing seems to be going on," the copilot said. "The landing strip looks like they've cleared some of the snow off of it."

"We'll be landing in a couple of minutes, Sergeant. You should go sit down," the pilot said.

"Will do, sir."

Dunn walked the length of the passenger area and sat down next to Cross, who watched him with a questioning expression.

"Landing in a couple of minutes. No movement on the ground."

Cross nodded.

Dunn tipped his head toward Goerdt and Schneider, who were a couple of rows forward, sitting across the aisle from each other. "Do you think this'll work?"

Cross shrugged. "They've been talking nothing but German to each other since we announced the plan Saturday morning. They've decided Rob should do the majority of the talking. They say his German comes across with no accent because he grew up speaking it at home and church."

The bottom fell out as the plane started its descent.

"Maybe we won't need their skills."

Cross grinned. "Okay, Pollyanna."

Dunn grinned back. "I sure as hell hope we can steal one of the trucks I saw. Be a damn long walk up the mountain."

"Ayup. I'm with you on that. A lot of 'ifs' on this one."

"Yep."

The plane touched down and a loud swishing sound came through the airframe walls.

"That sounds weird. We've never landed on skis before," Dunn said.

The Ju-52 already had skis attached for the winter when they first boarded her.

"Doesn't seem to be too bad," Cross said.

The plane's speed fell off quickly and the pilot turned it to the left to find a place to park. Its forward motion stopped, and it began to swivel left until it pointed back at the field.

"Hang tight, Dave."

Cross nodded.

Dunn went back to the cockpit and peered out. They were facing the landing strip, west, at the southern end of the field. The other two Ju-52s were lined up to their north. Two trucks were parked outside one of the black buildings not far from the other two planes. He swept his gaze north along the landing strip, checking for movement. He checked his watch: 2:58 am.

The copilot switched off the engines and the three big radials ran down, the two-bladed propellers coming to a stop.

"Thanks for a good flight, gentlemen," Dunn said.

"You're welcome," the pilot replied. "Welcome to Austria."

The vagaries of international borders put the airfield west of the Brenner Pass, but in Austria instead of Italy.

"Ha, nice, sir. I'm going to send some men over to the trucks and see if we can get one running."

"Good luck."

"Thank you, sir."

"By the way, the elevation here is just under forty-five hundred feet."

Dunn nodded. That matched what he'd seen on the map. That meant the difference from the airfield to the radar station's elevation was nearly 2,800 feet. Over a distance of three and a quarter miles that would represent a slope of? He calculated the percent to be 16. He figured the Germans had built a bunch of switchbacks in order to get construction equipment up there.

"Thank you, sir. You both have your sidearms?"

"We do," replied the pilot, patting his right hip.

The pilots would remain with the aircraft, but move from the cockpit to the passenger area. With the engines off, they'd have no heat, so a bundle of thick wool blankets awaited them. And some steaming hot coffee in quality thermos jugs. It was unlikely that anyone would approach the plane. It would just appear to be one of several parked on the snow-covered parking area. The contingency plan for bad luck was to surrender as soon as possible. Hopefully, Dunn and his men would return before they were transported anywhere and would rescue them. A rather important feat considering none of the Rangers could pilot a plane.

"Thanks for volunteering for this, gentlemen."

Both men nodded.

"We know what we signed up for, Sergeant Dunn. If you can pull this off, the Fifteenth Air Force will owe you big time," the pilot said.

"Good luck."

Dunn strode through the passenger compartment to Goerdt and Schneider. It was so quiet, something they rarely experienced in an aircraft. "You guys ready for this?"

Both men nodded. Goerdt rattled off something in guttural German, then grinned. Dunn only recognized one word.

"Okay, smart ass, what'd you say?"

"Merely asking if you know the way to Berlin, *mein herr*."

"Funny man. So are you?"

"Yes, Sarge," both men replied.

"There are two trucks north of us about fifty yards, parked outside a building. No lights are on. Martelli and Higgins will go with you, like we talked about."

"Okay, Sarge," Goerdt said. He and Schneider got to their feet and headed toward the rear door. Cross joined them.

Dunn turned around and tapped Martelli and Higgins on the shoulders. "Time to go, guys. Stay alert."

The men rose to their feet.

"Will do, Sarge."

When all four men were at the door, they put on their captured white German helmets that Dunn had scrounged up and had painted white on Saturday. Instead of their suppressed 9mm Sten Guns, they carried the captured German MP40. Unfortunately, they weren't suppressed. In order to complete the subterfuge, their clothing had no markings at all. Each man understood the risk they were taking. If captured, they could be shot as spies. Of course, on the other hand, they would be shot anyway under Hitler's automatic Commando kill order from a few years ago. So it was either half dozen or six, please.

They left their hoods down so the German helmet would be easy to spot. The initial part of the plan relied heavily on the fact that people see what they expect to see.

Dunn, standing behind Martelli, nodded at Cross, who unlatched the door and pushed it open. Cold air rushed in.

Not as bad as the Arctic, Dunn thought.

"Good luck, men."

They nodded and Goerdt led the way down the short stairs that Cross had put in place.

Goerdt stepped off the last step and his boot sank almost a foot in the snow. Even though they had snowshoes, he decided to forge ahead without stopping to put them on. They'd just get in the way when they got to the truck. He started north, the other three men behind him stepping where he had.

Cross lifted the stairs and closed the door.

Dunn and he ran forward to a window near the cockpit. They looked out and could easily see the four men traipsing through the deep snow.

Goerdt reached the first truck, the common workhorse of the German army, an Opel Blitz troop truck with canvas covering the cargo area. While he opened the driver's side door, Martelli and Higgins set up facing the building, trying to look nonchalant. Schneider went around to the other side and got in.

Climbing into the driver's seat, Goerdt looked around the dashboard. The moonlight was dim inside the cab, so he had to lean forward to see clearly. He found the start button and the choke. The keys dangled in the ignition switch. Why wouldn't they be? Who would steal a German truck in German territory?

Depressing the clutch pedal, he pumped the gas pedal three times to shoot some fuel into the engine. He pulled the choke out half way, turned the key to on and pressed the start button. The engine cranked over several times but failed to start. He let go of the button and pumped the pedal once more. He didn't want to do more because it might flood the engine. Pressing the button again, the engine cranked twice and coughed, then fired. It ran rough so he adjusted the choke. The engine smoothed out.

Glancing quickly at the fuel gauge, he was relieved to see that it was at three quarters of a tank. Ample fuel to climb the mountain's three miles and back. He leaned out the door and said, "All aboard!"

He felt the truck move as the men climbed up into the cargo area. Someone thumped the back of the cab.

He drove off, heading for the squad's plane.

RONN MUNSTERMAN

Chapter 9

Aboard a dinghy
Deep water harbor, Gothenburg, Sweden
11 December, 0307 Hours

After a fifty-three hour voyage inside a submarine, the men were happy to get into fresh air, even if it was cold and windy and wet. The sub had crossed the North Sea and entered the Skagerrak Strait between Norway and Denmark near the Jutland Peninsula. This was where a two-day naval battle took place in 1916 between the British Royal Navy Grand Fleet and the Imperial German Navy High Sea Fleet. Most historians believed England had been strategically victorious despite losing more ships than the Germans.

The sub slipped into the Kattegat Strait between Denmark and Sweden. Continuing in a mostly southerly direction would have taken the boat into the Baltic Sea.

The city of Gothenburg was split into north and south areas by the Klar-Göta River, which began its nearly 450-mile trip in Norway, passing into and out of the enormous Swedish Lake Väner, and down toward Gothenburg. The point the river entered the Kattegat Strait created a kind of double-sided harbor docks. Their targets were north of the river's mouth; two large cargo ships, which were docked facing northwest with their starboard sides next to the dock. Other smaller watercraft were tied up farther north.

Saunders sat in the back of the dinghy while Barltrop was at the bow, guiding the rowers with verbal adjustments. They were a little over a half-mile from the cargo ships. Saunders expected it to take ten minutes to reach the first ship, southernmost of the two. The temperature was below freezing and the north wind made it feel worse as it picked up water from the harbor and sprayed the men. The harbor water appeared black and the wind whipped it up enough to create waves about a foot high.

Prior to departure from the sub, Saunders and Barltrop had met in the sub's galley along with their temporary replacement, Sergeant Major Harry Kirby. Kirby's path to the Commando unit under Jenkins was different from Saunders' and Barltrop's. He'd been a lowly private at Dunkirk, but when he was rescued and returned to England an internal fire of hatred had ignited. He worked harder than everyone else in his company during their training stint, was an expert shooter, unbeatable in hand-to-hand combat, and smart. A quick rise to sergeant laid the groundwork for volunteering for Commando School in 1942. Born and raised in Harrogate, just thirteen miles north of Leeds, he'd joined the army right after Poland was invaded on September 1, 1939, about the same time as Saunders, although in separate units.

Saunders reached Sergeant Major about a month before Kirby, which sometimes became a source of a more or less friendly rivalry. When it came to missions where he got to kill Germans or at least damage their war effort, he was 100 percent focused on the task until it was done. That was why Saunders had wanted to bring him along.

At twenty-seven, he was a year older than Saunders. He was a slender man with a matching narrow, rugged face. He had dark brown hair and brown eyes that seemed to always be in motion.

Saunders had started the meeting with, "Colonel Jenkins confirmed just a while ago by message that our resource in Gothenburg has indeed arranged a big party for the crews of the two ships we're after. There will definitely be security left aboard, more than likely Germans." Saunders looked at Kirby, who grinned a wolf's grin. "I see that makes you happy, Harry."

Kirby nodded, still grinning. His hand slipped to the knife on his hip.

"The ships are both due out, fully loaded, at eleven hundred hours. Odds are high we'll catch them already done with loading. So much the better. But if not, we still sink them now."

The men discussed the departure from the sub, who would sit where in the rubber boat and which ship they'd tackle first. Afterwards, they passed on the pertinent information to the men to ensure everyone was aware of what their individual tasks would be.

A particularly large wind wave splashed water near Saunders, who like a cat, cringed to get away from it. Some of the men nearby chuckled. Their favorite sergeant hated water.

Since Sweden was a neutral country, the citizens didn't bother with conducting blackouts. Some lights were on at the dock, backlighting the darkened ships. Streetlights were on and sprinkled across the city. Now just a quarter mile away, Saunders could clearly make out the ships. They were over three hundred feet long and both had a single smokestack, just behind amidships. The bridge was forward of amidships. Each ship had three spindly cranes and two masts.

Saunders kept his eyes on the ships, but a sound of powerful engines caught his attention.

Barltrop turned around and yelled loud enough for all to hear, "Everybody down. That's an E-boat coming out of the river. They're going to pass within a hundred yards of us to the north."

All of the men stopped rowing and shipped the oars. They bent over so their faces, although blackened with grease, wouldn't show.

Barltrop ducked but positioned himself so he could just see over the lip of the dinghy.

The one hundred foot plus long E-Boat was moving fast. Its hull slapped the surface of the water hard and the bow spray was high. He estimated its speed at about forty knots.

It was headed out toward the strait. He hoped the sub had already moved away into deeper water and was safely out of sight. Maybe the boat was just on a routine patrol. It passed by them but stayed on its course. After a minute or so, the boat's wake hit the dinghy and it rocked back and forth until the water calmed down.

When the E-boat was about a half mile out, it keeled over as it turned due north still at high speed. Barltrop watched it carefully until it began to blend in with the water and disappeared from sight.

"Everybody up! Start rowing. We need to hurry. If it comes back, we might be in its path."

The men, wanting nothing to do with the heavily armed torpedo boat, rowed their hearts out.

Soon, the rubber dinghy silently bumped the target ship's hull just a few feet forward of the aft, right next to the aft anchor chain, a built-in ladder.

Saunders spotted the ship's name, *Trosa*, as they'd approached from the aft direction. It was painted in white in the center of the stern. It matched one of the two on his list.

He waved at Cyril Talbot.

Talbot had been elected to scurry up the chain, dragging a coil of rope to dangle for the rest of the men. Like everyone else, he wore all black: coat, pants, shirt, and watch hat. He wore rubber diver's gloves borrowed from the sub's stores to help give him a grip on the likely damp chain links. He slipped the sling of his Sten gun with the integrated suppressor over his head and onto his left shoulder. The fifty-foot coil of rope was tied to the left side of his belt.

He stood and as the dinghy rocked with the weight change, Dickinson grabbed his belt to steady him. Leaning forward, Talbot got both hands on the closest chain link which was two feet long. The gap between the two links connected to it was about six or eight inches and that space would be his hand- and foot-holds. He glanced at Saunders in the rear of the dinghy and received a nod.

Talbot started up the chain carefully. It was at an angle to the aft, so it was a bit like climbing a narrow ladder. It took him a couple of minutes to almost reach the top of the chain where he stopped to assess what to do next. The chain entered the hull about five feet below the deck level.

Gauging the distance and examining the top link of the chain for moisture—it was dry—he lifted a foot and stepped onto the top link, grabbing the frame of the anchor chain opening with his hands to secure himself. Raising himself quickly, he grabbed the edge of the gunwale just above him and pulled himself up with both hands.

He peered over the gunwale. The deck was empty of men in all directions. He grabbed the lower horizontal bar of the three-bar railing and pulled himself up far enough to swing a leg through the space under the bottom railing. He got the other leg through and pushed himself onto the deck. Rising quickly to his knees, he raised his Sten and looked around again, taking his time for certainty. Clear.

He turned around and tied the rope to the bottom rail. After tugging it to ensure it would hold, he leaned over the gunwale. The men were looking up. He raised a hand and waved. Saunders acknowledged with a wave. Talbot worked loose the rope and uncoiled it down to the dinghy. He watched Dickinson climb onto the knotted rope and start his way up. Satisfied his first task was completed, he turned around and raised his weapon again, his eyes sweeping back and forth across the deck.

Dickinson made it to the top. Talbot stuck out a hand and helped the squad veteran climb aboard. As soon as Dickinson had his feet under him, Talbot took off in a combat crouch toward the base of the aft crane, which towered above him. Dickinson took Talbot's spot by the rail as the rest of the men continued boarding the ship. Talbot moved farther forward to the aft cargo hold opening, which looked like a long rectangular box sitting on the deck. The duel hatch doors were open. Taking a kneeling position behind it, he watched the area in front of him. As he scanned the rear of the second level of the bridge structure, a torch light bobbed as a sentry strolled around the bridge's outer aft walkway. Talbot checked for a long weapon, but didn't see one in the man's other hand or over his shoulder.

RONN MUNSTERMAN

Chapter 10

400 yards north on the downslope from the German Radar Station
Elevation 6,640 feet
11 December, 0326 Hours

Rob Goerdt, who stayed in place as the truck driver, stopped the stolen vehicle in the middle of the road. Although road was probably wishful thinking. The path upwards had followed the crease in the draw from the airfield to this point, a quarter of a mile from the radar station. He'd been relieved to see there were a lot of, presumably new, switchbacks in order to handle the overall slope to the top, which was far too steep to just go straight up the draw. The surface of the path had been somewhat cleared by a road grader, so the snow wasn't as deep as it was on the sides, where it was over two feet deep. He'd had to stay in second gear most of the way with an occasional drop back into first.

The reason he stopped was the appearance of two German sentries at a checkpoint, the kind with a counterweighted arm and a little communications shack.

Schneider sat in the passenger seat next to him. Both wore their white German helmets, but had the hoods back for better visibility. They'd switched weapons from earlier. Goerdt's Sten lay on the seat next to him. Schneider's was held between his knees with one hand, barrel down.

The approaching sentry still had his rifle on his shoulder and his hands in his pockets for the cold. When he arrived outside the window, Goerdt rolled it down part way, as if trying to minimize the amount of cold air coming in.

"What are you doing here at this time of night?"

Goerdt opened the door and stepped out into the snow packed road. He rubbed his bottom. Speaking in German he replied, "Sorry. Had to stand up. The long drive is killing my ass. You were saying?"

The sentry nodded his understanding of that truth. "But why are you here at night?"

Goerdt shook his head, but was thinking his German must have passed muster. "Bad luck is why I'm here. My sergeant told me to transport a bunch of stuff up here for you and the rest of the men here. The asshole insisted it had to be tonight!"

The soldier's eyebrow went up, his expression hopeful. "What kind of stuff?"

"We've got winter gear like we're wearing for you. It'll be a lot better than those things." Goerdt pointed disdainfully at the long gray, greatcoat the soldier was wearing. "We also have rations, including *Scho-Ka-Kola* tins."

"You've brought us chocolate?"

"*Ja*, lot's of it. Ask your comrade to come over here. We can give you a little early taste. No one will know." Goerdt winked to seal the idea.

The sentry waved enthusiastically to his partner, who jogged over. When he arrived, his expression questioning, but not alarmed, the first sentry said, "Want some *Scho-Ka-Kola*?"

The man's expression brightened. *"Wirklich? Ja!"* Really? Yes!

"Ja!"

Schneider, who of course had been following the conversation, slipped out of the truck quietly and went around to the back, his suppressed Sten raised to his shoulder.

Goerdt started toward the back of the truck. "Right back here."

Half way down the side of the truck, he stumbled slightly and the two enemy soldiers walked on past him thinking about chocolate. It was their last thought.

As they turned the corner, they came face to face with a German soldier aiming a weapon at them.

Schneider fired four times, two each in the head. The sentries collapsed.

Goerdt ran back and helped Schneider pull the two Germans off the road and into the deeper snow on the side. They quickly covered the bodies by shoveling snow with their gloved hands. As they walked back to the truck, they kicked snow across the blood trails and the big splotch behind the truck.

"I'll get the barrier," Schneider said, taking off.

Goerdt got back in the truck.

Dunn poked his head in from the cargo area. "Nicely done."

"Thanks, Sarge."

"Pretty glib with the lies, there, Rob. Kind of scary . . ."

Goerdt just laughed.

Schneider raised the barrier. Goerdt drove past it and stopped. Schneider lowered the barrier, and climbed in.

Goerdt drove off again.

"That was some story you concocted, Rob," Schneider said.

"Oh, yeah. Just came out on its own accord."

"You should be a writer. Making stuff up on the fly like that."

"Nah, that's got to be way too much hard work."

Behind them, in the little guard shack, the phone rang and rang.

In the cargo space, Wickham was bent over, hands on his knees.

"Hey, Stan. Are you all right?" Dunn asked from the bench seat across from Wickham.

"Elevation's getting to me. Not much over a foot high in East Texas."

Dunn smiled. Even in distress, Wickham could create a hyperbole. "According to our map, we're about fourteen hundred feet higher than Denver right here. The radar station is another six hundred feet. Will you be okay?"

Wickham took a deep breath and held it the way a smoker holds the inhale. He let it out slowly. "Never been to Denver. Maybe this is why. That last one helped. I'm all right."

"Are you certain, Stan? I don't want you collapsing at an inopportune time."

Wickham dipped his chin. "I'm sure, Sarge."

Dunn was suddenly worried he and Cross, but mostly he himself, had made a mistake in bringing Wickham. If he needed medical help, that would take two possibly three men from the attack force. Wishing he'd at least brought along someone like Sgt. Newman, who'd proven himself in the raid on Hitler's dam, he prayed for Wickham.

Dunn leaned over so he could see into the cab and from there to the outdoors.

Because they had passed the tree line there was little cover. A few scraggly shrubs dotted the landscape but would be effectively useless as cover. Dunn scanned the snow ahead of him. It seemed to have a blue tint in the moonlight. He wondered whether that was some kind of illusion or if high elevation did something to the air particles causing the light to refract and provide blue light. It was beautiful. He imagined a painter trudging all the way up here to set up and capture that lovely hue.

Dunn lifted his binoculars and examined the mountain peak above him. He quickly found the three masts. Even from three hundred yards they seemed enormous. Each mast, which more resembled a large net, was fifty feet wide and the same in height. They were spaced apart perhaps ten feet or so. They were aimed directly south, where the Allied bombers would always be coming from. To the right of the masts was a two-story block-shaped building. Perhaps one level for the radar crew's living quarters and one for the work area with all the equipment tied to the masts. There were no windows, which made sense. That way there would be zero risk of accidentally exposing a lighted room and giving away their position from the air. He thought the door, which was just a darker space on the north wall, was likely a double door entrance, like shops in London used during the blitz so they could have lights on inside but still meet the blackout requirements.

A truck, identical to the one they'd stolen from the airfield, sat quietly to the right of the building's front.

"Rob, if there's room, try to park so that other truck is between us and the station."

"Will do, Sarge."

As they neared the top and were on the final switchback, motion caught Dunn's eye just in front of the building. Two shapes, wearing dark clothing like the sentries at the checkpoint, rose from their hidden positions. They'd evidently been hunkered down behind some sort of snowy hidey-hole. One of them marched toward the radar station's front door, while the other faced the arriving truck. He had his rifle part way up, but when he recognized the type of truck, slipped the sling back over his shoulder.

Dunn turned to Jonesy, who was right beside him.

"Pass the word: We're watching to see if one of the exterior guards is getting more men."

Jonesy nodded. Eventually the message made its way around the truck.

The lone enemy soldier entered the door, and as Dunn expected, no light leaked out, indicating the probability of a double door system.

"Rob, change of plans. Is there enough room so you can park facing the building?"

"Yeah, no sweat, Sarge, lots of room."

Goerdt guided the truck into a spot facing the building, parking just to the right of the shoveled walkway between the building and the parking area.

To the men in the back with him, Dunn said, "Be ready to roll out when I give the word."

Dunn returned to watching the building. A couple of minutes later, the door opened again. Two soldiers stepped through, one carrying his rifle at the ready, presumably the one who'd gone inside, and another, wearing an officer's peaked hat, who had a pistol in his hand. Both strode purposely toward the Americans' truck.

RONN MUNSTERMAN

Chapter 11

Aboard the Swedish cargo ship *Trosa*
Deep water harbor, Gothenburg, Sweden
11 December, 0327 Hours

The ship's sentry was using his torch to see where he was walking rather than shining it out onto the deck where trouble was lurking.

Talbot raised his Sten, just in case. The range to the bridge was a mere thirty yards on the outside, well within the weapon's range, spitting distance for a Commando. The sentry turned a corner and headed away from Talbot toward the front of the bridge.

Saunders slid into position next to Talbot.

"One sentry on the second level of the bridge. Out of sight now," Talbot whispered.

"Rifle?" Saunders asked.

"Negative. Could be wearing a pistol. Couldn't see his opposite side."

Sergeant Kirby, and the rest of the squad joined Saunders and Talbot behind the cargo hold's opening.

Saunders turned to the men and reminded them who had which assignments and gave the order to go. Holmes and Myers scooted around the cargo hold's opening and started down the metal stairs on the starboard side. Dickinson and Forster ran to the aft side stairs that led up to the rear of the bridge. Barltrop and Alders took off for the near side of the bridge. Their goal was the amidships cargo hold just in front of the bridge. They would have to wait for Dickinson and Forster to clear the bridge. Kirby and Bentley followed and would also wait. When it was clear, they would bolt to the forward cargo hatch and plant their explosives inside there.

Saunders stayed put. He would act as sentry for the port side of the ship keeping watch all the way to the bow. Talbot ran across to the starboard side of the hatch they were hiding behind. He would guard the starboard side to the bow.

Dickinson soft-footed his way up the metal stairs to the bridge's second level, his Sten tight against his right shoulder, aimed upward. Forster quietly followed three stairs behind. Dickinson reached the walkway and stepped onto it, staying low. This was because there was a huge rear window in the bridge structure and a red glow emanated through it. Just to the starboard side of the window was a door leading into the bridge compartment.

Motioning for Forster to stay put, he duckwalked to a post near the righthand corner of the window. Carefully he lifted his head and peeked. A lone sailor stood watch facing the bow from the instrument panel. He was smoking a cigarette. Every inhale brightened the entire bridge. Dickinson slid over to the right side of the door and put his left hand on the flipper-style handle. Slowly he pushed down on it and pulled gently. He opened the door two inches, which was all he needed. Putting his left foot next to the door, he inserted the Sten's barrel through the gap and fired two shots into the man's head. The sentry dropped straight down without so much as a grunt. Only the sound of his body thumping on the floor could be heard.

Dickinson pulled the door the rest of the way open and waved for Forster to join him. The younger Commando darted across the walkway and through the door right behind him. Dickinson ran past the dead man on the floor toward the windows at the front of the bridge. He looked out at the deck below him that stretched a good fifty yards to the bow. Between the moonlight and a few streetlights along the dock, the deck was awash in light. Seeing no one, he went out on the front walkway and turned left to go around the corner. From the side of the bridge, he leaned over.

Barltrop and Alders were watching him closely. He waved. Barltrop acknowledged with his own wave. Dickinson went back inside the bridge where he and Forster would maintain overhead watch of the bow and aft decks.

Barltrop took off at a run along the port side with Alders, Kirby, and Bentley following. When Barltrop and Alders reached the amidships cargo hold they prepared to go down inside. Kirby and Bentley ran on past heading for the forward hatch. Soon, both teams were headed down the stairs into their respective holds.

For Saunders, this was the hard part. Most of the men were out of his sight and there was nothing he could do to help them if things suddenly went bad. He continued to scan the ship for unexpected movement, but saw nothing. He glanced over at Talbot, the one man he could see. As if he felt his squad leader staring at him, Talbot looked at Saunders. He gave his boss the 'clear' hand sign and Saunders acknowledged.

The quiet gave Saunders plenty of time to think of all the things that could go wrong. The crew could come back early. Should he put a guard on the gangplank? He and Barltrop had decided against trying to clear the ship by checking every possible space believing it would take far too long. But what if there were more crewmen below decks doing who knew what? Would they just pop up to the deck for a stroll or a smoke?

He checked the time. He figured it should take the men five minutes to place and arm the explosives. They'd been told to locate a suitable spot where the port hull met the lower deck. If any fuel or ammunition containers were found, a satchel was to be placed amongst those, also. The resulting explosion would make it far more difficult or impossible for the Germans and Swedes to raise the sunken ship and repair it.

Saunders grit his teeth as his nerves continued to get to him. It wasn't as if he was having some flash of insight or a premonition, but he was uncharacteristically worried. Checking his watch every thirty seconds or so didn't help matters, but when the five minutes were up, he looked at each of the three cargo holds in turn.

Suddenly, to his relief, Holmes and Myers popped into view and clambered out of the aft hold. They made their way over to Saunders and knelt beside him.

"All set, Sarge," Holmes said. "We placed one satchel against the port hull on the floor, and found some crates marked in numbers 'eight point eight' and '*zentimeter*.' We opened one and sure enough it was full of those bloody eighty-eight shells. We put the other satchel right in the middle of those things. I have to say that was more than just a bit terrifying."

Saunders nodded. "Aye, I'm sure. Good job, lads. Do me a favor and carefully and quietly go find the gangplank on the other side of the ship. Check out the dock nearby. Come back and report in."

"Sure thing, Sarge," Holmes replied. He tapped Myers on the shoulder and pointed down the port side.

Myers nodded.

They took off at a run. When they passed the bridge, they turned right and headed to the starboard side. The gangplank was just forward of the bridge and of course tilted down to meet the dock. The two men ran crouched over and when they reached the gangplank, hit the deck in a prone position to reduce their silhouettes. They examined the dock. A couple of empty trucks were parked about fifty yards away, next to a dark warehouse. Mounds and mounds of wooden crates were stacked along the west side of the warehouse. Holmes thought it odd they were outside the building, but perhaps they were next to be loaded aboard in the morning. He wondered whether it would be worth setting charges on them, too, but recalled that their orders were specific: the ships only. They were not to step foot on Swedish soil. Blowing up the ships was probably bad enough as it was.

Seeing no one moving on the docks, he tapped Myers and they rose and took off the way they'd come.

Back with Saunders, on the port side of the aft cargo hold, Holmes reported what they'd seen.

Saunders seemed visibly relieved, but said only, "Right, thanks. Head back to the dinghy."

After the two men left, Saunders felt somewhat better.

Soon, Barltrop and the others who had gone forward reappeared and made their way back to him. Dickinson and Forster, who had seen the four dark figures emerge from the cargo holds, were on their way, too.

In just a few minutes all the men except Talbot had climbed back down to the dinghy. Talbot knelt and untied the rope everyone had used, letting it fall into the waiting hands of the men below. He climbed over the rail and went down the same way he'd come up, using the anchor chain as a ladder.

Saunders checked that everyone was ready and thought, *"One down."*

RONN MUNSTERMAN

Chapter 12

German Radar Station
Elevation 7,257 feet
11 December, 0341 Hours

Like the other sentry had done, the officer relaxed at the sight of the familiar truck. He holstered his sidearm and the sentry with him slung his weapon.

"Rob, that officer is going to ask for your papers, I'm sure. Stall for thirty seconds. Use *'Jawohl'* as code for the end of your stall."

"Roger, Sarge."

Dunn watched the approaching two Germans through the windshield. They were about fifty yards away. The other sentry was still standing by near the front door, apparently not concerned because his rifle remained on his shoulder.

Dunn tapped Jonesy. "Get out of the truck and be ready to shoot the German standing by the snow berm to the left of the front door. I'll take care of the two coming to the truck. You kneel, I'll stand behind you."

"Roger, Sarge."

"Everyone else, get your snowshoes on. Here's what we're gonna do."

He laid it all out.

"Questions?"

"No, Sarge," was everyone's reply.

Jonesy and Dunn put their own snowshoes on, and quietly made their way to the rear of the truck. Jonesy went out first, staying to the right side of the truck to have plenty of cover. Dunn joined him.

They crept along the rear of the truck, a neat feat with snowshoes on. Rather than take a peek and risk being seen, they waited, listening for the crunching of footsteps in the snow. When the Germans arrived, they would talk to Goerdt.

The crunching sounds started and got louder as the Germans came closer. Finally, they stopped.

Dunn assumed it was the officer speaking to Goerdt, who was answering politely as far as Dunn could tell, with the subservient tone reserved for enlisted men talking to officers.

"What the hell are you doing here?" demanded the officer.

"We're delivering supplies, including winter gear and rations with *Scho-Ka-Kola* tins, sir."

The officer's eyes narrowed. "What happened to the guards at the checkpoint? They didn't answer their phone."

Goerdt managed to look embarrassed. "Sir, I'm reluctant to say."

"You will tell me!"

"I gave them some *Scho-Ka-Kola* tins. They probably had a mouth full when you called."

The officer shook his head, obviously thinking about reprimanding the sentries. He held out his hand. "Your papers!"

"Jawohl!"

At the code word, Dunn tapped Jonesy on the shoulder.

Jonesy knelt and leaned out from behind the truck, searching for his target. He couldn't find him!

Dunn leaned out and shot the officer and the sentry standing outside the truck.

As the two Germans went down, a shout of alarm came from the other sentry by the building.

Jonesy could finally see his target. He sighted.

The sentry shrugged his rifle off his shoulder and raised it, aiming at the truck's cab.

Jonesy fired a long burst.

The German fired, the sharp crack of his unsuppressed weapon echoing across the mountaintop.

The German was thrown backwards into the snow.

"Everyone go!" Dunn shouted.

Dunn advanced to the front of the truck. He checked the two Germans making sure they were dead. He looked in at Goerdt and Schneider. They were staring at a hole in the windshield just above Goerdt's head.

"Pretty damn close, Rob," Dunn said.

"Uh, yeah."

"Well, come on. Get out and get your snowshoes on. Rob, come with Jonesy and me. Schneider, you're with Cross."

Both men acknowledged their instructions.

Cross appeared on the other side of the truck, his group of men with him. He waited for Schneider, and waved at Dunn, who waved back. They took off, aiming not for the building but a point about thirty yards west of it.

The new man, Brooks, fell in behind Goerdt. Dunn and his men took off in the opposite direction. Dunn fully expected more soldiers to come out looking for the cause of the rifle shot. He probably had a minute, maybe two to get into position to the east of the building.

The snowshoe slog around to the side of the building in two-foot-deep snow would have tired out Dunn and the men even without the thin air. Add that factor in and they were close to wheezing. He recalled the elevation of the station on the map he'd studied several times before landing was shown as 7,257 feet. That meant they'd ascended over 600 feet from the checkpoint. He turned to Wickham, who was kneeling beside him. The big Texan glanced up and gave him a thumbs up and a tired grin. Dunn nodded, relieved.

Dunn scanned the area just in front of the radar station where he knew the German soldiers had been posted. It was a snow berm about five feet high about ten feet in front of the building. His position was behind the berm, on a line drawn along the front wall and out into the snowy areas. He was about thirty yards away from the snow berm. He knew Cross and his men would be in the same relative position on the west side. This angle was crucial to the expected firefight. Without it, Dunn's men would all be caught in their own crossfire. This way, everyone would be firing slightly downhill and away from the other group. Dunn quickly arranged his men in prone positions, so they were lined up facing their potential targets.

The door suddenly slammed opened and a stream of Germans poured out of the structure heading for the berm of snow and spreading out in a defensive formation.

Dunn counted ten new arrivals. He saw the minute flashes far on the other side from Cross's men's weapons as they attempted to bring down the Germans.

Dunn ordered, "Fire!"

The Germans, realizing their crossfire predicament, burrowed deeper. Dunn patted Jonesy, who was on his left.

The sniper, working without his Springfield, jumped up and combat ran toward the northeast corner of the radar station. Although ran might be a misnomer with snowshoes on. Perhaps flippered his way was more accurate. He eventually reached the corner and peeked out, the barrel of his Sten aimed toward the Germans' location.

He was twenty yards from the dark mounds of men. He took a calming breath out of habit as a sniper, let it out, sighting on the German on the right. He fired a double-tap and moved on to the left. After killing three, the fourth figured out that the metallic sound he heard was a weapon and he rolled over aiming his rifle at Jonesy. Martelli saw the movement and fired, killing the soldier. The remaining six aimed their weapons at Cross's group and began firing uselessly as Cross's men dropped into the snow.

Jonesy, Dunn, and the others on that side, finished the Germans off.

Jonesy, still the closest Ranger, watched the Germans for signs of life. Seeing none, he ducked back behind the corner and crossed his arms toward Dunn, forming an X, signaling that all the Germans were down.

The entire firefight lasted less than two minutes.

Dunn rose, and moved to his right just far enough so he could turn his attention to the radar station's front door. Fully expecting another stream of German soldiers to come pouring out, he instructed his men to move beside him. Jonesy stayed put as did Cross and his men.

After about three minutes of waiting, Dunn stood and waved an arm. Across the way, a hundred yards off, Cross rose and waved back. Dunn gave a signal indicating for Cross to stay in place, and that Dunn's group would advance to the door.

To the men beside him, Dunn said, "Let's go."

They rose and the group clomped their way over to Jonesy.

"Jonesy, you and I will head straight to the door. You guys," he pointed at the other three, "check on the Germans. Here we go."

He took off, staying close to the station's wall. The rest followed him until they were closer to the German bodies. Goerdt, Wickham, and Brooks peeled off.

Dunn glanced over as his men began checking the Germans to make sure they were dead. Dark blotches on the snow appeared purplish in a weird color blend of red and the blue tint he'd noticed earlier. By the time he reached the entrance, the three men had finished their gruesome task and fallen in behind Jonesy. Dunn checked the closed door. Made of steel, it had no window. He crossed in front of it to get to the doorlatch side. He leaned out and signaled for Cross and the others to come forward.

Cross and his men rose and headed in.

Dunn turned back to the door and put a hand on the foot-long metal handle. That alone indicated the door was heavy and thick, as did the huge hinges. A steel door in a wood structure seemed odd, but it did add some security.

He tipped his head at his four men. They immediately moved into position behind him fanned out at an angle to the door. He glanced over his shoulder and waited until Cross and his men reached their positions farther back. He moved to stand more in front of the door.

Figuring he had a fifty-fifty chance the door was unlocked, he pushed down on the handle and pulled. He lost the bet; the door didn't budge. He bent over and examined the door around the handle. There it was.

Turning around, he said, "Jonesy, Goerdt, Brooks, check those Germans for a key. If a guy doesn't have one in a pocket, look for one on a chain around the neck."

While the men began searching each dead soldier's pockets, Dunn became increasingly nervous standing outside the station. When the larger group of Germans' Mauser rifles had been fired, why hadn't anyone else from inside at least come to take a look? He decided it was one thing: absolute instructions to never go outside. A second alternative came to mind. They had a way to see outside and someone was waiting just on the other side of the entrance ready to shoot whomever ran through.

A couple of painful minutes passed before Brooks, with his bare right hand, held up a chain with a large brass key dangling from it. "Sarge!" he whispered as he rose and walked over to his new squad leader.

When Dunn took the chain he noticed small streaks of blood on Brooks' fingers. The chain and key were clean however.

"Thanks, Brooks. Be sure to clean off your hand before you put your gloves back on."

"Yes, Sarge." Brooks bent over and stuck his hand in the snow and swished it around as if it were water. He pulled it out and examined it. Satisfied, he wiped his clean hand on his trousers. He struggled to get his hand back inside the glove because his skin was damp, but he managed it.

Dunn smiled at Brooks' solution.

Turning, he inserted the key and rotated it. A *clunk* came from inside the door. Once again, he worked the handle. This time the door opened. He stopped its motion when there was a foot-wide gap. He peered into the darkness within. Seeing no one, he pulled the door open the rest of the way.

An entryway about ten feet square greeted him. On the opposite side was a matching door. Grabbing the key from the outer door he stepped inside. The line of men moved forward to follow, Jonesy first.

He unlocked and slid open the inner door, but only about an inch. Bright light came from inside. The wall on the left held a large map of Europe with lots and lots of grease pencil markings. He opened the door a little more.

The bullet sparked off the door at chest height.

Chapter 13

Aboard the Swedish cargo ship *Askersund*
Deep water harbor, Gothenburg, Sweden
11 December, 0348 Hours

Saunders was relieved that the second ship's name also matched his list of two. He was impressed by the intelligence information. The two cargo ships were close to identical making Saunders believe they were "sister" ships. After the squad had climbed aboard the same way as before, Saunders and Talbot found themselves in the same positions as they waited nervously for the men to finish their work. Dickinson and Forster encountered and dispatched two armed sentries on the bridge.

Sergeant Major Harry Kirby and Corporal Ted Bentley were deep in the bow cargo hold. Bentley held a torch while Kirby attached the detonator wires to the timer, which was already set to go off at 0430 hours, just forty-two minutes away. This was their second satchel. As Kirby looked over the objects Bentley and he were standing beside, he reflexively swallowed. There were two sets of three rows by four high twenty-foot-plus torpedoes for a total of twenty-four weapons. He knew enough to be scared to death. The things carried over six hundred pounds of explosives each. He gently placed the satchel on the deck below the lowest torpedo close to the center of the stacks. He pushed it as far underneath as possible without touching the skin of the torpedo.

He backed away and looked at Bentley, whose face was pale in the torchlight.

"Ready to go, Corporal?"

Bentley just nodded and backed away from the torpedoes.

At that inopportune time, they both heard clanking sounds. Turning together they saw the round wheel on a hatchway to the aft of the cargo hold spinning.

Kirby grabbed Bentley by the arm and dragged him to the front of the torpedoes where they ducked out of sight. Bentley doused the torch.

Sounds of boots stepping into the hold came to the frozen Commandos.

Kirby raised his head. A man was walking toward the hold's ladder. He carried a torch and it lit his way. He seemed to be ignoring the torpedoes. Kirby looked back at the hatch, which the man had left open. Some light filtered through from the passageway beyond. He couldn't see anyone else.

Kirby motioned for Bentley to stay put as he duckwalked around the nose ends of the torpedoes so he could see the man from the opposite side. He was heading directly toward the only ladder. What if he was going to the deck to close and dog the cargo hatch?

Kirby gauged the distance the enemy was from the ladder at about twenty feet. It would come down to timing.

He waited until the man turned off the torch, slid it into a pocket, and placed both hands on the ladder to prepare to step up onto the first rung.

Dashing across the open space, he drew his deadly combat knife with his right hand as he ran. His soft rubber boot soles kept his advance quiet.

The man stepped onto the ladder. He lifted his other foot for the next rung.

Kirby leaped upward, snaking his left hand over the man's mouth. His momentum pulled the man off the ladder with a muffled scream.

As they fell from the ladder, Kirby twisted in the air so he would land on his back with the man on top of his chest. Even though he was prepared for the shock of the landing, he nearly let go as the collision with the lower deck knocked the air out of his lungs.

He tightened his grip as he gasped to take a breath.

As the man struggled to escape, Kirby raised the knife and slashed the razor sharp blade across the throat.

He rolled to the left to get the man off his chest, but maintained his grip on the man's mouth as blood gurgled onto the deck.

A minute later it was all over as the man convulsed once and became still.

Kirby disengaged himself, pushing the dead man over onto his front. He wiped the blade on the back of the dead man's coat, and sheathed it. He wiped his bloody hands there to get some of it off. They still looked streaked in red.

Bentley turned on his torch and shone it on the ladder.

In the pale light, Kirby waved him forward. When Bentley arrived, he motioned for him to ascend the ladder. While the younger Commando started up, Kirby turned on his torch and ran over to the hatchway the man had come through. He peeked quickly into the passageway and, seeing no one, carefully closed the hatch and dogged it. He looked around on the deck but finding nothing to use to jam the wheel, unshouldered the sling of his Sten. Unclipping the two connectors he tied the sling to a wheel spoke. Next, he tied the other end to part of the mechanism at the bottom of the hatch that pulled back to unlock it. He tested the wheel. It was frozen in place. Anyone trying to get in would have to retrace their steps and climb to the deck, cross it, and come down the ladder. They would find the dead man first, and might not think to look for explosives in the initial period of confusion.

He ran back to the ladder, avoided the dead man's mess, and jumped onto the ladder. Shortly after, he joined a kneeling Bentley on deck. They ran back to Saunders' position.

"Everything go okay?" Saunders asked. In the dim light he didn't see the blood on Kirby's hands.

"Had to kill a bloke who came out of a passageway down in the hold. It was silent and I jammed the hatch he came through."

"You okay?"

"I am. We also found twenty-four torpedoes down there. Set a satchel underneath them. We may want to be a considerable distance away when they go up."

"Bloody hell. Bob's your uncle! Maybe we can watch that one through the sub's periscope."

"I'd pay a quid or three for that."

Saunders grinned and patted his peer on the shoulder.

A minute or so later the other two groups returned, followed by Dickinson and Forster who'd remained on the bridge to provide cover.

"Time to go, lads," Saunders said.

In a matter of minutes, the men boarded their dinghy, Talbot released the rope again, and shinnied down the anchor.

As the men rowed away from the soon to explode ship, Barltrop, sitting in the bow again, faced the ship and gave directions relative to the ship to aim for their pickup spot.

It was getting colder as the north wind picked up even more. Barltrop had to redirect the rowers to adjust for the wind. When they seemed to be nearing the right distance from the docks, Barltrop had Alders turn on his torch aimed seaward and flash it twice, pause, and three times.

The men sensed rather than saw the sub's conning tower lift out of the water only thirty yards ahead.

"Not bad navigating for a landlubber," Saunders said to Barltrop, grinning.

Barltrop shook his head. "Just bloody grateful to see her."

The men rowed the dinghy close and a gaggle of British sailors, who had popped out of a hatch on deck, helped everyone get aboard. The Commandos wasted no time in getting below, except for Saunders and Barltrop, who went last as always, and were standing next to the hatch.

The sailors were lashing the still inflated dinghy to the deck.

A humming sound crossed the water.

Barltrop looked toward the sound.

"Oh bugger! Mac."

Saunders turned to look where Barltrop was staring and pointing.

The German E-Boat was headed at full speed toward them from about two miles away.

Before Saunders or Barltrop could yell a warning, the sailors, who had obviously heard the scream of the enemy torpedo boat's engines, dropped the dinghy's lines and darted toward the hatch, waving frantically at the two Commandos. Saunders and Barltrop didn't need to be told twice. They climbed down the ladder and made way for the sailors.

An alarm was going off all over the boat. One of the sailors grabbed a handset off the wall in the passageway and said something. A few seconds later, the boat began its desperate descent.

Saunders and Barltrop ran as fast as safely possible to the control room. They entered the busy room.

"Torpedoes in the water!" shouted the sonarman, who took his head set off, but held one of the earpieces close to his left ear.

The captain, standing next to the helmsman, ordered, "Steer three-three-seven."

"Aye, aye, sir, steering three-three-seven."

"Make full speed."

Another sailor pushed a lever forward and a double bell rang.

"Aye, aye, sir, full speed."

"High speed screws approaching. One hundred yards . . . fifty yards."

"Passing one hundred feet," someone else called out.

"Ten yards . . . zero yards."

High-pitched whines zipped overhead.

"Passing one hundred twenty feet."

"Steer two-seven-zero."

"Aye, aye, sir, steering two-seven-zero."

"Propeller sounds, five hundred yards behind us and fading," said the sonarman.

"Passing one hundred fifty feet."

"Level off," the captain ordered.

"Leveling off, aye, aye, sir," replied the planesman.

"Propeller sounds moving nine-zero and growing faint," the sonarman reported.

"All stop."

"Aye, aye, sir, all stop."

"Come to periscope depth."

Saunders and Barltrop were fascinated by watching and listening to the control room crew and their captain calmly working as a well-trained, precise team.

The submarine reached the correct depth.

Saunders checked his watch: 04:27.

"Up scope," the captain ordered.

The executive officer hit the button and the steel tube lifted out of the deck. The captain grabbed the handles and flipped them down while the scope was still moving upwards. He rotated the scope so it was facing east. He peered through for a full minute, and walked around in a circle as he scanned the surface in a three-sixty. He came to a stop finally, facing east again.

"No craft in sight. Have eyes on the target ships." He pulled his face back from the scope's eyepiece. He found Saunders. "Care to watch your work, Sergeant?"

"I would love to."

Saunders took over at the scope. It appeared they were a good mile from the docks, and northwest of them. The dock lights acted as backlighting for the two ships.

"You can zoom in and out with this button by your right hand," the captain said, pushing it for the Commando.

The view enlarged with a click as the lenses switched.

"Do you happen to have a camera in this thing, Captain?"

"Yes. That button is on your left in the same relative position. Up to twenty-four shots."

"Thank you, sir."

A bright flash appeared at the aft of the right-hand ship, the first one they'd boarded. Two more flashes appeared at amidships, and toward the bow. The smoke and fire boiled skyward.

Saunders snapped several pictures.

Two simultaneous flashes appeared on the left-hand ship's aft and amidships.

The sonarman laid down his headset and flipped a switch on his console. A speaker over his head began to rumble.

"Explosions sounds coming through, Captain."

"Very well, thank you."

A massive explosion in the periscope nearly whitewashed Saunders' view of the ships.

He snapped some more pictures.

A few seconds later the speaker seemed about to come off the bulkhead from the deep rumbling thunder coming through it.

"Torpedoes just blew," Saunders said.

The right-hand ship's stern began to go down.

Screeching sounds, unmistakable as anything but thick steel being twisted apart burst into the control room through the speaker.

"Breaking up sounds, Captain."

"Very well, thank you."

The left-hand ship's fireball disappeared, leaving smoke hanging above. The bow broke off and began to sink backwards. The rear of the ship tipped forward, filled up, and sank within a minute.

The other ship slipped beneath the waters.

Saunders snapped a long series of pictures. He had been counting and stopped at twenty, waiting.

A loud series of clanging and clattering came.

"Ships are hitting bottom, Captain."

"Very well, thank you."

Saunders took the last four pictures of the spots where the ships had been just minutes before. He stepped back and looked at the captain. "Thank you, sir."

"You're welcome. We'll have those photos processed for you when we get back to London."

"I'll be happy to have them. Thank you. If you don't mind, sir, I think Sergeant Barltrop and I will join the men for a debrief."

"By all means. Congratulations on a successful mission."

"Thank you, sir."

As Saunders and Barltrop were leaving the control room, they heard the captain issue orders to go deeper and head for home.

They were glad to hear them as they left the control room.

About an hour later, a knock sounded on Saunders' door. He rolled out of the tiny bunk and opened it. A sailor stood there.

"Yeah?"

"The captain wondered if you'd care to see something interesting through the periscope?"

Saunders rubbed his eyes. "Sure. I'll be right there."

"Yes, Sergeant."

A few minutes later, Saunders made his way forward and entered the control room again.

The captain gestured for him to take the periscope which appeared to be pointing to the port side of the boat.

"I thought you might find this intriguing, given your line of work."

Saunders grabbed the bars and leaned into the scope. In the distance he spotted a bright rotating light.

"Huh. Is that a lighthouse, sir?"

"It is. It's on the northern point of land near Skagen, Denmark. We're about five miles off. They use the lighthouse only when a convoy is near."

Saunders stepped back. "Interesting. Are we going to go after the convoy?"

The captain shook his head. "I didn't see it. It may have already passed. We're not going to go search for it because it could have been going in one of several directions. No, we'll head home. Just thought you'd find it interesting."

"I did, sir, thank you."

Saunders left and hit the sack again, lost to the world.

Chapter 14

German Radar Station
Austrian-Italian border
11 December, 0356 Hours

Dunn reeled backwards as another bullet smacked into the metal door. He left the door open as he put his back against the wall using the door as a shield. He looked at Jonesy who had concern all over his face. Dunn mouthed, "I'm okay."

Letting his Sten dangle from its sling, he pulled a pineapple grenade from inside a horizontally slit pocket on his coat chest. He pointed at Jonesy, who did the same thing. Each man grabbed the ring for the pin. Dunn mouthed, "One . . . two . . . three."

They yanked the pins. Jonesy pulled the door open a foot while standing behind it. They threw their grenades as far as possible into the radar station. Jonesy shouldered the door shut. It latched closed. They covered their ears and ducked away from the door.

The grenades exploded inside the station at the same time, sounding more like someone dropping a heavy pair of books on the floor. But immediately after, shrapnel slapped into the other side of the door sounding like someone firing an automatic weapon's short burst into it.

Dunn rose and turned around, leaning against the interior wall. Jonesy moved over behind Dunn on the right. The rest of the men scrunched in behind Jonesy.

Dunn opened the door about a foot and waited a moment before taking a split-second peek. When he pulled back he held up four fingers and pointed his forefinger at the floor: four men down. He looked around the door jam again for a longer span of time. The four men were the only ones he found. The room was the entire size of the building. At the rear of the building a stair set went up, presumably to the living quarters.

He faced his men. To Cross, who was just a few feet away in the tight space, he said, "Dave, take your men and set the charges on the supports for each of the three radar masts."

"Will do, Sarge."

Cross got his men on the move and they left the entryway, closing the outer door behind them.

Dunn kept the more dangerous task for his team: clearing the radar station interior, and setting the charges to destroy the equipment, and the structure itself.

Dunn gave instructions to his four men.

He and Jonesy darted through the door to the left and hit the floor, weapons ready. They searched the wide-open room visually. Still no one in sight. To their right was a series of darkened radar screens sitting on long tables. A couple were damaged by the grenades. Desks were set up around the room with lamps on them that were knocked over by the grenades' concussion. Lights hanging from the ceiling were the only ones on. A couple of them were dark and had also been hit by grenade shrapnel. In the center of the room stood a foot square support beam.

Dunn and Jonesy got carefully to their feet and stepped forward a few yards. Dunn bent over and checked the man nearest him. He wore a German army uniform and a Luger had fallen on the floor near his right hand. Jonesy checked the others.

"All dead, Sarge."

"Mine, too." Dunn faced the door and waved, pointing toward the right side of the room.

Wickham led Goerdt and Brooks inside. They took positions near the radar screens.

Dunn held up his hand for silence and the men froze in place.

Sounds of footsteps came through the ceiling, going toward the stairs at the far end of the room.

Dunn gestured for Wickham to take his two men to the bottom of the stairs. He moved toward the stairs also. It was odd moving inside with the snowshoes still attached, but he didn't want to waste time taking them off only to have to put them back on in a hurry. The men removed their gloves.

Jonesy followed Dunn.

When they all reached the bottom of the stairs, Dunn crooked a finger at Goerdt, who clumped his way over to him.

"Tell them to come down and surrender if they want to live. Tell them we're going to blow up this building. They can come with us or die inside here."

Goerdt nodded and leaned toward the stairs, looking upward. Raising his voice, he passed on Dunn's message verbatim in German.

No reply came from above.

"Again, but add 'last chance.' "

This time a frightened voice answered. Goerdt listened intently. "He says he doesn't believe us. That we'll kill them if they come down." He ran off a few German sentences trying to convince the men up there to come down.

He could hear a couple of voices, evidently discussing options.

Dunn said to the other men, "Start setting the charges like we discussed, but add a small one to the center post there. That'll collapse the upper floor and possibly the roof. Rob, tell them what I just said."

Goerdt nodded and repeated Dunn's words.

Jonesy, Wickham, and Brooks went about the deadly business of setting charges, with Jonesy taking care of the support post first.

The speaker upstairs said something.

"They're coming down," Goerdt said.

Dunn nodded.

Goerdt said something else to them. "I told them to come down with their hands to the sides, palms up."

A set of footsteps crossed the floor a few feet over their heads and joined the other man's as they started down the stairs.

Goerdt moved to the bottom of the stairs, facing up with his Sten at his shoulder. Dunn moved over by Goerdt and raised his weapon.

As the Germans came down the stairs and more and more of their bodies were visible, their empty hands were in sight by their thighs, palms up.

A good idea by Goerdt, thought Dunn.

When the Germans reached the bottom of the stairs, Goerdt told them to stand still. With Goerdt guarding, Dunn patted them down for weapons. Finding nothing, he nodded.

Goerdt gestured with his weapon and told them to sit on the floor with their legs crossed and their hands in their laps. The two frightened men followed the instructions, their eyes wide and following the weapons' barrels.

"I'll stay here. You get busy with your charges, Rob."

"Okay, Sarge."

Dunn moved in front of the two men and squatted. While aiming the Sten over their heads, he unzipped his coat. Reaching in with his left hand he awkwardly retrieved a pack of Lucky Strikes. He jiggled the pack in the way smokers do, and a few cigarettes worked their way out. He held the pack toward the men. Each gratefully took one and sniffed the American tobacco.

Pocketing the pack, he fumbled around in the same pocket for his lighter. He got the black, silver speckled Zippo out and flipped the top back with his thumb. He spun the flint wheel. The flame jumped to life and he held it out for each man in turn. When they finished getting their cigarettes burning, he closed the lighter and put it in his pocket.

He stood and took a step back. They still watched the barrel of his weapon with fear. He directed the muzzle away from them and smiled. This relaxed them and their expressions turned to hope. It wasn't the "last cigarette" for a condemned man after all.

Meanwhile, the four other Americans were working hard to get the charges laid.

About the time the two German prisoners finished their cigarettes, the men completed their work and joined Dunn.

Wickham spoke for the bomb laying crew, "All done, Sarge. Set for oh four-thirty."

Dunn checked his watch: 4:13. "Excellent. Let's get outside. Rob, you and Lindstrom shepherd these two. Get them some coats and stuff."

"Roger, Sarge," Goerdt said. Soon the two prisoners had on heavy parkas and gloves.

Dunn, his men, and the prisoners all stepped outside onto the cleared path to the parking area.

The prisoners gasped at the sight of their dead countrymen. They'd done the same when walking past the four inside. Dunn checked their expressions quickly each time to see if they were angry or afraid. Fear was the overriding emotion. Good, he didn't need a couple of guys trying to be heroes due to indignant rage.

Dunn told Jonesy to go check on Cross, but when Jonesy reached the corner of the building, he stopped.

"They're coming back. Almost here," he shouted at Dunn.

A moment later, Cross and the others appeared. Cross maneuvered next to Dunn. He eyed the prisoners for a second.

"All done. You?"

"Yep. Picked up some passengers."

"So I see."

"I'm hoping they'll cooperate with the British radar folks. Maybe learn something useful."

"Ayup," Cross replied in his best Nor'easter accent.

"You set yours for oh four-thirty?" Dunn asked.

"Ayup."

"We're out of here, gentlemen. Load up," Dunn said.

The men traipsed over to their truck. Goerdt jumped in the cab and started it.

They got their snowshoes off, helped the prisoners get in, and climbed aboard themselves. Dunn joined Goerdt in the cab.

A few minutes later they reached the checkpoint. Goerdt didn't bother stopping for it and it snapped off, flying into the snow like a javelin.

Dunn checked his watch. "Two minutes, guys." To Goerdt, he said, "Pull over there, Rob." He pointed.

Goerdt stopped the truck. They were facing north on the switchback, so the radar station was to their right.

"If you guys want to watch, raise the canvas on the right side."

Everyone wanted to see their work, so a couple of the guys rolled up the canvas side. All waited impatiently.

"Ten seconds." Dunn raised his binoculars.

Simultaneously, a series of explosions lit the night sky to the left of the radar station building. A few seconds later, the building exploded and caught fire. The explosions echoed off the mountain, lasting quite some time.

The masts, having lost their support, teetered for a few seconds, and tipped over backwards falling off the ridge, disappearing from view. Dunn knew they were probably sliding down the mountain peak on the Italian side of the border. *Won't they be happy?* he thought with a smile.

The building's roof peak sagged for a second, then collapsed as Dunn had hoped. Fire began to spread. An explosion from the other side of the building, the fuel for the generator, shot skyward. Flame engulfed the entire building. He figured it could be seen for miles. He lowered the binoculars. His men were watching the events raptly. He hated to interrupt, but . . .

"Got to go, men."

The same men rolled down the canvas to stave off the wind.

"Let's go, Rob," Dunn said.

Goerdt nodded and drove off.

"That was pretty damn awesome," Goerdt said.

"It sure was. We do very fine work, wouldn't you say?"

"I would, Sarge."

The drive down was marginally faster, but with the switchbacks, it seemed to take forever. Goerdt had to keep the truck in second gear to prevent it from building up too much speed, and to save on the brakes. Reaching the valley, he turned toward the airfield.

Dunn examined the airfield. He was a little surprised everything seemed the same as they'd left it. None of the buildings had lights on. No vehicles were moving. Their plane was still sitting where they'd left it.

Goerdt drove up near their Junkers. The rear door popped open and the copilot stuck his head out and waved. Dunn waved back through the truck's windshield.

While the squad got out of the truck, the pilot and copilot started the three engines. The men boarded and took their seats.

Dunn placed the two prisoners at the rear of the plane and assigned Schneider to guard them, telling him he would get relief in one hour.

Dunn stepped through the cockpit door. "Mission accomplished, sir."

"Great!" the pilot said. "We heard it, and saw the place go up from here. Rather spectacular fireworks."

"Yes, sir. Any problems while we were gone?"

"Ran out of coffee," the pilot said, smiling.

"I'll buy you some when we get back, sir."

"Deal."

Dunn left the cockpit.

The plane taxied to the far end of the airfield.

The copilot said urgently, "I see lights coming toward the field ahead." He pointed.

A truck was about a mile away headed right at them.

The pilot grit his teeth and turned the plane around as fast as possible.

He shoved the throttles all the way forward. The engines roared and the skis glided over the snow.

The copilot opened his sliding window and peeked out to watch the approaching truck.

"They're about a half mile back."

The plane picked up speed rapidly.

As they neared the rotation point, which was when the pilot would pull back on the yoke, the copilot said, "They're about a quarter mile back and seem to be giving up." He slid his window shut and sighed. "Thank God."

The pilot pulled the yoke backwards and the plane leapt into the sky. He kept the yoke back for a long time. They had a whale of a mountain peak to clear.

The pilot banked left and the plane soared over the obstacle.

"Tell Sergeant Dunn we're safe and on the way back to Rimini."

"Roger, sir."

Dunn accepted the news gratefully and passed the word.

He glanced out the port window and spotted the still burning radar station. It was like a beacon.

Everyone settled back in their seats, except for Schneider, and were asleep in a minute. *Mountain fighting is damn hard work,* was Dunn's last thought.

Chapter 15

The Farm, Area B-2, Catoctin Mountain Park
11 December, 0122 Hours, U.S. Eastern Standard Time

The ten women of The Farm's current class stood in a line outside the mess/classroom building. There were no lights on indoors or out. The dark sky was mostly clear with strands of wispy clouds laid across it like lint on a dark jacket. The stars were bright and twinkling. A helpful moon was a waning crescent, which amounted to about twenty-five percent of the moon being alight. Visibility on the ground was quite good because the ladies' eyes had dilated for thirty minutes.

Rick, the main instructor, stood in front of the women, waiting mostly patiently along with them for his eyes to reach maximum night vision. It varied of course by person, so they waited another fifteen minutes to make sure.

It was twenty-eight degrees out with a ten mile an hour northerly wind, which didn't help anyone stay warm.

When he thought the extra fifteen minutes had passed, Rick rolled over his wrist, keeping it some distance from his face. The luminous watch hands told him it was 01:37 hours.

"All right, ladies, time."

The women broke into two predetermined teams of five each. Gertrude led one of the teams and Edna the other.

The two teams lined up behind their leaders. Rick moved so he could see each woman's face.

"Night operations will make up the bulk of your work when you get to your assigned location. There's a good reason for this. No one can see you, at least if you're careful. But the opposite is true, too. You can't see the enemy if they're tucked away in a good hiding spot.

"Remember, look everywhere. Stay inside vegetation whenever possible. Never cross an open space. Instead, follow the vegetation around the perimeter. Never, ever look up at the sky when moonlight could shine on you. Your face makes a perfect reflective surface and will look like a headlight to someone who has their night vision in full force, like you do now."

"Each team has three goals. First, to safely reach the target without being spotted by our training staff who could be anywhere. Second, to take the object from the target location, and finally third, to reach this point, without being captured, and to drop your object in that red fire bucket."

He pointed at the bucket on the ground.

"Any questions?"

There weren't any.

Rick checked his watch: 01:43.

"You have forty-five minutes from now. You must return the object here no later than oh two twenty-eight hours." He clapped his hands together once. "Go!" He shouted.

Edna's team immediately broke into a run, heading directly west.

Gertrude gathered her women close. All the women wore black pants and jackets, plus black gloves and shoes. Each of her women pulled a watch cap out of a back pocket. Normally, one would wear the watch cap with part of it rolled up an inch or so, and place it so it covered the forehead. All of Gertrude's team pulled the watch cap down over their faces, adjusting them so the balaclava-like eye opening was correctly positioned.

Mildred wondered why Gertrude and her team were taking their time instead of running off right away. When she realized they'd created their own balaclavas, evidently with scissors earlier that night, she spoke up, angry, "Hey now. That's cheating!"

Rick glanced over and immediately realized what Mildred was complaining about. He stomped over to stand in front of Gertrude, who stared at him through the narrow opening in the watch cap.

"That's against the rules, Peggy."

"What is, sir?" Gertrude asked sweetly.

"Why you—"

Rick held up a hand to silence a sputtering Mildred.

"You aren't wearing the clothing you were given."

"Sir, I listened very carefully to your instructions earlier, after dinner. What you said was we had to wear the clothing we were given. You didn't say we couldn't alter anything."

"You—but—" Rick shook his head when he realized Peggy was right. He hadn't said anything at all about altering the gear in any way.

"Fine. Your clothing is approved."

"Sir!" Mildred protested. "You're giving her an unfair advantage."

"I'm rewarding her for adapting, Mildred. Something they'll all have to know how to do in the field. Team two, best be on your way."

Gertrude wasn't going to waste any more time. She did however throw a glance at Mildred as she ran past her. She got eyeball daggers in return. Unable to help herself, she laughed as she ran into the night, her four teammates right behind her.

Rick looked at Mildred, disapproval heavy on his face. "Mildred . . ."

She glanced at him, barely able to hide her displeasure. "What?" she snapped.

"You're making this personal between you and Peggy. You've got to cut it out."

"She just rubs me the wrong way."

"Oh, Mildred. Can't you hear yourself?"

"Well, it's true."

"It's one thing to be hard on a candidate and quite another to go out of your way to antagonize one. Repeatedly. It has to stop."

"What? Or else?"

"You are important to our work here. Up until now, you've conducted yourself in a very professional manner. So yes, this is an or else. Change your behavior or I'll have to talk to David about whether to reassign you elsewhere."

Although Rick wasn't the leader of The Farm, he naturally had the ear of David Walker, who was.

Mildred looked away in the darkness. Deciding she'd rather not be reassigned even if it meant putting up with the smart aleck young woman, she turned back to Rick. Taking a deep breath, as if it pained her, she said, "It won't happen again. I'm sorry, sir."

"Good. I need you here."

"Okay."

"Let's go inside and get some coffee while we wait."

The two instructors went inside.

Gertrude led her team toward the nearest woods on the right. This put them about fifty yards north of the building they'd just left, home base, it was called for the exercise. As soon as they entered the darker confines of the woods, she halted the team and had everyone kneel in a tight circle.

The women each carried a .38 Police Special with no ammunition, not even blanks. The idea was simply to get them used to the weight of a weapon on their hips. A rubber practice combat knife was in a sheath on their offhand side. For Gertrude, that was her left.

"Does everyone know exactly where we are relative to the target?" she asked, whispering.

All four replied with a soft, "Yes."

"Great."

Gertrude was quite happy with her teammates. Although the teams had been created at random by Rick, she'd drawn her tall friend Ruby, Pearl, who sounded like she was from the Deep South, Marjorie, the obvious New York City woman, and Anna, who was likely from the Midwest like Gertrude.

"We're going to stick to the plan. Everyone ready?"

The women nodded, which Gertrude could just barely see in the moonlight filtering through the naked tree branches above.

"You have your whistles?"

They nodded again.

"Good. Remember to use them."

Gertrude rose and strode off without looking back. Each woman would leave thirty seconds after the previous woman departed in a prearranged order, but would take a slightly different route. Splitting up seemed to Gertrude a good way of increasing the possibility that at least one of them would reach the target. The team had agreed and they'd made plans for several eventualities.

She moved lithely through the woods stopping behind large trees to examine the way ahead before continuing. After traveling about two hundred more yards in this start and stop fashion, she halted for a longer period, kneeling. She should be only fifty yards from the target. Since no one knew where the other instructors would station themselves, it was difficult to guess where they could be, although, to her, it stood to reason that the area around the target would be rich with adversaries.

As she looked around the dark woods, she couldn't help but wonder how humans had survived against predators like big cats and wolves, who could see at night as if the sun was shining. She used her ears instead of her vision, tuning in to the slightest sounds. Some of them were the result of the north wind pushing branches around that scraped against each other and creaked under the weight shift. It was far too cold for insect life sounds, but she did hear a small squeak a few yards away and a patter of tiny feet across some fallen leaves. She wondered whether there were any owls out here looking for a dinner. She also wondered whether she would even hear it if it flew down to grab the furry snack.

Focusing ahead with her eyes, she let them relax and examined the periphery of her sight line, since that part of the eye was far more sensitive to light. A human shape moved not ten yards away, a little to her right. When she looked directly at it, she lost it and had to resume using her peripheral vision. She reacquired the person, who was kneeling behind what might be a large oak tree. The person was facing Gertrude's line of travel. If she hadn't stopped when she did, she'd have stumbled right into the trap.

She smiled to herself. Had she been lucky or had some sixth sense warned her? She shrugged silently. Didn't matter. She knew where the enemy was. All she had to do was take him or her out.

She started moving stealthily, making sure before she stepped down, that her foot wouldn't break a twig or rustle a pile of leaves. She moved far to the right of the person, ninety degrees from her previous position, due east. She knew she was getting close to the line of travel for Ruby, who would have left after her. Hopefully they wouldn't collide and give themselves away.

Judging she was south-southeast of her enemy, she turned left and stopped behind another tree. She eyed the person's location and found the shape in the same spot. Selecting the next tree to use, which was only four yards ahead, she made it there soundlessly. She advanced to the next one, which put her directly east of the enemy, who was still facing west. Gertrude was behind the tree, and looked out from the right side. She gauged the final distance to the person to be three yards. Two long steps. Examining the ground between them, she found it clear of leaves and twigs.

She slowly pulled her revolver from its holster, careful not to create noise against the leather.

Taking a quiet deep breath, she let it out slowly.

She pounced. In just two long steps, and as quick as a cat, she was behind her enemy, dropping to her knees and snaking her left arm around and covering the mouth with her gloved hand. She yanked back and jammed the barrel of the revolver into the back.

"Bang," she said softly. "You're dead."

The person raised his hands. "Well done, Peggy," he whispered, through Gertrude's gloved hand.

Gertrude nearly let go out of surprise. She turned the man around. "David?" She almost forgot to whisper.

David Walker smiled in the moonlight and nodded.

She let go and holstered her weapon.

Walker sat down, leaning against the tree, crossing his legs.

He saluted her.

According to the rules, he would have to stay there, and remain quiet until the exercise was finished. If another enemy combatant found him, he could not speak or in any way give them any clues.

She nodded at him and took a position behind the tree so she could see ahead. She patted him on the shoulder, and started moving stealthily through the woods. She reached a small clearing, one that was perhaps five yards across. In the center, on the ground sat a black box with a handle. Rather than just dashing out to grab the target, she started slowly walking clockwise around the clearing at a distance of two yards.

Suddenly, from somewhere to the east a whistle blew sharply three times. That was Anna's signal as she'd been third to leave. She'd been caught. The rules said that a person capturing one of the trainees must take that prisoner directly back to the building and wait there. That meant there would be a gap in that direction, if anyone needed it.

She finished her circle and found no one, which surprised her. Had she missed someone?

She thought it over for a short time, planning her next steps.

Making her decision, she crept closer to the edge of the clearing and stopped once more. She watched and listened. Nothing. Still she was wary. It would be about four running steps to reach the box and four more to exit the clearing. Perhaps five seconds in total.

She lowered her body almost to a runner's starting position and drew her revolver.

Dashing across the clearing, she bent over, snatching the box off the ground in mid-stride. She reentered the woods, but didn't stop. She continued to run south. She streaked past a surprised— again—David Walker.

She ran another hundred yards and suddenly turned left, east, going a couple of more steps before stopping suddenly, leaning against a tree. Breathing hard and trying to be quiet about it, she eyed the woods in all directions. Nothing. She started walking, carefully now.

Another whistle went off behind her. Two blasts: Ruby caught.

She estimated she was only seventy-five yards from the building. She looked ahead, using her peripheral vision again. Another shape materialized not far from her, to the left. It had moved in response to the whistle and stopped. The person appeared to be looking right at her, but she didn't think they knew she was there.

She got down in a prone position and began to crawl to the left. She periodically stopped to raise her head slightly and check on the person. Still there. Before too long she had maneuvered herself behind her second enemy. She rose to her feet quietly.

This time, she stopped a couple of feet from the person's back. This one appeared to be female. She pointed her gun at the woman's back.

"Bang!" she whispered.

"Oh heck."

The woman, who went by the name of Norma, turned slowly and stared at Gertrude. Surprised by the makeshift balaclava, Norma leaned closer. "Who is that? Peggy?" She whispered.

"Yep."

"Off you go." Norma, like Walker, sat down and leaned against the tree.

Just as Gertrude started to leave, Norma whispered, "I have five bucks on you. Don't let me down."

This surprised Gertrude. The instructors were betting on who might win? Huh.

She refocused and moved to the south edge of the woods, which placed her only fifty more yards from home base. This might be the most difficult part: running across the clearing before someone could catch her. She examined the sides of the building where someone could be hiding, but the left side was all in shadow. She could see no one.

What was the best way? To dash the distance? Or to advance in a crawl to get closer before a shorter dash? She elected to crawl half the distance. If it backfired, so be it.

Her slender dark form snaked across the clearing, moving slowly and smoothly. She kept her eye on the red fire bucket, although it looked black in the moonlight. She stopped and prepared to leap to her feet. She still saw no one.

She jumped up and ran.

A dark shape broke away from the side of the building she'd worried about, the shadow side. The form streaked toward her.

She sped up.

The form altered directions to intercept Gertrude just before she could reach the bucket.

Gertrude measured the distance. It was going to be close.

When the form was a couple of yards from intercepting Gertrude, it dove for her, trying to tackle her at the knees.

Gertrude timed her leap and hurdled the person's outstretched hands. She landed hard near the bucket, twisted her body and slammed the box into the bucket. It made a huge clanging sound.

Rick opened the door and stepped out. He ran over to Gertrude, who'd stopped and turned around to face her enemy, who was still on the ground.

She stepped over and held out her hand.

Mildred looked up with steam in her eyes. She suddenly seemed to calm down, grabbed Gertrude's hand and got up.

The three women from the other team appeared and the one in front dropped her box into the bucket.

Rick blew his whistle, stopping the exercise.

Ruby and Anna exited the woods behind Gertrude, followed by their captors. Gertrude had beaten them through the woods. They ran over and hugged her. Soon, all the women were gathered around in a loose circle.

Rick stepped closer. "Well done, ladies. You nearly broke the record on time. Maybe the next time, huh?"

The women cheered.

"Anyone want some ice cream?"

He got no argument there and everyone trooped inside.

Gertrude was happy to have won the challenge for her team.

But she was far happier to have bested Mildred.

Again.

RONN MUNSTERMAN

Chapter 16

Sardinia's east coast
Between Muravera and San Priamo
14 December, 0442 Hours, 3 days later

As the German U-boat sank beneath the waters of the Tyrrhenian Sea, *Sturmbannführer, SS* Major, Erich Becker and his men set about hiding their two rubber dinghies under a camouflage net and loose sand. When finished with that task, the men knelt behind the sandy ridge hiding them from view of anyone on the road that ran parallel to the beach. Sunrise would begin at 6:34 am and become fully lit an hour and four minutes later. He planned to be at his base camp location well before then.

He'd felt honored to have been selected by Skorzeny for this mission. When the colonel had told him that he was leading the mission in his place, he was quite surprised. When he asked why Skorzeny wasn't going, the colonel had simply said he was working on something else important for the *Führer*.

The whine of large tires carried on the southerly breeze. A moment later, he lifted his head to peer over the sand ridge and spotted two farm trucks headed his way from the south.

"Get ready, men."

He'd brought nineteen of his best Waffen SS soldiers with him, none with a rank lower than *Oberscharführer*, Staff Sergeant. They were elite combat veterans who had a history of superior performance in some of the toughest campaigns including Russia and Italy. They ranged in age from twenty-six to thirty-one, and all were at least six-three in height. Any one of them could have been a poster boy for the Aryan Nazis with their blond hair and blue eyes.

The men wore clothes matching what a farm laborer on the island of Sardinia would wear: dark trousers, boots, tan shirts, and dark brown or black coats. For weapons they each carried a 9mm MP40 submachine gun that could fire at a rate of 500 rounds a minute, a 9mm Luger named for its inventor, Austrian Georg Johann Luger, a combat knife, and a steel-wire garrote. Four potato masher grenades were located in pockets sewn into the inside of the coat, two on each side. Extra magazines for both weapons were carried on the belt. Two smoke grenades were in the outside coat pockets. A canteen was also hooked to the belt. Some tins of food were in a small pack, but only enough for a few days.

The trucks slowed as the drivers, recruited from amongst the German spy Heinz Schulz's group of trusted men, recognized their first destination. Becker stood and stepped over the ridge toward the road, a hand raised as if flagging down a taxi in Berlin. The lead driver spotted Becker's large frame and pulled over to a stop on the side of the road. The second truck stopped right behind the first, leaving room behind for the men.

Becker pulled his Luger from its holster, holding it by his thigh, and stepped up onto the running board. He spoke to the driver in unaccented Italian, "I hear Cagliari is wonderful this time of year."

The driver, a man in his thirties with dark hair and dark eyes, replied, "You'll enjoy your stay at the Savelli."

Becker nodded and stepped back down, holstering the Luger. He turned and waved at his men. Nine men separated from the group and headed toward the back of the first truck, while the other ten aimed for the second one. Becker joined the group going to the second vehicle.

While nine of the men climbed into the back of the truck, Becker spoke to his second in command, *Hauptsturmführer*, Captain, Horst Messer. The man was Becker's size but a few years younger. They'd been together for two years and the major explicitly trusted him with his life.

"I'll see you at our gathering point, Horst. I know you'll be careful."

"Yes, sir. I will be. Have a safe trip yourself."

Becker nodded and the two men shook hands.

Becker walked back to his truck.

Both leaders doublechecked that their men were sitting down in the back and as comfortable as they could be. They also checked to make sure their MP40s were hidden from view. Afterwards, they stepped up and got in the truck cabs.

"Ready," Becker said simply.

The driver nodded and drove off, headed north for Muravera. From there he would follow a mostly east-west road through the mountains and come out north of Cagliari. He would turn south until it was time to turn off toward the base camp location, which was a few kilometers northwest of Villa Bellavista, the eventual target.

Messer's driver did a three-point-turn on the empty road and headed back south. He would drive through San Priamo and on to Cagliari from the southeast, making his way through the city to the north. He would turn off at the same point, and close to the same time as the first truck, and take his passengers to their destination.

Becker had spent considerable time preparing the mission. He was confident that splitting up the team and sending each squad by a different route improved the odds for at least one reaching the destination and successfully assassinating the president and the prime minister. He felt that the odds were high both groups would make it to the base camp location.

Friends in America had provided some information about Roosevelt's protection detail called the Secret Service. The one thing that stood out was the background of all the men: they were either former police officers or had worked for the FBI. They were not soldiers. They wouldn't have the experience needed to defend against a firefight initiated by his superior fighters. He had seen one photograph of the men standing on the steps of a large building, perhaps in the American capital, Washington, D.C. They looked more like bankers with their long coats and bowler or fedora hats. The youngest man looked to be forty or more while the rest were ten to twenty years older. As for Churchill, the egomaniac only had one bodyguard, a detective inspector with Scotland yard, who was in his mid-fifties. Even if he brought extra men and they all came with the president and prime minister, they would stand no chance against his Waffen SS.

Not a chance in hell.

Chapter 17

Colonel Mark Kenton's office
Camp Barton Stacey
14 December, 0600 Hours, London time

A bigger than usual crowd gathered in Colonel Kenton's office. Kenton took his usual place behind his desk with his aide, Lieutenant Tanner, seated on the colonel's right. Colonel Rupert Jenkins and his aide, Lieutenant Mallory, sat to the left of Kenton's desk. In front of the desk from Kenton's left to right were Dunn, Cross, Saunders, and Barltrop completing a kind of oval shape of soldiers.

Dunn and his squad had arrived back from the Rimini, Italy airfield around dinner time the same day as the attack on the radar station, which was three days ago. He'd debriefed the colonel on the Alps mission including the handing over of the radar station prisoners to Intelligence. Kenton enjoyed that almost as much as the blowing up of the station and its masts. A few days off helped the men get fully rested after such a physically demanding adventure up a mountainside.

Saunders and his men had returned the previous morning after a little more than two days traveling by sub. Fortunately, with nothing to do on the submarine trip back, they were all caught up on sleep, too. That afternoon, Saunders had given Jenkins a mission debrief and passed on the spectacular periscope pictures of the two cargo ships exploding and sinking beneath the harbor's water. Jenkins had made a somewhat in jest comment about framing one or two for his office. He told Saunders that the Swedish government had officially and indignantly complained about the attack on their sovereignty. The British reply had been sent back in two parts, one official and one through the back channels. Officially, "We don't know what you're talking about." Back channels, "That's what happens when a neutral country aids a belligerent country. Don't do it again or suffer the same."

Saunders had received the call from Lieutenant Mallory announcing this meeting just before he was about to give the men a day off. He postponed saying anything about leave until he found out what the meeting was about.

"Thanks for being here at this hour, gentlemen," Kenton began. He opened the lone manila folder on his desk. It was about a quarter-inch thick, which made Dunn lift an eyebrow. Thicker than most.

"This all started with the Nazi *Operation Rösselsprung*, which translates to 'Long Jump.' You'll recall that Roosevelt, Churchill, and Stalin met in Tehran, Iran a year ago in November."

Everyone nodded. It had been in the news.

"What's not publicly known is the SS planned to assassinate all three men."

"Son of a bitch," Dunn said.

"Bloody hell," Saunders said.

Kenton nodded. "My sentiments exactly. Obviously, it was a failed mission, but Intelligence just stumbled onto a second plot. This time it's to assassinate Roosevelt and Churchill. They're having another conference, without Stalin, in Sardinia.

"They arrived late evening the day before yesterday, the twelfth. Our problem is, through Bletchley Park, we just learned a German SS unit arrived a little more than an hour ago somewhere on the island, so we have to move fast. Even though they both have their own security detail, they're concerned about having the manpower to fight off a concerted effort by the Germans. The location they've jointly selected is a villa on about fifty acres. The house is on a hilltop that is perhaps two hundred yards long by a hundred and fifty. It overlooks the small town of Sinnai."

"Can't their security detail move them back to the airbase?" Dunn asked.

Kenton shook his head. "They're deathly afraid if they leave the location, they might get ambushed on the road down. In addition, there's only airbase security, not any army units. They'd rather stay put."

Dunn nodded thinking, *oh, crap.* "Understood, sir," he said.

Kenton stood and pointed at the large pinewood map table behind Lieutenant Tanner. "Let's go see what you're up against."

Everyone else got up and migrated to stand around the table where a detailed map of Sardinia lay spread out. Dunn and Saunders took positions beside Kenton. Cross and Barltrop stood to the side of the table near Dunn and Saunders

Using a pencil he picked up from the map table, Kenton tapped a spot just north of Sinnai. "Here's where the villa is located. It's called Villa Bellavista, which I gather means 'beautiful view.' It was built in 1903 and is something like ten thousand square feet, so a mansion."

Dunn whistled at the size. "And they thought they could secure a place that big?"

Kenton shrugged.

Dunn and Saunders leaned over the map.

Kenton stepped back to give them room to work. He glanced over at Jenkins, who smiled and nodded. The two men had come to truly respect each other after a rather fiery beginning that resulted from Jenkins' belief that the British way was the *only* way. Naturally, that was in strict opposition to Kenton's way of thinking. Over time, and after many successes by their respective units, their stubborn beliefs fell to the wayside and they currently enjoyed perhaps one of the better Anglo-American relationships amongst their peers.

Dunn stood upright and turned to face Kenton. "Sir, is it safe to say you want us there yesterday?"

Kenton smiled at the old standby army phrase for "urgent." "You're correct."

Dunn looked at Kenton's aide. "Lieutenant Tanner, could you get a few things for us, or tell me where they are and I'll go get them."

Tanner appreciated the way Dunn phrased the question with respect to their different ranks. He nodded. "I'm more than happy to gather whatever you need, Sergeant."

"Excellent, thank you, sir."

He rattled off a list of things that included, perhaps most importantly, lots of hot black coffee.

Tanner wrote a list. "I'll be back." He left the office.

Kenton nodded at Jenkins. "Colonel, we may as well have a seat." He waved at the chair where Jenkins had been sitting.

"Thank you."

The two men sat. They'd learned long ago to give the two sergeants the mission goal and get out of their way. Lieutenant Mallory joined his boss.

Cross and Barltrop edged closer for a better look at the map.

Tanner returned pushing a cart with a steaming pot of coffee and some cups. The men swarmed the coffee cart while Tanner laid out on the table the notebooks, papers, and rulers Dunn had requested.

After the Rangers and Commandos had gotten their coffees, and settled back into their work, the officers rose to leave the office, taking their coffee and cigarettes with them.

Dunn glanced up as Kenton reached the door. The colonel looked back, winked and went out the door. Dunn smiled and went back to work. A few friendly arguments arose during the planning of the mission with Dunn, Saunders, Cross, or Barltrop disagreeing ardently over some point or other. When they were done, though, they had a comprehensive security plan as well as several contingency plans.

Dunn took the last sip of his now cold coffee and set the cup back down. He checked the time on the wall clock to his right: 6:52. It had taken around forty or forty-five minutes to get it done.

"I'll go get the officers," Cross offered.

"Okay, thanks," Dunn said. He turned to Saunders. "How's Sadie doing, Mac?"

"She's feeling pretty good. Morning's are still pretty rough. Going through all of our biscuits pretty fast."

Dunn nodded grimly. He remembered Pamela's morning sickness bouts, which had finally faded away. "Glad she's okay, though."

"Aye, thanks."

Dunn looked at Barltrop. "Any news about you and Kathy?"

Barltrop shrugged, but smiled gamely. "Still going steady. Not much else to tell."

Dunn nodded.

"How's Pamela getting along?" Barltrop asked.

"Real well. She's in her fourth month, so the morning sickness has gone away. She's just so happy that's over. She's shopping for, uh, larger dresses. Starting to show and everything is getting tighter."

Saunders and Barltrop nodded solemnly.

Cross burst back in with the officers in tow. Everyone resumed their previous spot around the map table.

Dunn and Saunders went over the mission plan and the contingencies in thorough detail. Jenkins or Kenton asked questions here or there for clarification. When Dunn and Saunders were done, Kenton asked one last question: "You really want to capture at least one of the attackers?"

Dunn shrugged. "We might get names of who's authorizing these missions."

"I get it. As long as the mission isn't compromised."

"No, sir, of course."

"Do you need anything from Colonel Jenkins or me?"

"Just transportation, which I'll work out with Lieutenant Tanner. Oh, and one question. Are the security details expecting us?"

Kenton chuckled. "You might say that. You were requested by Roosevelt himself."

Dunn's eyebrows shot up. "Really?"

"Really. And Sergeant Saunders was requested by Churchill. When you arrive at the airfield, you can request a couple of trucks for transport to the villa. Lieutenant Tanner will arrange it. The man heading up the president's security is Agent Elmer Perkins and the one for Churchill's is Detective Inspector Walter Thompson. You should expect their full cooperation."

Dunn somehow didn't think so. He was about to infringe on their area of expertise from the outside. But he said, "That's great to know, sir."

The meeting adjourned with Dunn and Saunders grabbing up their notes, and the map—with permission from Kenton.

Once outside standing near their separate cars, Dunn asked, "Mac, you want to bring your guys over for a mission brief?"

"Aye. We can be there in maybe fifteen minutes."

"Great, see you all soon."

The four men shook hands all around and got into their cars; Dunn and Cross in a jeep with its canvas cover on, and Saunders and Barltrop in an Austin 8AP Military Tourer staff car.

As the men drove off, Saunders in the lead, Cross said as he drove, "Never thought we'd be protecting the president of the United States."

Dunn shook his head. "Me neither, buddy, me neither."

Chapter 18

Villa Bellavista
1 mile north of Sinnai, Sardinia
Elevation 1,100 feet
14 December, 1440 Hours, later the same day

Dunn, Saunders, and their men jumped down from the two massive deuce and a half trucks that had transported them the eight miles from the U.S. airfield located three miles north of Cagliari. It had been uphill all the way since the city was mostly at sea level and the villa was perched at 1,100 feet.

Cross and Barltrop had driven the behemoths.

The Rangers and Commandos had gotten their weapons and gear ready, and traveled to Hampstead Airbase in less than two hours. The nearly five-and-a-half-hour flight had been uneventful.

Dunn set down his two travel bags and looked out at the bay directly south. It was breathtaking, and the villa certainly lived up to its name "beautiful view." A ribbon of brilliant turquoise followed the shoreline. Farther out, the glittering Mediterranean Sea followed the Earth's curvature. Dunn recalled the formula for distance to the horizon and calculated it was around forty miles. The north coast of Africa, near Tunis, the capital of Tunisia, was perhaps another ninety.

The temperature seemed to be in the mid-fifties and a pleasant, sea smelling breeze blew across the hilltop from the south.

Cross sidled up next to him. "Incredible. Nothing quite like this in Maine."

Dunn chuckled. "Nor Iowa."

The rest of the men lined up with Dunn and Cross and stared at the sea in wonder.

Footsteps sounded on the gravel driveway behind the men, but no one was interested in shifting his view.

"Who the hell's in charge here?" growled a low voice.

Dunn and Saunders turned around to find a man in his fifties scowling at the men taking in the panorama.

"We are," Dunn said, stepping forward. He was about to offer his hand when the man spoke again.

"You're not paid to enjoy the view." The man's eyes had zeroed in on Dunn.

Stifling a reply in kind, Dunn simply stared at the man. He was about five-ten and wore a gray suit and gray fedora. Dunn spotted the bulge in the suit jacket in front of the left armpit. *A large pistol, probably a .38 Police Special,* he thought. The man's eyes incredibly matched his suit and seemed just as cold. Lines crinkled around his eyes. Dunn was certain they weren't laughter lines.

He decided to offer his hand anyway. "Tom Dunn, sir."

Reluctantly gripping Dunn's hand, the man shifted his gaze for a moment to Saunders, taking in the red hair and mustache, then looked back at Dunn. He let go disdainfully. He eyed the M1 slung on Dunn's right shoulder and he sniffed as if it was an unworthy weapon.

"Agent Elmer Perkins. I'm in charge of the president's detail."

"Glad to meet you, sir. This is Malcom Saunders, our British counterpart."

"I already figured that out, Dunn."

Saunders grunted. Dunn recognized it for what it was. His friend was sorely pissed off. He related.

Again, rather than rising to the bait of the rude remark, Dunn remained calm. "Congratulations on selecting such a good place, sir."

Perkins looked down his nose—a neat trick for a man four inches shorter—at Dunn for a few seconds longer than was polite. "I don't need your approval."

Ignoring yet another insult, Dunn said, "Where do you want us to park the trucks, sir?"

Perkins pointed to the west where a gravel parking lot was located, accessible from the front drive.

"And where do you want us?"

"Not here." Perkins snapped around and stomped off toward what appeared to be the villa's main entrance.

Dunn wondered whether the man meant not to discuss it here, or actually "don't want you here at all." He decided on the latter. He was surprised they hadn't been told to use the servants' side door.

When Perkins was safely out of hearing distance, Saunders muttered, "Never did like Yanks."

Dunn laughed. "That's okay, we don't like you either."

Saunders punched Dunn in the arm.

Cross and Barltrop climbed back into the massive trucks and parked them. They double-timed back to the men.

The two squad leaders corralled their men and formed two columns. As they marched toward the door, Dunn was thinking he was glad the men hadn't heard the unfriendly comments Perkins made. He fully expected them to quickly learn of the man's obvious anger at their presence.

As he led the men he took in the villa. A monstrosity of a structure, it was three stories tall and was at least seventy-five feet wide. On the drive in, he'd estimated the depth of the villa at forty to fifty feet, making its three floors easily total the 10,000 square feet Colonel Kenton had mentioned. The stucco exterior was painted pastel yellow. Bright white paint trimmed the doors and windows. Above the wide entrance was a second-floor porch supported by white posts. French doors opened onto the porch. At ground level, clay pots of all sizes were filled with multicolor flowers. Towering palm trees surrounded the house. The double front doors wore a huge Christmas wreath above.

He spotted several suited men walking around the villa, their eyes outward. Dunn nodded mentally. At least Perkins had sense enough to post guards.

Perkins disappeared through the double door entrance where two more men in suits stood guard. At the bottom of the stairs leading to the entrance, Saunders halted his men to allow Dunn and his men to go first. The men trooped up the stairs and entered the villa's foyer. The floor was white tile and the walls a turquoise that nearly matched the ribbon of water in the bay. A winding square-shaped staircase to the upper floors began to the left. A gold and crystal chandelier hung from the three-story ceiling inside the staircase's open-air square. Underneath the chandelier stood a twenty-foot tall decorated Christmas tree.

Perkins stood impatiently at the foot of the stairs, his arms folded. Another man stood beside him, but he wore a noncommittal expression.

Dunn stopped the squad when he reached a point near Perkins.

Perkins tipped his head toward the man with him. "This is Agent Bryant. He'll show you where you'll be sleeping. After you put your stuff away meet us in that room." He pointed to a large room to Dunn's right. It appeared to have been set up for a lot of people with wooden chairs arranged like a classroom.

"Will do, sir," Dunn said. Without waiting for another comment from Perkins, he nodded to Bryant, who turned and led the way up the stairs. The Rangers and Commandos followed as he led them to the third floor. He stopped in the hallway at the top of the stairs.

Pointing to Dunn's right he said, "Americans down this way. First three rooms on the right, two on the left. Two men per room. Bath is at the far end of the hall. British the other way, first three on the *left* and two on the *right*. Another bath at that end of the hall."

Dunn nodded, and said, "Thank you, Agent Bryant."

"You're welcome."

Bryant, a slender man in his late fifties with gray hair gave Dunn a smile. He lowered his voice, "Most of us are glad you're here, Sergeant."

Dunn grinned. In an equally low voice he replied, "Thank you for saying so, sir."

Bryant stepped back against the wall to make room for the twenty men to get by to their respective rooms.

Dunn set down his travel duffels and directed traffic as the men paraded by him. He passed on Perkins' meeting room request to the men asking them to meet him right here in five.

After the last man passed by, he grabbed his duffels and went down the hall to the third room on the right, where he'd told Cross to go. He walked into the small room. Two utilitarian beds were set up on the right side a few feet apart. One window let in the bright afternoon sunshine. On the left stood a wooden wardrobe.

Cross had his bags on the bed. His rifle stood in the corner between the bed and the exterior wall. He was already busy unpacking the duffel with clothes in it. The other bag carried a Thompson .45 submachine gun, magazines and clips for his weapons, a half-dozen pineapple grenades, and a combat knife all wrapped carefully in cloth. His 1911 Colt .45 was on his right hip.

"Not bad, huh?" Cross asked.

"It'll do in a pinch. Nice of you to take the bed by the window. The mosquitos will find you first."

Cross grunted. "Thanks ever so much," he said, mimicking Wickham's Brit-Tex accent.

"My pleasure."

The two friends finished their unpacking and left the room. When they arrived at the top of the staircase, all the men were there waiting. Saunders and Barltrop stood closest to the stairs.

"You ready to go meet with your friend?" Saunders asked, grinning. His mustache twitched as he chuckled.

Dunn shook his head. "Not my friend. Let's go."

He started down the stairs and a stream of Rangers and Commandos followed.

RONN MUNSTERMAN

Chapter 19

Major Becker's mountain base camp
2.9 kilometers northeast of Villa Bellavista
Elevation 365 meters
14 December, 1459 Hours

Heinz Schulz took his hat off and wiped his brow as he approached the encampment's location. It had been only a kilometer's hike from his car, but it was all uphill. The rise in elevation had been about sixty meters over that span of distance making it about a six percent grade. Steep, but not unmanageable. Still, enough to cause him to sweat even on a cool day. His ankle began to throb even though he was using his cane.

Unknowingly, he'd passed by two farm trucks that were hidden in a grove of trees, covered with branches. A dead body sat in each one behind the steering wheel.

A tall man he assumed to be a German soldier emerged from a hiding place, his angry-looking submachine gun aimed at Schulz's chest.

The soldier didn't tell him to stop advancing, so Schulz continued walking toward him. He stopped a couple of meters away. He gave the soldier a code phrase. The soldier immediately and silently turned and led the way. Schulz followed a few meters behind. They wound their way through some thick shrubs and entered the forest. After a time, they popped out into a large clearing. Schulz spotted about fifteen more soldiers sitting on the ground eating. He assumed there were other men forming some sort of protective perimeter around the clearing.

Another tall man, wearing the same nondescript clothing as the others, walked toward Schulz, his hand extended.

Schulz met him and shook hands.

"I'm Major Becker," the man said, his eyes boring into Schulz's.

"Pleased to meet you, sir."

"You have the plans?"

Evidently Becker was done with the niceties. He didn't even care to know his contact's German name.

"Yes, sir." Schulz held up the small satchel he was carrying.

"Come." Becker nodded and took off. He stopped on the other side of the clearing and sat down. With a glance, he invited Schulz to sit beside him, which the spy did.

Schulz set the satchel on his cross-legged lap and opened it. Digging inside he removed a sheaf of folded papers and gave them to Becker.

Rather than attempt to explain the floor plans he'd taken from the governmental archive, Schulz just sat quietly. He watched the men eat their meal. There was little conversation. The only sounds were nearby birds in the trees and Becker rustling the papers.

Schulz turned his attention to what Becker seemed to be doing with the architect's floor plans of the Villa Bellavista. He had unfolded the plans for the first floor and set them on the ground to his right. Next came the elevation drawings, the view from a person looking at one of the four primary facades of a building. Becker intently examined each of the elevation drawings, and touched each wherever there was an entrance.

Suddenly, two more men seemed to appear out of the air from the south side of the clearing. They were dressed the same as the others, but were covered in leaves and twigs for camouflage. They carried automatic weapons over their shoulders.

Becker stopped what he was doing to look at them.

They joined Becker, nodding to Schulz, then seemed to forget he was there.

The major gave Schulz a stern look. "You've told no one we're here?"

Shocked by the question, Schulz replied tersely, "Absolutely not!"

Becker nodded, and rose. "*Herr* Schulz, thank you for these drawings. They should prove quite useful. I'll be sure to pass along to *Obergruppenführer* Kaltenbrunner just how helpful you've been."

Surprised and disappointed to be dismissed, Schulz was smart enough not to show it. He rose. "It's my pleasure to be of assistance, Major Becker. Do you care for me to leave you a telephone number in Cagliari where you can leave a message for me?"

"*Ja, Herr* Schulz, that's very gracious of you."

Schulz pulled out a crisp business card and handed it over.

"Thank you."

"Of course, Major."

"I'll have one of my men escort you back to your car."

"Thank you." Schulz offered his hand and Becker took it.

As Schulz walked away, the same man who'd met him outside the encampment joined him.

Schulz was looking ahead and didn't see the man turn to look over his shoulder and give Becker a questioning look.

Nor did he see the affirmative nod Becker gave.

Becker absentmindedly shoved the business card in his trousers pocket.

Major Becker and Captain Horst Messer sat down across from each other.

"Any problems?"

"None whatsoever. We were able to make a complete circle around the villa unseen. There were some guards walking a short perimeter, very close to the house, in fact. They all wore business suits and no weapons were visible which leads me to believe they are carrying pistols under their jackets, but that's all. Their patterns were regular, which I thought was careless and will be to our advantage."

"Dogs?"

"None."

"What about snipers?"

"None sighted. We looked very closely, sir, through our field glasses. Every window and every part of the roof top."

Becker nodded. He pointed at the elevation drawings. "Do these appear to reflect what you saw?"

Messer took the first elevation, which was from the south and showed the main entrance. He pulled a notebook from his jacket pocket and flipped a couple of pages. He had sketched the villa from each of the four cardinal compass points. He spent several minutes comparing each of his sketches to the architect's formal drawings. Whenever he spotted a discrepancy—only three—he penciled it in on the architect's drawing. He sat back when he finished.

"Overall, it is the same. As you saw, I noted some minor changes, all of which were the widening of three windows that face south. Presumably to take greater advantage of the Mediterranean sunlight."

Becker looked at the main entrance elevation and read the name of the architect and the date.

"The villa is quite young. Only forty-one years old. I'm surprised someone made those changes."

"Perhaps the original architect passed away or moved away and another one was brought in."

"Could be." Becker set the drawings aside and gazed at his second in command. "What's the road to the villa like?"

"Wide enough for three vehicles. Graded dirt and gravel. Appears to be fairly smooth. Leads away at roughly south-southwest."

"Any trees close enough to fell one or two to block reinforcements?"

Messer nodded. "Plenty to choose from. A grenade pack in the right place should do the trick."

"Good. That's good to know. How much time did it take you to get there?"

"Going was a bit slower, of course, at forty-two minutes, coming back thirty-eight."

Becker looked away, staring at the trees on the other side of the clearing to think.

Messer relaxed and waited for his commander to make his decision.

The man who "escorted" Schulz out of the camp returned. He walked straight to Messer after noticing that Becker appeared to be in his thinking mode.

"Captain, I put the body into one of the trucks and covered it again. I drove his car into a different clearing and also covered it with branches and such. No one will find any of them for a long time."

"Well done, thank you."

The man left and rejoined the others to relax from his task.

After a few more minutes, Becker, still looking at the trees, said, "In the morning, we'll leave in time to arrive and set up the initial attack so it coincides with the early stages of dawn. Give us some decent invisibility as we prepare, and sufficient light to make the attack. Let's get the squad leaders over here to review the plan."

Becker had divided his twenty-man roster into four units: two of seven men, one of four, and one of two. He would lead one seven-man squad, Messer the other one, and two *hauptscharführers*, master sergeants, the two smaller groups.

"Schulz has been taken care of, sir," Messer said.

"Yes, thank you. I heard."

"Yes, sir."

Messer rose and quietly gathered the two master sergeants. When the three men arrived at Becker's position, they sat down.

Becker looked at his men one by one before speaking.

"We have high expectations upon us, men. We are going to do what has never been done before in recent history, perhaps ever: the decapitation of two belligerent nations' leadership. The chaos that will follow, the fear this will generate, will be what the Fatherland needs to hold out in this war, perhaps it will be enough to win as our enemies lose the will to fight from the shock we are about to lay on their heads and in their hearts.

"Whatever it takes, we will do it to ensure this mission concludes in only one way: the assassinations of Roosevelt and Churchill!"

RONN MUNSTERMAN

Chapter 20

Villa Bellavista
14 December, 1502 Hours

Dunn entered the meeting room and was surprised to find President Roosevelt and Prime Minister Churchill sitting at the front, facing the rows of chairs. A man in his late thirties sat next to the president. Perkins stood near the president. About a dozen and a half men wearing suits sat in the front two rows, leaving the back three rows for the soldiers. Another man in his mid-fifties stood stock still beside Churchill. He wore a gray pin-striped suit with a colorful cloth in his breast pocket.

Dunn did some quick math and arrived at a total of thirty-eight men present to defend the president and prime minister. That was almost four squads worth, a platoon.

As Dunn walked toward the third row, Roosevelt spotted him and waved at him cheerfully, wanting him to come forward. Churchill was also looking his way and smiling. Dunn raised a hand in return and smiled back. He turned and gestured for Cross and the men to take their seats. Dunn waited until Saunders was about to go down a row and stopped him.

"They want us to go up there, Mac."

Saunders looked at the front of the room. "Sure, why not?"

Dunn stopped in front of the president who beamed up at him. He wore a double-breasted white suit, and held a long black cigarette holder in his left hand. Smoke curled toward the slow-moving fan blades above their heads.

"Sergeant Dunn! I'm so glad to see you again," Roosevelt boomed as he offered his hand.

Dunn shook it, surprised again by the strength of the grip. The first time had been at the White House.

"Hello, Mr. President. It's good to see you again, too."

"How's that pretty wife of yours? Pamela."

Dunn was surprised and pleased the president remembered her name. "She's doing very well, sir."

"Good to hear. How's her father? Recovering well?"

Dunn was dumbfounded. The president knew about Mr. Hardwicke getting shot?

Roosevelt noticed Dunn's nonplussed expression and with a twinkle in his eye said, "I am the president, you know. I know everything."

Dunn laughed. "Yes, sir. May I introduce Sergeant Major Malcolm Saunders, the Commandos' squad leader?"

Dunn stepped aside so Saunders could shake Roosevelt's hand.

"Very pleased to meet you, Sergeant."

"You, too, sir."

"Why don't you say hello to your Prime Minister?"

Saunders looked at Churchill, who rose and offered his hand.

"I'm honored to meet you, Prime Minister."

Churchill, also smoking, but a cigar instead, talked around the stogie.

"You're the lad who helped capture that German jet bomber, aren't you?"

He shook hands with Saunders, who blinked in surprise.

Colonel Kenton had mentioned that Churchill had specifically requested him, not why. Churchill was talking about the time he had gone to Germany and landed at the Horten Brothers' airfield with the intention of blowing up their Horten 18 jet bomber. However, the squadron leader of his P-51 escort flight had another idea. He'd talked Saunders into helping him steal the bomber. As a result, the bomber now resided in American aeronautical engineers' hands. They were working at a plant in Missouri to reverse engineer the aircraft and produce their own.

"I just gave a helping hand to the pilot who flew it out of Germany, sir."

Churchill grinned around his cigar. "Of course. Teamwork, eh?"

"Yes, Prime Minister."

"You're here to stop the Nazi bastards from killing us?"

"Aye, sir."

"Glad you're here. Nice to meet you at last."

"Thank you, sir," Saunders said.

Churchill turned slightly toward the man next to him. "Permit me to introduce Detective Inspector Walter Thompson. He takes care of my safety when I'm wandering around. Detective Inspector Thompson, this is Master Sergeant Tom Dunn and Sergeant Major Malcolm Saunders."

Thompson immediately offered his hand.

Each soldier shook it and said, "Nice to meet you, sir."

While Saunders was exchanging handshakes with Thompson, Dunn and Churchill did the same.

"You, too, gentlemen," Thompson said. "I've brought along five of my best men."

"Excellent, Mr. Thompson," Dunn said. "We'll need all the help we can get."

Perkins frowned at Dunn's remark and Saunders caught it.

Roosevelt introduced the young man next to him as Jim Burns, his aide.

Dunn and Saunders left the two world leaders and found seats with their respective squads. On the way, Saunders had whispered, "Lad, that Perkins fellow really doesn't like you."

Dunn snorted softly. "No kidding."

Perkins moved to a large easel to the left of Roosevelt and Churchill. He lifted a cover sheet and flipped it over the back revealing a large floor plan of the villa's exterior walls, stairs, and the grounds around it. It had been expertly drawn and someone must have had possession of a topographic map as well because the drawing included contour lines showing the elevation. Dunn studied those lines carefully for just a few seconds. They matched what he'd seen on the map Kenton had, and on the way into the villa. What lay behind the villa to the north told him what he needed. It confirmed his initial thought about where the enemy would come from.

Perkins cleared his throat.

"Gentlemen. I've studied this floor plan and drawing of the grounds for some time with my assistant, Agent Adkins." He paused to point at the man on the front row, and waved for him to stand.

Adkins rose part way, twisting as he lifted a hand to the audience, and sat down quickly.

Dunn shook his head to himself. It figured that the full-of-himself agent would make defensive decisions without consulting men who'd been in combat.

Perkins picked up a rubber-tipped pointer and tapped the north side of the villa.

Dunn knew that area was steep downhill from the villa. He counted the lines and figured the bottom of the hill to the north was a good three hundred feet below the villa.

"We've determined that the assassins will attack the rear of—"

Dunn jumped to his feet and interrupted, "May I, sir?" He didn't wait for Perkins to answer the question and headed toward the front.

Perkins seethed.

When Dunn was close enough, he stopped and leaned in near Perkins' ear. He whispered, "Begging your pardon, sir, that is tactically incorrect." Dunn wanted to spare the unlikable agent the embarrassment of correcting him loudly in front of his men.

Sadly, it appeared Perkins was unable to discern Dunn's kind motive.

"Who do you think you are to come up here?" Perkins snapped, obviously angry that a mere sergeant dared interrupt him.

Dunn ignored the man's anger. "Let me help you here, sir," he whispered.

"What the hell do you think you're doing?"

"Protecting the president and prime minister. I'm afraid your plan is headed for failure . . . Sir."

Perkins straightened up as if he'd stuck his finger in an electrical socket. "You can't talk to me that way."

Roosevelt took his cigarette holder from his mouth. He looked at the audience and smiled. "Gentlemen, why don't we take a five-minute smoke break. Head on outside. When you come back in, we'll resume our briefing."

All the men in the audience rose and quickly left the meeting room. As Perkins was about to pass by the president, Roosevelt said, "Stay on a moment, Elmer."

Dunn walked by, stopped himself from glaring at Perkins, and exited the room, too.

"Have a seat there, Elmer." Roosevelt pointed toward a nearby front row chair.

Perkins looked at the president warily. Something had gone amiss, he knew. He sat down, his back rigid.

"Sergeant Dunn isn't just some ordinary G.I. You know I handpicked him to come here and help?"

"Yes, Mr. President."

"Perhaps I was remiss by not telling you more about him. He earned the Medal of Honor and I presented it to him not too long ago. I believe you were on a trip to check security for that trip to Chicago."

"Yes, Mr. President, I recall the trip."

"I cannot tell you exactly why he earned the medal because it's classified, but I can tell you that he personally saved this country from an evil and unbelievable national catastrophe. Hundreds of thousands of Americans would have died."

Perkins said nothing, but his eyes grew wide and his face paled.

"He has a track record *in addition* to that one event that is unparalleled in our military. He is a professional, consummate soldier, a Ranger of the top rank. I think it would be a good idea for us to listen to what he has to say with respect and trust. What do you say?"

Perkins tried to recall a time when he'd been dressed down so effectively and by a man who hadn't even raise his voice.

"Absolutely, Mr. President. I'm sorry. I'll take care of it when the men return."

Roosevelt knew immediately what Perkins meant by "take care of it." "Good man," he said.

"Thank you, Mr. President."

A few minutes later the men returned and took their seats. Dunn decided it might be kinder to take a seat first, but he selected an aisle chair.

Perkins went back to the easel. He spotted Dunn and smiled.

Dunn nodded back at him, surprised.

"Sergeant Dunn, I'd appreciate it very much if you'd rejoin me up here."

Dunn did that and stood on the right side of the easel again.

Perkins turned slightly and offered his hand. "My apologies, Sergeant Dunn. I made some erroneous assumptions."

Dunn shook hands. "No need, sir. Just here to help."

"And we are grateful." Perkins held out the pointer. "Would you care to lay out a defensive plan?"

"Certainly, sir, thank you. As I go, please feel free to ask questions or make comments. That includes you guys." Dunn swept a hand to the audience. He received a lot of nods from the security details. He caught Saunders and Cross both grinning, but refrained from grinning back.

"The enemy is made up of Waffen-SS soldiers. These are experienced combat veterans who've seen and done many horrific things over the past three or four years, perhaps longer. They are exceedingly dangerous. They fully understand how to attack a stationary target like this villa. Remember, they have just one goal: to assassinate our president and prime minister." He glanced over at the two targets and mouthed the word, "sorry."

Both men waved it away.

"Therefore, they can shoot everything in sight. They will attack with a ferocity you'd associate with a man-killer tiger. They will not stop unless we kill them or wound them so they're incapacitated."

He paused for a few seconds to let it sink in.

"They follow no rules. They'll use subterfuge and misdirection, as well as overwhelming force when possible. We'll have to be prepared for many contingencies."

Dunn paused to examine the faces of the Secret Service agents. They looked extremely worried.

"We do have two things going in our favor, however. We know they are coming, but they don't know we're here unless they happened to be watching the villa when we arrived. Surprise is likely on our side. We just have to manage it properly." He turned to the agent in charge. "Mr. Perkins, by any chance did your men bring extra suits?"

Perkins smiled at this, realizing immediately what Dunn was interested in doing. "Well, yes we all did. I'm sure we can find some close enough matches."

"We only need a few for our recon trips around the property."

"Whatever you need."

"Thank you, sir."

"First things first. No Rangers or Commandos go outside today unless they are wearing a borrowed suit. Only sidearms are to be carried during this period, none of our bigger weapons that would give us away. Also stay away from open windows when indoors and in uniform."

Dunn looked at the bottom of the easel. He found what he wanted and picked up a black grease pencil.

"First, I'm going to show you how I would attack this villa. Next, I'll show you how I would defend against that. Any questions or comments before I start?"

Several of the agents shook their heads, their expressions open and curious. The Rangers and Commandos were so used to mission briefings their expressions were of men totally focused and prepared to hear from Dunn.

Dunn marked a small X at a point due south of the villa and another to the southeast. "The elevations here and to the southeast are the same as the villa. The Nazis will . . ."

RONN MUNSTERMAN

Chapter 21

Villa Bellavista
14 December, 1603 Hours

Dunn and Saunders looked at each other in amusement. Finding a suit that could sort of fit the big Commando had been a challenge. Finally, one of the agents who was in his sixties and of a certain size offered one of his. Saunders managed to squeeze into it without tearing the sleeves off. Only thing was, he couldn't quite button it closed. The man's fedora fit remarkably well, though, and completed the charade. He strapped his .455 Webley's holster on around his waist. The bottom of the jacket just barely hid the end of the long barrel on his right hip.

"Sadie would love to see you like this."

Saunders gave a wry chuckle. "You look dashing, too, lad."

Dunn laughed. His suit fit pretty well, and he wore a black derby. His Colt .45 was also hidden by the jacket.

He reached over to his friend and patted his lapels flat. "You ready?"

"Aye. Let's go on a walk."

The mission briefing had gone well, after the false start with Perkins, who, to give him credit, completely changed his tune.

Dunn wondered what the president had said, but he wasn't about to ask.

Tasks had been assigned, specifying who would be where and when. What-if scenarios were worked on as a group. The Secret Service agents had loosened up and began to participate with what turned out to be surprisingly intuitive suggestions. By the end, the plan of defense was complete. They also discussed what to do with any captured Germans. This became heated as the soldiers, who had to adhere to the Geneva Convention, and the agents had differing views: capture versus kill. Dunn had won the day by simply saying that if a German was down, incapacitated, he would be captured, although care would be taken not to get tricked into helping him and he triggering a grenade. Germans who raised their hands would be treated the same as long as they dropped all of their weapons and followed instructions to the letter. Dunn also pointed out that capturing the commander of the German unit could become a public relations coup by reporting that the Germans had attempted to assassinate the president and prime minister.

Dunn grabbed a small notebook off the dresser in his room and pocketed it. He found a couple of sharpened pencils also and slipped them into the jacket's breast pocket, point down. *"Don't you run with scissors, Tommy!"* his mom often shouted at him. The memory made him laugh.

"What's so funny?"

Dunn told him.

"Aye. That's my mom, too." He looked at Dunn, crossing his eyes. *"Stop that, Malcolm, or they'll get stuck like that. Don't you come cryin' to me if they do!"* he said in a high-pitched voice.

Dunn snorted, which almost started a laughing jag. He contained it at the last possible moment by taking great gulps of air.

Both men looped their binoculars over their heads.

"Okay, enough. Let's go, Ollie."

"What?"

"Ollie Hardy of Laurel and Hardy."

Saunders looked indignant. "Wait . . . I'm the round one?"

"If the shoe fits . . ." Dunn shrugged and ran to safety down the hall. Next to the bathroom was another door. He opened it and went up the narrow stairs. Opening the door at the top, he stepped out onto the villa-wide-and-deep flat roof. Saunders was right behind him, muttering something about squishing a skinny "Stanley."

The late afternoon sun cast long shadows to the east.

The men went directly to the wall on the south side. They put their hands on the wall's surface, which was about four feet high, and leaned against it.

Dunn examined the road they'd arrived on. It went in a left-hand curve toward the north, and then a reverse right hand to go south and down the hill toward Sinnai. The small city lay spread out in front of them, a mile distant. Following a ridgeline northeast, another road led away from the villa and was lost to sight about a half mile away when the ridge petered away and the terrain began a descent.

"Where do you think they are?" Saunders asked as he, too, studied the land around the villa. Maps were great, but eyeballing made a huge difference.

Dunn had thought about that for some time. "Let's go look north."

"Aye."

They made their way to the roof's north wall and again leaned against it. Rolling hills covered the ground clear to the horizon miles away.

Dunn pointed to the northeast. "That's Punta La Marmora, the highest place on the island at six thousand feet."

"Yeah, saw that on the map."

Dunn knew the peak was over forty miles away, but it stood far above the surrounding terrain.

Dunn's eyes searched for and found again the ridgeline road.

"I don't think they'll come from Sinnai. Too many prying eyes. It's got to be that way, maybe two or three miles." He pointed northward. "I'm really interested in that road on the ridge." He changed his point. "See it?"

"Aye." Saunders stared along the road for a bit. "Do you see that spot where the ground to the southeast of the road falls away sharply?" He helped Dunn by pointing with a massive finger.

Dunn followed the point. He immediately saw what Saunders meant. He raised his binoculars and examined the area. Saunders did likewise.

"Better do a right-to-left sweep while we're up here in case someone's watching us," Dunn said. He lowered his field glasses and said, "Look here." He pointed at nothing far to the left to emphasize where he was supposedly interested. Saunders glanced sideways at his friend and aimed his binoculars. He lowered them and nodded vigorously to add to the act.

The men moved to the west wall and pretended to be interested in some other spots in that direction.

"Had enough?" Dunn asked after a time.

"Aye. Want to walk around the grounds?"

"Yep."

A few minutes later, the two men exited the front door. They started walking slowly around the villa's property, circling clockwise at a distance from the villa varying between fifty to seventy-five yards. The property was oval in shape. Dunn estimated the long east-west axis measured about 200 yards and the short axis at about 150 yards, which matched what Colonel Kenton had said. The villa lined up parallel to the long axis. The hilltop was nearly flat with some areas undulating a few feet.

When they reached the north area, they walked close to the spot where the ground fell sharply away.

Dunn looked down the steep hillside following it all the way to the bottom. "The map is correct. That's a three-hundred-foot drop."

Saunders nodded. "Aye. Be a bloody fun sleigh ride."

Dunn chuckled. "Fun going down, hell coming back up."

Saunders snorted.

Dunn stared at the ground for a while. It was covered primarily by grasses and weeds, plus an occasional lone tree. He gauged the distance to the bottom horizontally and guessed it to be about 350 yards or so. He did some quick math. "That slope is close to thirty percent overall, with the part closest a little steeper than that. It's not impossible."

Saunders looked at Dunn. "You think they actually might try coming up that way after all?"

"Not all of them. I might send a team of three or four who could act as a decoy for the real thing."

"So we have to watch this way, too?"

"Don't you think we should?"

"I do. Just wish we didn't have to."

"Yeah, me, too."

They continued their travels, making their way to the front of the villa. Directly in front of the villa just past the driveway a grove of thick trees spanned twenty yards. Dunn and Saunders stared at it briefly.

"That'll be one location for a fire team."

"Yep," Dunn replied.

Dunn scanned to the west of the grove about fifty yards. The ground appeared to drop off at that point.

"We'd better go check out that spot." Dunn aimed with his eyes, rather than pointing.

Saunders followed the gaze. "Yes, I see your point. We'll mosey-like our way."

They walked toward the grove of trees and began to curve right, following a line that would take them within a few yards of the spot. As they passed it, Dunn, who was on the left, eyed it with side glances. They walked another fifty yards, bending more to the right, and ended up west of the villa, a point they'd already examined.

"That spot back there would be good for a few shooters. They'd be below the ground and out of sight, like they had a built-in trench," Dunn said.

"Right. That's what I thought, too."

Saunders turned to face south. The blue Mediterranean Sea sparkled in the early evening sunlight. He shook his head.

"Hard to believe what might happen here in such beauty."

Dunn compressed his lips. "It is. Maybe someday we can bring Sadie and Pamela here along with the kids."

Saunders let out a deep sigh. "That would be wonderful, my friend." He clapped Dunn on the back.

"I'm hungry. Let's see if they can put on a decent meal."

"I'm with you."

They headed to the front door at a brisk pace.

"What are we doing with the staff here?" Saunders asked.

Dunn told him.

The small, but efficient Sardinian house staff had been contracted to work during the conference. When the Secret Service met them, they interviewed each one and with the help of the local police department got a look at anyone with a record. Only one did, a twenty-year-old gardener, and it was as a juvenile for stealing another kid's bicycle. He'd returned the bike and got a stern talking to by the judge. That was the end of his criminal career.

The cousin of the concierge the German spy Schulz had met with, was still the main chef. The head of the household staff, the butler, was a dignified man in his sixties. The cleaning and serving staffs were women.

The one thing the Secret Service had insisted upon, was that the phone service be turned off, and all of the staff would stay at the villa for the duration. This was to prevent gossipy mouths from spilling important beans.

The other thing the agents had insisted on was that should there be any trouble—not saying there would be, you see—the staff was to immediately go down to the basement room where the president and prime minister, and the British bodyguard detail would lock themselves in for safety.

Chapter 22

Villa Bellavista
14 December, 1735 Hours

Dunn and Saunders found their men already eating in a large ballroom decked out with tables and chairs enough for everyone, including the Secret Service agents and the British bodyguards. Several long tables were set up along a wall. Trays of food were laid out, some with little Sterno cans burning underneath. Roosevelt and Churchill sat across from each other at a four-top table. Two empty places were set.

The windows, facing south, were covered by closed drapes to prevent any unwanted eyes from seeing the Rangers and Commandos in uniform. Perkins had stationed guards on the roof and Dunn had assigned Lindstrom and Higgins to walk the perimeter. They borrowed a couple of suits, too, and carried only their Colt .45s. Those on guard duty had grabbed a quick bite to eat first.

The two soldiers went straight to the food tables. The meal included fried chicken and mashed potatoes. They also spotted American grilled cheese sandwiches and hot dogs. At the end of everything was a big pot of soup. When Dunn checked it out, he discovered it was some kind of fish chowder. He filled his plate with chicken and hot dogs, but bypassed the potatoes and chowder. He scanned the end of the table and found bottles of Heinz ketchup. Grinning at them he grabbed one, checked to make sure the white lid was screwed on tight, and shook the bottle vigorously. Satisfied any watery liquid at the top was mixed back in, he opened the bottle and poured the contents over his hot dogs and a large puddle of ketchup next to his chicken.

Saunders stopped to watch, shaking his head. "Would you like some meat with your ketchup?"

Still grinning, Dunn looked at Saunders. "It's a food group for me."

"So you keep saying. Your vegetable, I take it?"

Dunn raised an eyebrow. "I believe you're correct."

Dunn grabbed a bottle of Coke from a tub, used an opener to pop off the crimped-on lid, and picked up his plate. He spotted a couple of empty chairs next to Cross and Barltrop who were sitting across from each other at a long table almost full of soldiers.

He picked a seat and put down his meal and Coke, and pulled his chair out. Saunders took the place across from Dunn.

Motion caught Dunn's eye and he looked that way.

Roosevelt was waving a hand at him. Dunn nodded. To the three men nearby, he said, "I'll be right back, guys."

Cross lifted a drumstick in answer as he chewed a bite.

"Yes, Mr. President. What can I do for you?" Dunn said when he stepped up next to the president's table.

Roosevelt waved a hand at the other two places set at the table. "We were wondering if you'd join us for dinner. You and Sergeant Saunders."

Dunn quickly looked over his shoulder at the tables filled with Rangers and Commandos. A pang of guilt struck him. When he looked back at Roosevelt, his expression must have given his thoughts away.

"Rather be with your men, would you?"

Dunn swallowed and his face pinked up at being so transparent. "Uh, I'm sorry, sir. Of course, we'll join you."

"I have a better idea. Is there room over there for a couple of old farts like us?"

Dunn grinned at the president. "I'm sure we can work that out, sir."

Dunn spotted a couple of serving staff ladies, who were watching the crowd. He waved at them and they sped over. In just a matter of minutes, the Rangers and Commandos near Saunders, Cross, and Barltrop rearranged the seating. Roosevelt rolled himself into a spot on Cross's right, and next to Schneider. Churchill sat across from the president and between Barltrop and Dickinson.

As soon as everyone was settled and comfortable, the men resumed eating. Every now and again they glanced toward the two leaders as if surprised the very important men would deign to dine with them.

Roosevelt, with decades of dinner conversation under his belt, started with Schneider.

"You're a good-sized fellow. How old are you?"

Schneider hurriedly swallowed his bite of food. "I'm twenty, sir."

"What's your name, son?"

"Bob Schneider, sir."

Roosevelt paused for a moment, looking at nothing in the distance. "You're the man who brought Sergeant Dunn back to life aren't you?"

Schneider looked confused. "Sir?"

"When you performed chest compressions on him."

"Oh." Schneider tilted his head and frowned. "You know about that, sir?"

"Just between us," Roosevelt said conspiratorially, "since I met the good sergeant, I've had all of his after-action reports sent to me. They give me insight that I truly appreciate. Besides, he's a natural storyteller."

Schneider stared at the president. "You've read all of our AARs, sir?"

"Going back to the big one in June. Operation Devil's Fire."

"Wow. I'm not sure what to say, sir."

Roosevelt patted him on the shoulder. "Nothing at all. I'm just terribly proud of you all."

"Well, thank you very much, sir."

"Not at all."

Roosevelt turned his attention elsewhere and the dinner progressed with seemingly everyone getting some attention from

FDR. Churchill accomplished the same thing with those around him.

The two squad leaders and their second in commands, forming a square of seats at the table, plus Perkins and Thompson, who were seated near Dunn, began discussing the plan Dunn had presented earlier.

"You still think they won't come tonight?" Thompson asked.

"We'll have to be prepared for a night attack, although with it being a new moon, visibility will be just about impossible with only starlight available. We'll want to have lights out no later than twenty-two hundred so they can't see the villa well.

"But like I said, we think they'll actually come right at first light. They'll attack with a few men from one direction as a feint, and the remainder of his force will come at us from one or two different directions."

"Did you learn anything new on your walk?" Perkins asked.

Dunn filled them in on a couple of things of note. "Did any of your men have any questions afterward? They asked some, but I wanted to make sure nothing gets left behind."

"None," Thompson said. He turned back to his meal, rightfully thinking the meeting was over.

"No, they seemed to fully understand your plans and, to be honest, pleased with your level of detail. Personally, Sergeant, I wanted to tell you I appreciated that you didn't talk down to the men," Perkins explained.

"You're welcome, Mr. Perkins. I figured we're all here for one reason only and I'm happy to work with you and your men, and DI Thompson's, too."

Thompson nodded his thanks.

Perkins nodded. "I apologize again for how I spoke to you. I'm afraid I was protecting my turf. It's quite embarrassing."

"No need, sir. That's all behind us." Changing the subject, Dunn asked, "Are you married, sir?"

"Call me Elmer, would you?"

Dunn cleared his throat and looked uncomfortable.

Perkins smiled. "Too ingrained now, is it?"

"That would be correct, sir. Three years of it."

"Okay. Yes, I'm married, Wonderful woman. Never understood what she saw in me."

Dunn grinned. "I often wonder the same about my wife. How long, sir?"

"Coming up on thirty-one years in March. Her name's Ethel."

Dunn smiled. "Well, congratulations in advance."

"Thanks. Your wife?"

"Pamela. Married last July. Expecting a baby in May."

"Congratulations! Maybe the war'll be over by then."

"Can only hope so, sir."

Perkins looked out the window briefly, evidently somewhere else mentally. Dunn said nothing. The agent sighed and said, "Our daughter is married to a sailor in the Pacific, the *Enterprise*. Works on deck using those paddles to help the pilots land."

"Your daughter an only child?"

"A son, too. We lost him at Pearl. The *Oklahoma*."

Dunn laid a hand on the man's shoulder. "I'm so very sorry, sir."

Perkins, unable to speak, merely nodded his thanks.

The moment passed and conversations shifted.

When everyone was finished eating, Dunn checked his watch: 18:20. He pushed back his chair and rose. The sound of his chair scraping along the tile floor caught everyone's attention and they looked at him expectantly.

"Gentlemen. I hope you enjoyed your dinner and the friendship and conversation. It's time to get ready." He turned to Roosevelt. "Mr. President, thank you for joining us for dinner. And Prime Minister, thank you, too. We are grateful."

The two leaders smiled and raised a hand acknowledging the comment.

Roosevelt backed his wheelchair out and rolled toward the table where he and Churchill were first seated. Churchill rose and followed. The two men took their places at the table. Staff came over and filled their glasses and offered them cigars or cigarettes.

The Rangers, Commandos, and the protective details gathered around at the other end of the room. Dunn spent a few minutes reminding everyone of the plan for the night. Afterwards, the group broke up and set about getting ready. Dunn grabbed Saunders, and found Perkins talking with Walter Thompson by one of the south-facing, draped windows.

"Pardon us, gentlemen," Dunn said as he strode up to them.

The two older men turned to face Dunn and Saunders.

"Yes?" Thompson asked.

"We have a question. I'm sure you've already thought of this, but," Dunn paused to tilt his head slightly, "since we're certain of an impending attack, should we simply move the president and prime minister to a safe location under the cover of darkness? My boss, Colonel Kenton, mentioned concerns over an ambush, but darkness might make that unlikely."

Thompson shook his head ruefully. "Indeed a good question, Sergeant. I can't speak for Mr. Perkins here, but since I took over guarding Mr. Churchill, I have, and believe me, this is no boast, saved his skin over a dozen times. From various organizations like the Irish Republican Army, Nazi spies, Indian and Arab nationalists, and Greek communists. Oh, and don't forget the occasional barmy person. In a word, Mr. Churchill is stubborn. It would, of course, be inappropriate of me to share my personal description of his behavior, but just between the four of us, the word 'foolish' seems to come to mind often. 'Careless' being the other. So no, moving the prime minister would not be an acceptable, to him, alternative."

Thompson took a deep breath as if recovering from the long speech.

Dunn looked at Perkins, who shook his head. "Already asked, as you thought, and the answer was, 'hell no, Elmer!' He went on to say something about if you men were going to be in harm's way to protect him, the least he could do would be to actually be here to protect."

Dunn looked from one guardian to the other. "Thank you, gentlemen. It sounds as though you both have difficult . . . no, impossible jobs."

"You're right, there, young man," Perkins said as Thompson nodded. "Welcome to our world."

"We'll do everything in our power to protect them."

"We appreciate your help very much," Thompson said.

Perkins nodded.

Chapter 23

Dunn leaned against the villa's roof wall trying to examine the terrain. Starlight cast some illumination across the ground, but it was nowhere near as helpful as the quarter moon of four nights ago would have been. He swept his gaze left and right hoping that if anything was out there, any motion would catch his eye.

Saunders, Cross, Barltrop, Perkins, Thompson, and Dunn had collaborated on creating the defensive positions on the large paper Perkins had used in the briefing. Cross showed some unexpected artistic skills with his drawings of the penciled-in assignments for everyone.

The villa itself was at the center of the top of the hill, laid out longwise east-west. The driveway, ten yards from the villa, ran across the entire length of the front, ending in a small parking area that was perpendicular to the drive. The two trucks that had brought the Rangers and Commandos were still parked there, plus the half-dozen or so army staff cars that had transported the conference attendees and their staff.

Continuous four-foot-tall shrubs bordered the entire south edge of the driveway, forming a complete green wall. Dunn's men started digging their foxholes after it grew dark, so as to not give away their positions. Although time consuming, the dirt they dug up was spread out over a wide area around the foxholes to prevent creating a telltale berm. They were located on the south side of the shrubs, placed so the men inside them could escape through the ground level gaps between the individual shrubs. Fox hole number one was at the west end of the driveway, number two was directly in front of the entrance, and number three was southeast of the villa.

Dunn and Saunders had four areas of concern. The first was southeast of the villa about sixty-five yards. The ground dropped away enough so a large force of men could position themselves there and have excellent lines of fire at the villa with good cover. The second was the smaller and similar spot to the west-southwest at about fifty yards range that Dunn and Saunders had noticed earlier. It was only big enough to hide three or four men. The third location was due south of the entrance, the grove of trees about twenty yards wide at a distance of fifty yards. Dunn expected men in either or both of the last two areas to be the initiators of the attack. Fourth was a second grove directly east only twenty yards way which also presented a good place for secondary attack.

Dunn and his men, plus half of Perkins', took the first watch. Saunders and his men, plus the remaining agents would sleep, relieving the first watch at midnight. Walter Thompson and his men were resting as well.

Now that darkness had settled across the landscape, his men wore their uniforms and carried either their M1s or Thompsons, depending on where they were positioned. Those on the roof had the long guns while those in the foxholes had the shorter-range but much higher firing rate submachine guns. Perkins' men were paired up with Dunn's machine gunners in the foxholes. Because they'd had considerable experience firing the Thompson .45 as a part of their Secret Service training, they each had one in addition to their .38 Police Specials.

For communications and fire control, each Ranger and Commando carried a five-pound walkie-talkie. All were set to the same frequency. They wore it over their left shoulder on canvas straps, with the radio resting against their upper left chest. This allowed them to use their left hand to trigger the talk button. The volume was set very low, but they could hear it without touching it.

Dunn crouched as he moved over to kneel next to Jonesy, who had an M1 and his scoped 1903 Springfield with him. He'd told Dunn earlier he wouldn't be able to make much use of the sniper rifle in such darkness. What little he could see would be better suited for the open wing sights on the Garand.

They were positioned on the roof's south wall. Higgins was behind them at the north, Goerdt at the west, and Lindstrom the east. Dunn would rotate around the roof, keeping low to prevent even the slightest possibility of being seen under the starlight.

Lights from Sinnai just below them were visible as were those from Cagliari. No need for blackout there. German bombers wouldn't make it anywhere close to the island. Plus, why would they bother?

"You okay, Jonesy?"

"Yeah, Sarge."

"Get enough to eat?"

"More than I should have, I think."

"Yep, me, too."

Dunn patted him on the back. "Stay sharp."

"Will do."

Dunn quickly checked in with the other three men, eventually settling in next to Lindstrom on the east side.

He peered over the wall. It was exceedingly difficult to differentiate the ground from the sky at first. He took to using his peripheral vision. He could make out the lighter long strip of ground that was the road on the ridgeline. That was where Saunders and he decided the Germans would come from, sliding out of sight below the ridgeline.

As time passed, he naturally began to think about Pamela. As he'd said to Perkins, he was often flummoxed by what she saw in him. But whatever it was, he was grateful because he loved her so much. They were alike in some ways, interest in learning, a strong sense of right and wrong, a commitment to others in need— something she excelled at as a nurse. Their differences made their lives more interesting, not difficult. Growing up in two different countries. For as much as the States were similar to England, there were many differences in language, which was odd since it was after all, English, and Dunn truly had trouble grasping just how important "class" was in England. While he hadn't experienced prejudice based on class, he knew Pamela's parents had throughout their lives. They were tenant farmers, which put them in a position lower than some who obviously believed being born right was incredibly more important than living right.

Where Dunn was a whiz at math, Pamela, who was an intelligent woman, thought math was merely created solely to torment her. She loved the arts, he loved baseball. She'd agreed to attend some games when they moved to the States, and she was trying to get him to, at a minimum, appreciate paintings. He'd given it a try a few times on weekend passes to London, but he was pretty much mystified by portraits of people who looked like their lives were nothing but a misery. And being able to discern that *this* painting was by so and so, but *that* one was by another so and so was completely beyond him.

So they worked together on their differences and celebrated their similarities. The big one was wanting to be parents. They fully hoped to have four children. He was one hundred percent certain the baby she was carrying was going to be a boy. When pressed to explain his belief he could only say it was just a feeling.

Dunn switched gears and thought about Pamela's dad, Mr. Hardwicke. *Call me Earl,* he always insisted. Hard for Dunn, but he'd finally been able to do that after Earl had been shot in his own front yard. Dunn shuddered at how close it had been. Even though he'd been in countless firefights and had experienced fear during them, it was nowhere near as terrifying as the attack at the Hardwicke Farm. The thought of losing the woman he loved deeply struck his heart horribly. It had turned out all right, but only because things went their way. He felt responsible for what had happened because the Nazis had decided to hunt him. Both Mr. and Mrs. Hardwicke had told him that was nonsense and not to worry about it.

He shook his head in the dark. He was a fortunate man to have in-laws he loved, and to be loved by them. Having parents who loved him and two sisters who did, too.

He paused his thinking long enough to lift a quick prayer of thanks for all his blessings.

He sighed deeply feeling content for the first time in a good while.

RONN MUNSTERMAN

Chapter 24

The Farm, Area B-2, Catoctin Mountain Park
14 December, 1310 Hours, U.S. Eastern Standard Time

Even though the temperature was thirty-three degrees under a gray sky, the ten OSS recruits were warm having just run two miles, as was the custom every day after calisthenics. They'd run through a heavily wooded area on a narrow animal trail. It had rained the day before and the trail was still wet. A couple of the women had fallen, their boots slipping out from underneath them. The recruits running behind a woman who went down, kept on going, forbidden to help anyone. This was to instill self-dependency.

The morning had been devoted to weapons training. Since they'd started weapons training eleven days ago on the .38 caliber Police Special, they'd been firing all kinds of other pistols daily. Among them were the American 1911 Colt .45, the British Webley .38, the German 9mm Luger, and the Japanese 8mm Nambu, which roughly resembled the Luger. Gertrude found she favored the big American Colt. She liked the weight and feel in her hand, and enjoyed the sheer power of the big round. Plus, it held seven rounds in the magazine. Lately, they had been taught to use what Rick called instinctive fire instead of the prepared range-style position. This meant crouching and drawing the weapon quickly, and firing two rapid shots at the target, lovingly called the "double-tap." The purpose was to kill or wound the enemy before he or she could kill you. Gertrude liked it and scored well.

"All right, ladies. Form a column facing the ravine," Rick the instructor said. He used military terms for formations since they were precise.

The women formed a line perpendicular to the ravine in front of them. It spanned twenty-five yards and was about ten feet deep. The bottom was grassy, although of course it was brown for winter, and at least fifty percent covered with leaves. Stretching across was a rope bridge, which was constructed of three ropes: one for the feet, and two at waist height for the hands. Every five feet, a vertical support rope connected the waist ropes to the foot rope, forming a V for the students to pass through. In essence, a tightrope with handholds. It was something you might see in a Tarzan movie. If it had been summertime, they'd have used a different location, one with a creek running through it that was about five feet deep. Extra punishment for falling.

This was their first time on this particular obstacle. Gertrude happened to be first in line. Whether that was good or bad luck was yet to be determined.

Rick looked at her and said, "Get ready, Peggy."

She stepped forward and grasped the two hand ropes with her gloved hands.

"Go."

She put one boot on the lower rope and a second, about a foot or so in front of the first one. Her toes were pointed to the outside and her heels to the inside like duck walking. She took another step, sliding her hands along.

After she'd traveled only one yard, she heard Rick yell, "Go!" at the next woman in line. The next trainee stepped onto the rope, which Gertrude immediately felt through her feet and hands. Her breathing grew faster as she advanced, and as new trainees were stepping onto the rope bridge. It was hard work because the lower rope kept trying to sway one way or the other and slip out from beneath her. She stopped once to reduce the swaying. It didn't work because of the other recruits' movements.

Rick immediately shouted, "No stopping!"

She instinctively knew better than to either try to look at him or to speed up. She got back into a rhythm and was almost halfway across. The ten feet of drop below her didn't particularly bother her, although it looked far deeper from above. But her muscles were burning from the strain. Nevertheless, she continued her rhythm of stepping one foot at a time and sliding her hands.

She reached a point that was only four yards from completing her crossing of the difficult bridge. She lifted her left boot to advance another step, focusing entirely on the rope at her feet.

The three nearly simultaneous explosions startled her so much she nearly lost her grip on the hand ropes. Dirt and leaves shot into the air and drifted with the wind onto her. The devices had been buried about ten feet from the bottom rope, to her right.

A scream behind and a thump on the ground below told her, and everyone, that someone had fallen. Ignoring that person, whomever it was, Gertrude looked up and tightened her grip on the top ropes. She thought her heart was going to pop out of her chest and run across the bridge by itself, it was beating so fast.

"Gee whiz," she muttered to herself, gasping for breath.

She sped up carefully and made it to the other side of the ravine. She darted off the small wooden platform at the end, running into the grass, where she turned around.

She walked over to the ravine on the south side of the bridge looking down. The young woman known as Rosemary, a petite brunette, was being helped to her feet by Mildred. It looked like one of Rosemary's ankles was hurt. Gertrude hoped it was just a sprain. The two women disappeared from view as they traveled south presumably to a point where they'd be able to climb out more easily. She watched the remaining eight trainees finish their crossing.

The women gathered around and looked at Rick, who had just stepped out onto the bridge.

They began clapping their hands rhythmically and shouted, "Go, Rick, go!"

He ignored them as he concentrated on his foot- and hand-work. He crossed the span quickly, much faster than the women had done. No surprise. He'd probably done it fifty times.

He stepped near the gaggle of trainees and smiled at them.

"Well, done, ladies. Not a record time, but you all passed. We'll work on this little gem now and again so you can get better at it. If you're wondering about Rosemary, she should be okay. The doctor will examine her." He paused to point down the trail leading away from the rope bridge. "You'll be happy to know in that direction, just a quarter mile away, I have a truck waiting for you. We'll wait for Mildred and Rosemary to join us, and we'll ride back to camp."

The women smiled. A truck. Sounded like heaven. They started jogging toward the free ride back to the camp.

1345 Hours

Back at the main camp, the women jumped down from the back of the truck. Mildred and Rick helped Rosemary down, and Mildred escorted her inside the main building where the infirmary was located.

"Column formation!" Rick ordered. He pointed at a spot on the ground near him. "Right here!"

When the women were in the column, Rick marched them around behind the main building, down a hill and to the edge of a meadow big enough for two football fields side by side. Several tables were set up on which were placed small brown suitcases, just a little bigger in all dimensions than a briefcase. There were no chairs.

At the opposite end of the field several objects were placed about ten yards apart. Gertrude peered at the things a hundred yards away and decided that the vertical ones were telephone poles. Also at the far end was a mound of earth that traversed the width of the field. When she peered at it for a time, she realized train tracks were laid down on top of it. The exercise's purpose suddenly clicked in her head.

She sidled over to Ruby and whispered. "Demolitions."

Ruby glanced over at her friend and noted her eyes were dancing with excitement. They'd been talking about this training for a couple of days. Both of them truly wanted to learn how to blow stuff up.

Rick walked around in front of the tables to a small table that also had a suitcase on it. "Pick a suitcase, ladies."

The women simply went to the table closest to where they happened to be standing. Gertrude and Ruby ended up next to each other.

"This lesson is about explosives."

Gertrude had to stifle a cheer, but she smiled.

"Open your cases. Slowly!"

Gertrude opened the suitcase and stared inside. The interior was divided into sections by cardboard inserts. In the top left section was a block of grayish white stuff about the size of two packs of cigarettes placed end to end. In the upper right was a timer. In the lower left was a small coil of black wire. Snuggled in with the wire was a pair of wire cutters. A small pocketknife for trimming the insulation off the wire lay next to the wire cutters. In the lower right, additionally segregated in small containers were slim silver pencil-shaped objects about two inches long with a pair of short wires coming out of one end.

Rick picked up each type of object from his own suitcase and gave the women all the details they needed to know about it. This went on for a half hour as he repeated the process several times to drill the information into their heads. He spoke constantly about the inherent dangers in working with plastic explosives, or other common explosives, like dynamite.

First, they practiced setting the timer for various numbers of minutes. He taught them how to cut two lengths of wire about a foot long from the coil using the wire cutters. Next, he showed them how to trim an inch of insulation off both ends of the wires with the knife. They attached the wires to the timer. He had them remove the wires and do it again, and set the timer for five minutes, but leave it in the off setting.

"Pick up your timer. Hold it in your right hand."

The women complied.

"Pick up one and only one detonator in your *left* hand. Do not let it touch anything."

He turned and walked away about ten yards, and stopped, turning back around.

"Come out here and join me. Stay in your relative positions but put five yards between you. Take a kneeling position."

After the women set up, he said, "Push the detonator into the ground so the top shows a half inch of silver."

The women did that.

"Set your timer on the ground away from the detonator."

When the women finished setting down the timer, he said, "Carefully attach the bare ends of the timer's wires to the detonator's two leads."

Rick walked along in front of the trainees watching them closely for safety rules and accurately following his instructions. He turned around and waited a moment.

"Anyone *not* done?"

No one raised a hand. He walked the line again, peering intently at the way the wires were twisted together. He reached the end of the line and went back to the center position.

"Very good, ladies. Everything you did looks correct. When I say 'go,' switch on your timers, stand up, run back and duck behind your tables." He paused a moment to check that everyone was paying attention.

He nodded to himself. "Go!" He checked his watch.

With a flurry of motion, the women switched on their timers, rose and scrambled back to their tables. On the way there, they noticed for the first time that there was a piece of wood nailed to the front of the tables that gave them cover.

Rick ran with them and joined Gertrude on the far right of the line.

He looked at his watch. Time moved slowly.

"Here we go, ladies," he called out, "Ten seconds, eight . . . five, four, three, two, one."

A second later a bunch of popping sounds came their way, much like firecrackers. It was over in a second.

Gertrude glanced over at Rick. "That's it?"

"Yep, that's it. All right everyone. You can stand. I'm going to go check to make sure all the detonators blew up, so wait here."

He jogged out to the line where the timers were still sitting exactly where the women had left them. Small craters gave evidence of the detonators going off. He counted nine, the correct number, since Rosemary was with the doctor.

"All clear. Come on out and look at your handiwork."

The women ran out and stared at their own personal crater. Some smiled, some frowned at the small size.

"Okay, pick up your timer and go back to your table. Unhook the wires, coil them, and place them and the timer back in their proper sections. Close your suitcases and form a column. We're going back to the main building for debriefing."

The women grumbled, disappointed.

One of them in the center asked, "When are we going to get to actually blow something up?" She pointed at the far end of the field.

"Soon, Faye, soon. Trust me," Rick answered.

Gertrude muttered, "Dang it."

RONN MUNSTERMAN

Chapter 25

Sergeant Major Malcolm Saunders carried his M1 in his right hand while he opened the door leading to the stairs to the roof with the other. Right behind him were Alders, Holmes, Myers, Talbot, and Sergeant Major Kirby. Barltrop was stationed on the second floor northeast with a Secret Service agent. Dickinson, Forster, and Bentley drew duty in the foxholes paired with rested Secret Service agents.

At the top of the steps, Saunders stopped. He glanced behind him. Kirby had shut the door to the hallway making it total darkness in the stairwell. Instead of opening the roof door, he rapped twice, and said in a low voice, "Saunders."

Dunn, who had positioned himself just outside the door, opened it and stepped back to make room for the arriving men to pass by. As they filed by, he patted each on the shoulder. He closed the door quietly and turned to Saunders, who stood facing south. The door entered the roof from a small shack-like structure that was positioned near the northeast corner.

"How're things?" Saunders asked.

"Nothing happening. Visibility is tough in the starlight. Thought we saw movement on the ridge road, but it was smaller than a man and moving fast, so probably a dog. Or I suppose a deer. I guess they have those here."

"Nothing from the ground?"

"Nope. Only heard from them when they checked in on the half hour."

The Rangers had been clicking their walkie-talkies a certain number of times, one through three times, to indicate all was well at each foxhole.

"Good." Saunders took a deep breath of the fresh air. It had fallen into the mid-forties and a breeze from the south carried the salt smell from the sea. "Nice up here."

"Yep."

"I'll get the men settled. You and your guys go get some sleep."

"We're ready."

Saunders quickly swapped out the Rangers for the arriving Commandos.

Dunn and his men quickly left the roof, heading for a welcome sleep.

Saunders walked the perimeter of the roof, stopping in many places to eye the dark terrain below. If only he could see in the dark like a cat.

Finding nothing moving, not even Dunn's dog or deer, he chose the northeast corner and leaned against the wall, staring intently so *his* peripheral vision could find the lighter-colored road running away at the northeast. He mentally shrugged. If there *was* movement on the road, he'd at least be able to spot that.

His other men had taken over for Dunn's in the foxholes. Rested Secret Service agents replaced Perkins' men who'd been paired with the Rangers. Thompson's men were helping defend from the interior of the villa.

Like Dunn before him, although he didn't know it or even wonder what his friend might have been thinking while on duty, Saunders' thoughts drifted to his wife, Sadie. He recalled the horror of that phone call from Mr. Hughes, her dad. It had been close to 3:00 am on July 11th. Barltrop had answered the barracks phone and woken him. Barltrop had driven him to the hospital over an hour away in Enfield, at the north of London's metropolitan area. Just recalling the fear that had gripped him at the sight of her damaged body lying in the hospital bed made his eyes tear up.

She'd been shopping for a new dress to impress him, of all things. It still made him feel guilty. A V1 rocket, a buzz bomb, had landed nearby. Her injuries included a broken femur and tibia, which created the need for a thigh to ankle cast. A concussion had pushed her into a coma and the doctor had given her a terrifying fifty-fifty chance of waking up.

He'd spent a week at her side in the hospital until she awakened. He focused on that moment for a bit. His heart had nearly burst from happiness and relief. Sadie had worked hard with her physical therapist so she could walk down the aisle with her father. Her other injury was caused by shrapnel cutting her face leaving her with a thin scar that ran two inches from the right corner of her lips toward her right ear. While the surgeon had done a remarkable job, it was still visible. Pamela Dunn had given her some make up and it hid the damage quite well.

Sadie had accomplished her walk down the aisle on September 23rd, two and a half months after her injuries. Saunders had barely made it to the church in Cheshunt in time.

He'd been on a mission to Poland to get V2 rocket components captured by the Polish Resistance. On the parachute jump, he'd ended up on the wrong side of the Vistula River, separated from his squad. While trying to find a bridge to cross back over, he'd come upon some Germans about to execute two Russian soldiers. He'd intervened, killing the Germans. In gratitude, the Russians captured Saunders and took him to their camp. An interrogation by a general with English speaking skills had led to an unexpected solution. The general had family in London. Could Saunders get a letter to them if the general found a way home for Saunders? With no time to spare, he'd arrived at the church.

He'd grown close to Sadie's family, especially her three little brothers, who adored the huge redheaded Commando. When he had leave, they would often drive up to visit. He suddenly realized they hadn't been to visit his family in London's East End since the wedding. He had three sisters, all married to servicemen. Perhaps everyone could get together at their parents' flat. He smiled at the thought. When he got back, he'd call his mother and see if she could help set that in motion.

Major Becker's mountain base camp
0450 Hours

Major Becker and his men worked in silence in the near total darkness. Starlight gave them some help but not much. They checked their MP40s and Lugers by feel. The only sounds were the weapons' clicks of metal against metal. Loaded and ready. When the men were finished, they formed a column. Starting at the rear, Becker walked the line, patting each soldier on the shoulder as he passed. He took the point position and immediately started marching, the column moving with him. He estimated a one-hour trip. That was longer than his recon force had used, but they'd had sunlight. Once they arrived at their line of departure, which was about 400 meters northeast of the villa, they would hunker down and wait until ten minutes before first light.

They would move into their positions.

Next, they would attack.

Finally, he would personally assassinate Roosevelt and Churchill from close range with his Luger. A camera in his pocket would record the proof of death.

He pictured the *Führer's* expression, which would be one of glee, he was certain.

Chapter 26

Villa Bellavista
15 December, 0634 Hours

The sun was rising and the first gray light that came with its arrival made visibility a hundred times better than the night had been.

Peering over the top of his foxhole, Sergeant Christopher Dickinson touched his American counterpart on the arm. When Secret Service Agent Tucker glanced over, Dickinson pointed at a spot about forty yards away. It was the area to the southwest that Saunders and Dunn had been worried about and had specifically pointed out to the defenders during the briefing.

Whispering, Dickinson said, "Movement. Two men." He grabbed his walkie-talkie and clicked four times—his position's call number for trouble. He knew Saunders would move carefully along the roof to take a look. This also alerted everyone else on the defensive team that something might be about to start.

He lifted his binoculars and focused the lenses.

Ducking down, he keyed the radio and spoke as softly as possible. "Dickinson here. Confirmed. Two men. Not in German uniforms. Armed with MP40s."

"Roger," Saunders replied. After a moment he said, "Confirmed from here. Be ready, lads."

Dickinson looked over the rim of the foxhole. He swept his gaze, turning his head as he went, from right to left. He paid a lot of attention to the grove of trees south of the driveway directly across from the main entrance. He found nothing there. He focused on the two enemy soldiers to the west again.

Saunders, kneeling beside Myers at the west wall, pointed out the two Germans.

"I see them, Sarge." Myers said. The British squad's sniper was armed with his scoped bolt-action Lee-Enfield .303, so it would be an easy shot.

"If they advance toward Dickinson, let them continue. If they go a different direction, kill them."

"Roger."

Saunders worked his way over to join Kirby at the south wall.

"See any movement?" he asked.

"No. Nothing."

"I'll stay here with you. We'll keep an eye on the grove and the road right down there."

"Right."

A long burst of automatic gunfire broke the morning silence. Nine-millimeter rounds peppered the west wall at the first floor. Glass shattered as the rounds pierced some of the windows.

None of the defenders fired, waiting.

Another long burst from the southwest struck the area around the main entrance.

Saunders keyed his radio. "Dickinson. Fire."

Dickinson nudged Tucker and said, "Ready."

Both men raised their Thompsons.

"Fire."

Their heavy .45 caliber rounds slapped into the ground just in front of the two Germans to the west. As the barrels naturally lifted, the rounds came closer.

The Germans scooted backwards to get farther below the ground line.

"Cease fire," Dickinson said.

The Thompsons grew quiet, smoke trailing from their huge barrels.

Dickinson turned left and eyed the grove. Motion.

Into his radio, he said, "Movement in the grove. Western edge."

"Roger," Saunders replied. He repeated the information to Kirby, who nodded.

"I heard."

The two men turned their attention to the west edge of the grove.

A couple of bright flashes and the sound of gunfire came from there. The rounds struck the villa below Saunders in the area of the entrance. Glass shattered in the door.

"Forster, fire," Saunders said to his radio.

Directly in front of the main entrance, Forster and his American partner fired long bursts from their Thompsons shredding bark and tree limbs in the grove.

Myers spotted the two men on the west side get up and start running. One went to Myers' left, while the other ran to his right, apparently heading for the back of the villa. He tracked that German for a few seconds, setting the lead.

His rifle bucked into his shoulder.

The German went down, sprawling, unmoving.

Dickinson and Tucker mowed down the other German.

More than a dozen MP40s opened up from a point to the southeast, the one Dunn and Saunders had noted.

Bullets struck the roof line, stone chips flying. Everyone on that side of the roof ducked.

The windows on the front of the villa shattered.

The ground around Forster's foxhole exploded as rounds struck there. He ducked, grabbing the American on the way. Bullets continued to whine and zip overhead.

Heavy German fire came from the grove straight ahead.

All of this kept the defenders' heads down.

Heavy fire erupted again from both the southeast and grove positions forcing the defenders to stay under cover.

Dunn pounded up the stairs. He'd had a rude awakening at the first shots. Everyone was up and on the way to their secondary positions either inside the villa or with him to the rooftop. He opened the door at the top and eased out onto the roof. He glanced around quickly and found Saunders. Running low, he joined the Commando.

"Southeast and the grove," Saunders said. "Just like we expected. Two more are already down at the southwest."

"Roger."

Dunn waved at the four men with him to take up positions along the south wall from the midpoint to the southeast corner. Jonesy had his Springfield in his hands.

Dunn and Saunders had decided the Commando would do fire control from the roof while Dunn would be a rover, pitching in wherever needed.

Fire from the southeast concentrated on Bentley's foxhole keeping his and the American's heads down. It was as if the Germans were trying to punch a hole in the line there.

Saunders spotted Bentley's predicament and radioed, "Bentley prepare to withdraw."

"Roger."

"All guns fire at the southeast position or south grove." The men would automatically target the location nearest to them.

The defenders' weapons lit up. The noise was deafening.

The Germans disappeared behind the ridge. One looked like he might have been hit.

Fire from the south grove ceased.

Bentley and his partner scrambled out of the foxhole, never getting more than six inches above the ground and slithered through the shrubs as fast as possible. Once on the other side and out of view of the Germans, they ran along the shrubs to the parking area. Using the trucks and cars parked there as additional cover, they made it to safety to the villa's west side. From there, they ran to the back, checking the north as they moved, and into the rear entrance at the midpoint of the back wall. They ran through the villa's hallways, up the stairs to the second floor, and to the southeast corner. They took positions by a window and waited for instructions with their weapons aimed out the window. Below them on the first floor and in the same relative position were Rangers Cross, Brooks, Martelli, Schneider, and Wickham.

Saunders called a cease fire. The men would fire at targets of opportunity only.

Dunn moved over next to the big Commando and they peeked over the wall at the southeast target area.

Two long objects tumbled through the air. One landed five yards south of the east grove. The other hit the ground somewhere behind the same grove. Dense gray smoke began to pour from them. In just thirty seconds, enough smoke was present to obscure both the southeast target area and the south edge of the east grove.

Major Becker had fourteen of his men, well, thirteen, thanks to the unexpected ferocity of the enemy fire, divided into two groups, A and B. He was with B, which was the one more west. Group C was stationed in the south grove and D was in the southwest area, although he hadn't been able to see any gunfire from their location in the past couple of minutes. That didn't bode well. That could put him down a total of three out of twenty or fifteen percent of his force already out of action in a matter of minutes.

Part of his mind was trying to understand why his intelligence had been so bad. He had recognized the sharp crack of the American M1, and the deep-throated roar of their damn Thompson submachine guns. He'd expected only the president's protection detail of perhaps ten or twelve men plus a half dozen for the English leader. He estimated the actual defending force to be at least thirty men. How many were inside? He'd expected the defenders to react heavily to the fire from the south grove and the west positions. They appeared to be extremely well-disciplined fighters and hadn't fallen for the bait.

At the moment, he was regretting the decision not to bring any panzerfausts, the famed anti-tank weapon. He'd chosen against it because he was worried about killing his two targets with one. That could make taking good identifiable photographs of the bodies impossible. With what he now knew, he was going to have to rely on good battlefield tactics. The smoke grenades were the first stage of that.

Taking six men with him, he ran crouched over behind the group to the right, staying low enough to be out of sight even without the smoke. The men ran fast, knowing the smoke screen would clear in less than two minutes. They crossed the driveway and headed north for a time. Turning left as soon as the east grove hid their movements along with the curling smoke, the team stopped and knelt.

Becker tapped the soldier next to him and gave him a hand signal. The soldier, a brute of a man at two meters in height, nodded and pulled a smoke grenade from his coat pocket. The average soldier could throw the stick grenade about forty meters. He could toss it ten more. His long arm drew back and he launched the grenade over the grove so it would land about halfway to the villa, which still remained out of sight due to the previous smoke grenades. Becker lost sight of the grenade, but when it went off the roiling smoke thickened into another screening wall of gray cloud.

Becker signaled to the men and they rose and ran forward. When they reached the grove, they slowed to a walk and moved quietly through the trees until they were at the west edge. There, they knelt behind trees and waited for the smoke to clear. In all, they'd covered about seventy-five meters.

Group A, down to six men, fired long bursts in the direction of the villa, sweeping their barrels left and right. Whether they hit anyone was secondary to their purpose, which was merely distraction. Sounds of some glass breaking indicated they'd done well. When they stopped firing, Group C in the south grove did the same for several seconds, and they, too, stopped. All was quiet.

Saunders and Dunn watched the third smoke grenade's innards spread out and block their view of the grove.

"Now we know where they're coming from," Saunders muttered as he pointed at the east grove.

"Yep."

Saunders raised his radio and told everyone on the roof and the interior of the villa to focus on the east grove, while the foxhole inhabitants were to watch their respective fronts.

Becker glanced along the line of his SS soldiers. They were focused on the direction in front of them, waiting impatiently for the smoke to clear so they could begin firing and start the next phase of the attack. He'd been surprised by whomever was commanding the defenders. He hadn't panicked at the first shots from the west position and the south grove. It was as if he'd expected the main force to be right where it was. Someone knew what they were doing.

Well, so did he.

So did he.

RONN MUNSTERMAN

Chapter 27

Villa Bellavista
15 December, 0645 Hours

Silence continued to drape the battlefield. The birds that had been singing to their hearts content earlier had flown away, distressed by the loud human noises. The southerly breeze picked up and began dispersing the German laid smoke.

Dunn and Saunders knelt behind the east wall on the roof. They rose together, taking a quick peek, and ducked again.

"I'm sure some of those soldiers from the southeast position have made a flanking move and are in the grove somewhere," Dunn said.

"Aye. No doubt about that."

"That leaves some men at the southeast position and others in the south grove. We need to counterattack."

"I agree, mate. What'd'ya have in mind?"

Dunn suggested one of their contingency plans.

"That's one of the riskier ones," Saunders said. "But I don't see another way."

"We'll see how much more damage we can do from up here first."

"Right."

The two men carefully raised their heads again.

A tree branch moved near the front of the east grove. "I have movement on the right side of the east grove," Dunn said into his walkie-talkie.

In addition to Saunders and Dunn, those along the east wall were Commandos Alders and Holmes, and Rangers Higgins, Goerdt, and Lindstrom. Commando Kirby and Ranger Jonesy, with his sniper rifle, were positioned at the south wall overlooking the driveway and the south grove. Commando Myers with his sniper weapon was still on the west wall, and Commando Talbot held fast on the north wall.

Inside the villa at the southeast corner on the first floor were Rangers Cross, Brooks, Martelli, Schneider, and Wickham. Commando Bentley and Secret Service Agent Goodman were located one floor directly above Cross. Also on the second floor, Commando Barltrop and his partner, Agent Conner, guarded the villa's northeast corner. Still in their foxholes were Commando Forster and his partner directly in front of the villa, and Dickinson and his agent at the west end of the shrubs.

Dunn clicked his radio on and said, "Smoke is clearing. Get ready."

As if he'd spoken directly to the enemy commander, automatic fire poured from the three German locations: the east grove, the south grove and the position to the southeast between the groves. The fire was concentrated on the roof line and the villa's southeast corner.

Dickinson, realizing he wasn't taking fire, popped up to ground level with his weapon as did Agent Tucker. They fired long bursts at the south grove driving those Germans back down. The Commando yanked a Mills Bomb grenade from his shirt, pulled the pin, waited one count and threw it. The dark oval grenade tumbled through the air on a high arc, hit the ground about five yards from the edge of the grove, bounced once and stopped short. Its explosion threw dirt into the air in a conical shape.

Fire started again from the south grove chipping away at the earth around Dickinson's foxhole as he and the agent ducked.

Dunn heard the grenade and ran over to take a spot next to Jonesy, who was searching for a target. Dunn eyed the grove, thinking about the plan of counterattack he'd suggested to Saunders.

German weapons fired from the grove. He spotted four muzzle flashes, but not the enemy soldiers firing.

"Can you see anyone?" he asked Jonesy.

"I get glimpses, but nothing worthwhile yet."

"Stay on it. Be right back."

"Will do."

Dunn ran over to Myers and said, "Ira, come with me."

Myers pulled his Lee-Enfield back from the wall and ducked, turning to look at Dunn.

Dunn took off for Jonesy's spot and Myers followed.

Dunn pointed to a place two yards to Jonesy's right. "Here you go, Ira."

He knelt between the two snipers. They joined him.

"I need you guys to take out those four Germans in the grove. As soon as possible. If you have to, take low-percentage shots. Even winging someone in there will help. Understood?"

Both snipers replied, "Yes, Sarge."

Dunn clapped both men on the back and ran to a position beside Saunders.

Jonesy leaned over and said, "I'll focus on the left side, if you'll take the right."

"Right, Jonesy."

The two men were friends in the sense they were the same type of soldier, a sniper. Since their firing range competition, they'd grown close and often spent time discussing their world of killing from a great distance. Snipers were often disliked by the average soldier, as if they were some other kind of creature not to be trusted. Fortunately, Rangers and Commandos were completely accepting of them because they fully understood their value to a mission.

They lifted their rifles onto the roof wall and scanned the grove through their scopes.

Jonesy caught motion behind a tree. A dark shape leaned out with a weapon up, presumably to fire at Dickinson. At such a short distance, Jonesy didn't bother with waiting for the perfect stillness he needed for a six-hundred-yard shot. He fired and worked the bolt action, the expended shell flinging up and over the roof wall.

The dark shape snapped backwards and disappeared.

"One down," Jonesy said.

Instead of answering, Myers fired his rifle.

"Two down," he said as he worked his bolt.

Jonesy, while keeping an eye on the grove, used his radio, "Jonesy to Dickinson. Can you launch another grenade to the west side of the grove?"

Dickinson replied he would.

Jonesy watched the Commando throw his grenade. It was right on target, bouncing into the grove. When it exploded, Jonesy already had his eye back on the scope.

Neither sniper spotted movement. The Germans were staying put.

Jonesy lifted his radio. "Jonesy to Sarge."

"Dunn here."

"Only two are down."

"Roger. Two are down. Keep looking."

"Roger, Sarge."

They signed off.

Dunn noted a lull in the action on the east and southeast. What were they up to?

His answer came in the form of a fusillade from the east grove and the southeast position. He ducked down as rounds tore into the villa's wall just below him. When the Germans stopped to reload, he shouted, "Fire!"

Everyone on the rooftop facing east or south fired at their nearest target. Tree limbs in the grove snapped off under the onslaught.

On the first floor, Cross directed his men there to fire at the grove adding to the fury of bullets tearing the trees apart.

This attracted the attention of the southeast position German soldiers, who fired at Cross's location. Bullets tore into the window frames and the men ducked behind some overturned furniture.

A smoke grenade landed near the villa's wall and came to rest a few feet away. The released smoke swirled upward obscuring the grove.

Dunn radioed Cross. "I'm gonna need Brooks to meet me at the front door."

"He'll be there," Cross said.

"Roger, out."

"Out."

Dunn grabbed Higgins, Goerdt, and Lindstrom, leaving Jonesy in place on the south wall with Myers looking for targets in the south grove.

The four Rangers pounded down the stairs into the villa.

Becker sent four men forward from the east grove, leaving himself and two others to provide supporting fire. The west edge of the grove was only fifteen meters from the villa's southeast corner. The men ran crouched over in an assault line with a meter between them until they were five meters from the villa's southeast corner.

Becker opened fire, aiming at the roof, which was partially visible through the smoke trails.

The advancing Germans dropped to a knee. Two pulled stick grenades from their jackets and unscrewed the bottom cap. They yanked on the porcelain ball, which pulled the striker that ignited the fuse.

They tossed the grenades toward where they thought the first floor windows from which the Americans were firing were located. The Germans rose and ran to the villa's south wall, ducking down and covering their ears.

Martelli was firing through the southeasternmost window. He had no visible targets, but knew something was up. To his left were the others, Brooks, Schneider, and Wickham at the other larger window, firing their M1s. Cross was moving toward Martelli, shifting from the other window.

Something came tumbling out of the smoke and struck the bottom of the window frame.

Martelli stared in horror as the potato masher grenade bounced straight up and seemed to hang motionless in the air just outside his window.

"Grenade!"

Something hit the outside wall to his left and fell to the ground.

He pivoted to the left and saw everyone diving to the floor.

Except Cross, who evidently didn't hear him.

Martelli body tackled the much bigger sergeant.

The grenade, falling back to Earth, exploded just below the bottom window frame.

The grenade on the ground exploded.

The double concussion waves seemed to make the room expand as if it was breathing.

Wood chips from the shattered window frame shot into Martelli's back like miniature daggers.

Across the room, the glass doors in a china cabinet exploded.

Martelli grunted.

Chapter 28

Villa Bellavista
15 December, 0654 Hours

Cross, lying on his back, had dropped his rifle when Martelli tackled him. The lighter weight Bronx boy had groaned in pain and gone still, his breathing shallow.

"Al! Al!"

"Unnh," Martelli groaned again.

Cross put a hand on Martelli's back and it came back bloody. He couldn't just push Martelli off. He might roll onto his back where he was wounded.

"Bob! Give me a hand!"

Schneider, who'd risen to his knees to peek out the window, turned and saw why Cross was calling for help. Staying low, he ran over, grabbed Martelli under the armpits and lifted. Cross wriggled out from underneath.

Schneider leaned close to Martelli's ear and said, "Al, I need you to sit up. Can you do that for me?"

"Yeah."

Schneider rolled the wounded man onto his left side, and lifted him into a sitting position.

"You okay, here?" Cross asked.

"Yeah, Sarge. I have him," Schneider replied.

Cross bent over and spoke into Martelli's ear, "Al, thanks. You saved my ass."

Martelli opened his eyes. "Youse welcome."

Cross retrieved his rifle and moved over to the larger window with Wickham. He looked out. The smoke was finally clearing. He raised his weapon.

"You okay, Stanley?"

"Yeah."

"Let's get ready."

Wickham already had his rifle aimed at the grove. "I'm always ready."

Cross radioed Dunn. When Dunn answered, he told him about Martelli being down and being looked at by Schneider. Dunn acknowledged and asked him to keep him posted on his condition.

Dunn raced across the villa's foyer to the front door. Brooks was already there waiting.

"Okay, men, we have to go out low. I'll take point."

Without waiting, he pushed open the right-hand door of the double door entrance. Raising his M1, he stuck it out and leaned forward, looking right, straight, and left. What he saw on the left shocked him.

Just ten yards away, four Germans were kneeling, weapons at the ready, at the southeast corner of the villa, facing away.

The one closest to the corner pulled a long object from a pocket and yanked at the bottom. He raised his arm and Dunn saw the grenade.

He aimed at the German with the grenade and fired. He quickly fired three more shots. The Germans pitched forward, dropping their weapons and falling face first. The grenade hit the ground.

Dunn dove back inside the villa.

The grenade went off with a muffled *boom*.

Dunn waited a few seconds. Over his shoulder he told Lindstrom, "Cover me, Eugene. I'm gonna check those guys."

"I got you, Sarge," Lindstrom replied as he stepped into the open door and knelt, swinging his rifle around to aim at the four Germans.

Dunn ran low to the ground and close to the villa's south wall. He quickly checked the condition of the four men lying face down. All were dead. One shot in the center of the back through the heart. No doubts. Maybe that's why they called it 'dead center.' Immediate. Or so it was said. The one who'd dropped the grenade was a red and gray pulpy mess from the shoulders up.

Running back to the doors, he waved for the men to wait inside the foyer. He joined them, turning around to watch through the door.

On the radio he said, "Dunn to Dickinson and Forster."

"Dickinson here."

"Forster here."

"Withdraw from your position carefully. Meet me at the main entrance."

"Dickinson acknowledges."

"Forster acknowledges."

Dunn watched the shrub line closely. A moment later, two pairs of men were scrambling through the wall of plants and streaking toward the front door in a crouch. Bless their hearts, the two older Secret Service agents were keeping up with the soldiers.

All four men darted through the open door.

Dunn gave them a second to catch their breath. He explained what they were going to do. The new arrivals nodded.

"We have almost a full squad with the nine of us. I'll take point. Goerdt will take last spot." He pointed at the Commandos. "You two and your agents will be in the middle behind Lindstrom. Follow me."

He took off toward the two trucks parked not far away. He circled behind them and ran due west until he crossed the rounded ridgeline. He slowed and went downhill about five yards, enough to put their silhouettes below the ridge.

Turning south he followed the contour of the ridge. When he was southwest of the villa, he came across the bodies of two more Germans. Continuing around to the south he stopped and dropped to a knee when he had eyes on the south grove, which was only thirty yards away. Jonesy had confirmed two kills, but Dunn had definitely seen four muzzle flashes.

Dunn reminded Dickinson, Forster, and the agents they would provide cover fire. They were to start shooting when Dunn and the other four men had reached a point due south of the grove. A standard flanking maneuver.

The Commandos and agents dropped to prone positions and made their weapons ready.

Dunn took off straight south, putting the ridge above him again. He and the other four Rangers turned east at a distance of twenty-five yards from the men left behind. They ran another thirty-five yards until they were due south of the south grove. He and the other men got into a prone position and combat crawled forward until they could see the grove. He raised his head just enough for Dickinson to see him.

The deep sounds of four Thompson submachine guns came from the supporting fire position.

Dunn watched the grove. After about thirty seconds, he spotted motion near the grove's west edge.

Two MP40s fired several long bursts at Dickinson and crowd, all of whom pressed deeper into the ground.

When the two Germans stopped to reload, Dickinson and his men fired their entire magazines in two-shot bursts.

Dunn and his men jumped to their feet and charged the grove.

SS Major Becker, kneeling behind a large oak tree, was reaching the worry stage. The two men in Group D on the far side of the villa were most certainly dead. The four men who had charged the villa through the smoke, and thrown grenades, were likely dead. He'd heard the crisp four shots of an American M1 and a grenade going off outside the villa. The south grove team could be down from four, but to what he had no way of knowing. Including himself, he only had three soldiers in the east grove. Plus the six survivors in Group A, which was the position southeast of the villa, gave him just nine men on this side of the villa. He realized, too late, that he'd severely underestimated the enemy's capabilities. He decided he would make one more attempt to knock out some of the enemy. He pulled a whistle from his shirt pocket and blew it twice.

Saunders' ears perked up at the whistle coming from the grove to the east. "Get ready, lads."

MP40s unleashed bullets from the southeast position and they chipped and slapped at the wall surrounding the roof. The men there had no choice but to duck.

From their second-floor northeast position, Barltrop and the American Secret Service agent fired their Thompsons at the Germans in the southeast position. Cross and Wickham on the first floor southeast also fired at the southeast position forcing the Germans to dive behind the ridge.

Dunn and his four men ran forward and entered the south grove from the south side. Once there, they spread out facing west, finding cover behind trees. He could hear the chatter of the MP40s just ahead of him.

Moving forward one tree and a few yards at a time, the five Rangers advanced toward the two Germans firing at the support team. Dunn spotted the Germans from a distance of ten yards. He glanced to the right at his line of men. They were watching him closely. He pointed at his eyes with two fingers, then pointed one straight ahead at the Germans. He held up two fingers. He gave a signal telling them to wait for him to fire first. They nodded their understanding.

Raising his M1, he took aim and fired, as did the other four Rangers. The two Germans' coats erupted in blood and they crumpled to the ground.

Dunn ran forward to check on the bodies, and confirmed they were dead. He stepped through the tree line and waved at Dickinson, who waved back. He and his men ran on a direct route to the grove to join Dunn. Dickinson clapped the Ranger on the shoulder and nodded. Dunn returned the nod.

"Follow me," he said.

He turned and ran through the grove, the mixed squad of Rangers, Commandos and older Secret Service agents charging after him.

At the east end of the grove, he stopped and knelt behind a tree. The other men knelt where they could maintain cover.

He recalled what he'd seen of the German positions from the roof. Straight ahead of him had been a large group of over a dozen, the southeast position. He suspected it had split and those coming from the east grove had originally been at the southeast position. That meant the remaining force there, since he couldn't see them, must be farther along the ridgeline. He glanced left at the villa. Sporadic fire was still coming from the east grove, the southeast position just out of his view, and from various points in or on the villa. Judging from the shots he heard from the east grove, the number of Germans there must be quite small. The four he'd killed near the front door had surely come from there. He pictured everything in his mind and decided on the action necessary.

A shrill pair of whistle blows pierced the morning Sardinian air. All of the German weapons ceased firing.

Dunn frowned. He grabbed his walkie-talkie and keyed the button. "Dunn to Saunders."

"Saunders here."

"See any movement?"

"Negative. Where are you?"

"South."

"Roger."

"Heading to the east in a moment."

"Roger."

They signed off.

Dunn told his men how the next attack would go.

Becker told the two men near him, "Target the second-floor window, right side."

The men shifted the barrels of their MP40s.

He blew his whistle twice.

MP40s in the east grove and the southeast position opened fire.

Bullets ripped into the window's wood frame and sprayed to the left across the opening.

Barltrop, who'd been peeking outside beside Agent Conner, grunted as he went down.

Agent Conner could say nothing. A bullet created a third eye just above his nose.

Cross, Wickham, and Schneider, who'd finished patching up Martelli, were exchanging fire with the southeast position, as was Saunders' group on the roof. The three ducked back as bullets shredded the wood in the window that survived the potato masher.

Cross leaned into the opening and fired. An incoming 9mm round found its mark.

RONN MUNSTERMAN

Chapter 29

Villa Bellavista
15 December, 0705 Hours

Dunn led the men along the ridgeline, staying low. When he reached a point about thirty-five yards east of the south grove, he stopped and lowered himself into a prone position. He waved at his men to get down and wait.

Combat crawling forward, he advanced slowly staying alert for motion. After about ten yards of this, he spotted a German, who was firing at the villa from a prone position.

Inching forward, he gained view of several other Germans, also firing.

Seeing enough, he backed up until he was out of sight, and turned around, looking somewhat like an awkward bug changing directions. He made his way back to the men.

"As I thought. There's at least four there, although I think there must be a few more from the weapons sounds. The plan stands. Let's go."

Lying on his back and gasping from the pain of the gunshots, Barltrop grabbed his walkie-talkie with a trembling hand. He pressed the button with a bloody finger. In a weak voice he said, "Barltrop to anyone. We're shot. Need help. Second floor northeast." He let go of the radio and closed his eyes. He'd just rest for a minute.

"Kathy . . ." he whispered.

Saunders' knees went to jelly at Barltrop's weak call for help. He struggled to think clearly. Who was closest to his best friend? It finally came to him, seemingly after minutes of thought, which was actually only a second or two.

"Bentley. Go help Barltrop. ASAP, lad!"

"Roger, Sarge."

Schneider dropped to his knees next to Cross, who had fallen on his left side.

"Sarge! Where are you hit?"

Cross grunted as he rolled onto his back. That was when the big man could see blood soaking through Cross's shirt sleeve. The outer side of his right bicep had been hit.

"Let's get that shirt off."

"No, you get back to firing at those bastards."

"You sure?"

"Go on."

Schneider rejoined Wickham and the two continued firing.

Cross used his left hand to push himself upright and leaned against a chair that was tipped over on its side. He unbuttoned his shirt and shrugged it off, grimacing as he did. He examined his wound. It appeared to be a deep graze. It was a little more than two inches long and was bleeding pretty heavily. It wasn't as bad as Wickham's had been, he was relieved to see. He raised his arm so his bicep was above his heart. That seemed to help slow the bleeding a bit. Awkwardly, with one hand, he struggled to open his first aid kit on his belt.

A hand came out of nowhere. "Let me help youse," Martelli said, in his Bronx boy accent.

Cross nodded his thanks.

Martelli set about taking care of the squad's beloved second in command. As he moved, he hid the grimace caused by the wounds in his back from Cross.

Four of Dunn's men, Dickinson, Forster, Brooks, and Higgins crawled directly east to a position south and behind the Germans. Dunn, Goerdt, Lindstrom, and the two Secret Service agents moved along the ridgeline until Dunn could see about half of the Germans.

No one ever figured out why, but one of the Germans in the middle of the unit suddenly turned and looked over his right shoulder to the south. He spotted movement and raised the alarm.

Before Dickinson could order his men back, the Germans had all pivoted one-eighty and fired at his group. He yelled, "Fire!"

Dickinson's group and Dunn's men all opened fire at the same time.

Brooks took a round through his body. Being in a prone position meant the bullet entered left of his neck and traversed through his chest, cutting his ascending aorta in two before piercing his heart. He simply died without a sound.

The Germans, caught in a crossfire, began crawling backwards to the northeast to get out of view. They fired as they moved.

Higgins raised up slightly to get a better shot at one of the retreating Germans. Before he could fire his M1, a 9mm round struck his right shoulder, bore through and snapped the collar bone, and lodged in his side, just missing his right kidney as it streaked past. He dropped his rifle and cried out.

The Germans retreated far enough so they could get out of sight and out of the firing line of both enemy groups. Several of them threw smoke grenades between them and the villa, and one between them and the enemy behind them.

Dunn and Dickinson lost sight of the Germans.

Under cover of the smoke, Dickinson and one of the Secret Service agents jumped to their feet, grabbed Brooks and dragged him back to Dunn's position. The other agent helped Higgins to his feet, retrieved the dropped M1, and they slowly made their way back to Dunn.

Bentley ran across the room and fell to his knees beside Barltrop. He glanced at the American Secret Service agent, who was lying on his side. His condition was clear. Dead.

Barltrop's eyes were closed.

"Sarge! Wake up!" Bentley shook Barltrop gently and was relieved when the senior Commando's eyes fluttered open.

Bentley tore open Barltrop's shirt and examined him. There was blood all over his right chest.

He stopped himself just in time, so he didn't blurt out what he was thinking, *Bloody hell, Sarge!*

Instead he calmly said, "We'll take care of you, Sarge."

Barltrop nodded his head, and grimaced.

Bentley opened his first aid kit and set to work.

Barltrop had been shot twice in the upper right chest, the puncture wounds about an inch apart. Blood was pouring out. He leaned close to examine the holes. No bubbles.

"Right. Sarge, looks like they missed your lung."

"Two?"

Bentley nodded.

" 'kay," was all Barltrop could manage to whisper.

Bentley poured sulfa over the wounds and placed a large bandage over the two punctures. He pressed hard, causing Barltrop to groan.

Taping the bandage in place, Bentley said, "Got to roll you over."

" 'kay."

Barltrop cried out when Bentley rolled him left. He slipped Barltrop's right arm out of the shirt and pulled it back. There were two holes there. He held Barltrop on his left side using his right leg as a leaning post. He examined both for bubbles. Again nothing. He quickly treated the wounds, covering them with a bandage.

Gently lowering Barltrop onto his back he wiped his bloody hands on his pants. He grabbed his walkie-talkie and said, "Bentley to Saunders."

"Saunders."

"We need to get Sergeant Barltrop to a hospital. He has two gunshots in the upper right chest. Through and through, but no air bubbles. I bandaged him up."

"I'll send someone to help you carry him downstairs."

"Roger. The American agent is dead."

Saunders hesitated at the news. "Roger."

"Bentley out."

"Saunders out."

Bentley didn't hear anything over the radio, so he assumed whomever was coming was on the roof with Saunders.

Becker heard his men from the southeast position enter the east grove behind him. It was time, he decided. He told the two men with him to follow.

A sudden burst of fire from the rooftop struck the giant of a man who'd thrown the grenade over the grove.

Becker turned in time to see him collapse onto his back. He ran over and checked on him. It was bad. Very bad. His chest was riddled with bullet holes. Still breathing, but that was a struggle.

He touched the man's shoulder and he looked up at him. The giant nodded and closed his eyes.

"I'm sorry, old friend," Becker said, rising.

Leading the way east, he met the surviving six men. All together he'd lost twelve men, leaving him with eight. Less than a squad.

He pointed at four men and said, "Smoke grenades, so we can leave."

The men nodded and threw their grenades.

A minute later, a wall of smoke rose and blocked all view of the villa and the southeast position.

The Germans ran at full speed back toward their route to the base camp.

As he ran, Becker worried about what in the world he was going to tell Kaltenbrunner. Furious at himself for his failure, he knew this was going to be a black mark against his otherwise stellar record. Frowning, he ran on.

Dunn looked down at the body of Brooks and shook his head. Forster was giving first aid to Higgins, the young man from Lincoln, Nebraska. He tapped Dickinson on the shoulder.

"Let's go see what's happening."

"Right, Sarge."

The two men moved forward slowly in a combat crouch, their weapons ready. They advanced to the position where Dunn had been able to see the Germans not long ago. Inching forward, they made their way to where the Germans had been. They found nothing. They'd completely missed them.

Dunn peered over the ridgeline toward the east grove, but the smoke obscured everything. He dropped to a knee, tugging Dickinson down with him.

"Better stay out of sight so our own guys don't plonk us."

Dickinson nodded.

Dunn got on his radio. "Dunn to Saunders."

"Saunders here."

"We're at the southeast position, don't shoot us. No Germans here."

"Roger. We'll target the east grove as soon as we can see the bloody thing."

"Roger. I have Brooks killed and Higgins wounded."

"Sorry to hear that. Steve . . ."

Dunn waited briefly for Saunders to finish his sentence, but only silence came.

"I heard the news, Mac. I'm sorry. Let's send Higgins with him to the hospital. I think a bullet is still in him."

"Roger. Bentley is taking care of Steve. Do you think they're retreating?"

"As soon as the smoke clears, Dickinson and I are going to make our way to the east grove to make sure they're gone. Keep your eyes open for us."

"Roger."

They signed off.

"Ready, Christopher?"

"Yes."

The two men carefully lifted their heads over the ridgeline and peered north, and northeast. The smoke was beginning to waft away on the southerly breeze. Dunn could see the treetops and some of their upper trunks.

"Should be clear soon," he said.

"Right."

Finally, they could see clearly. They examined the area to the north, and the northeast again.

"No movement," Dickinson said.

"Nope."

Dunn lifted his radio to his lips. "Dunn to Saunders."

"Saunders here."

"See anything anywhere?"

"Not a bloody thing. Been checking through binocs, too."

"Roger. Heading to the grove now."

"Roger. Saunders out."

"Dunn out."

Dunn glanced at Dickinson, who'd been keeping an eye out while Dunn was talking to Saunders.

"Ready for the dash?"

"Yes, Sarge."

The men climbed over the ridgeline, again staying in a crouch. Once on level ground they sprinted the thirty yards to the grove and stopped just inside, taking cover behind the trees. Cautiously, they advanced from tree to tree until they'd made their way to the west edge of the grove. There were no Germans so far.

"Let's walk through the grove some more to search for any dead or wounded Germans. We should split up to cover more ground faster."

"Sure thing, Sarge."

Dickinson walked off to the northeast.

Dunn headed north through the grove finding no one until he was about ten yards from his starting position. He spotted some feeble movement on the ground. Raising his rifle and aiming at the form lying in the grass beside a tree, he advanced using a slide step, never letting his eyes leave the form. As he got closer, he could tell the man was severely wounded, but still breathing, lying on his back. He approached the man from a direction that kept the man's head closest to him and the feet the farthest. This way the man couldn't easily raise a weapon and fire at him.

The man heard Dunn's soft footsteps and he opened his eyes looking upside down at Dunn, who was standing directly above him.

He made a weak move toward the Luger's holster on his belt.

Dunn bent over and grabbed the man's hand, saying, "*Nein*." He removed the pistol from the holster and threw it to the side in the grass.

Dunn examined the wounded man, who seemed extraordinarily tall, even lying on the ground. He was bleeding profusely from several bullet wounds in his torso. Kneeling, Dunn gently grasped the man's bloody hand. The man's breathing suddenly grew ragged. Dunn bent his head and recited the Lord's Prayer out loud.

The man watched and listened as if he understood. He struggled to take a breath, but managed to whisper, "Thank you."

Dunn nodded. "*Bitte*."

The German's eyes closed. He took one more shuddering breath and became still.

Dunn folded the man's hands across his chest. He rose to his feet and turned to find Dickinson standing a few feet away. He hadn't even heard him approach.

They stared at each other for a moment.

"You're a good man, Sarge."

Dunn tipped his head. "Find anything?" he asked.

"Nope."

Dunn called Saunders. When the big Commando answered, he said, "The grove is clear."

With a "roger," Saunders signed off.

Into his radio, he said, "Dunn to everyone. Make your way back to the villa. Keep your eyes open. Forster, get Higgins ready for transport to the hospital. Bentley, do the same for Barltrop."

He received two "rogers" to his individual instructions.

"Hang on a minute. I want to check this man's pockets." Dunn knelt and went through all of the German's pockets. He rose. "Nothing there. Let's get on over there, Christopher."

"I'm ready."

The two men strode off, side by side.

Chapter 30

Villa Bellavista
15 December, 0732 Hours

Dunn and Saunders stood together in the room where the planning meetings had taken place. Saunders had left Jonesy and Myers, the snipers, Kirby, Talbot, and Holmes on the roof to watch for a potential return of the enemy. Dunn had sent a detail of Wickham, Goerdt, Lindstrom, and Forster to gather the dead bodies and take them to a central point on the lawn by the blown out southeast window.

Saunders had sent Barltrop, Higgins, and Martelli to the airbase hospital with Dickinson driving the big truck down and back. Cross had refused to go explaining it was "just a scratch."

The redheaded Commando looked particularly upset to Dunn.

"Worried about Steve?"

"Aye."

"I wish I could help you. He'll be okay, right?"

Saunders turned his blue eyes on Dunn. He gave a tiny shrug. "I don't know for sure. I think so, but there's no guarantee."

Dunn put a hand on Saunders' shoulder. "I understand."

"This is our life now, lad."

Dunn nodded, but could think of nothing to say.

The room's main door opened and a disheveled Agent Elmer Perkins entered. He spotted the two soldiers and headed their way.

"Are you all right, Mr. Perkins?" Dunn asked gently.

Perkins' expression was quite sad. "Agent Conner was a good man. I've never lost a man before." He frowned. "Well, I've lost friends before in the first war. But this . . ."

"Is different because he was your responsibility."

Perkins nodded slowly. "Yes . . . I suppose that's it. How?" He looked from one soldier to the other. "How in the world do you handle it?"

Dunn rubbed his chin. He sighed. "That's a good question, sir. We all deal with it in our own way. One thing that helps us is knowing we were all doing our job the best we could."

"I see. Do you . . . get used to it?"

Dunn glanced at Saunders, who swallowed hard. Turning back to Perkins, he said, "No, I don't think we ever do."

Perkins nodded. "Thank you for keeping the president safe. We're very grateful."

Dunn tipped his head. "Just doing our job, sir. But you're welcome. Is he coming upstairs soon?"

"I sent some men to do that. I'd better go get ready for him." He offered his hand and the two men shook it.

After Perkins left the room, Saunders stepped over to a chair and collapsed onto it, elbows on his knees. He put his head in his hands. Dunn sat down next to him. There was no need for conversation and the two men sat in dark, worried silence.

1/2 kilometer north of Villa Bellavista
0737 Hours

Sturmbannführer, SS Major, Erich Becker, sat with his seven surviving men in a small circle. They'd stopped running when they'd entered a large wooded area to rest and for him to think. None of the survivors had been wounded, so they were in good shape physically, but they'd lost twelve brothers in arms, good, close friends. They were frightened. They were angry.

Becker looked at each man, making sure he made eye contact. When he was done, he said, "We had bad intelligence, gentlemen, but we almost pulled it off anyway. We ended up walking into quite the buzzsaw with the soldiers who were there. I don't know about you, but I saw Americans and Englishmen fighting us. I caught a glimpse of a Ranger patch on one of the Americans, and based on the way they fought, I'd say the English were Commandos."

The men nodded at this assessment.

"We are severely outnumbered. However, our mission is far from over. We just have to outsmart the enemy. I have an idea."

The men leaned forward as he spoke. After a short while, they were all nodding, their expressions grim.

Villa Bellavista
0742 Hours

The door to the meeting room opened again. Dunn and Saunders looked over. Roosevelt wheeled into the room, followed by Perkins, who was pushing the president's wheelchair, Churchill, and last Detective Inspector Thompson. Dunn and Saunders jumped to their feet.

When the two national leaders reached the two soldiers, both men offered their hands. Everyone shook.

"Have a seat, gentlemen, won't you?" Roosevelt said.

Dunn and Saunders sat.

"Thank you for fighting off the enemy. You've done a superlative job keeping everyone safe," Roosevelt said.

"Here, here," Churchill said, smiling.

Roosevelt's expression grew somber. "Mr. Perkins told me we have lost some men, and others have been wounded and are on the way to the hospital. I am so very sorry about your men."

"Thank you, sir," Dunn said.

Saunders nodded his agreement.

"I'd appreciate a list of names, and what in particular has happened to them."

"The same goes for me," Churchill said.

"Will do, sir," Dunn replied.

"Aye, I will, too."

"If you'll excuse us, we're going to have our conference that this was all about in the first place," the president said.

Dunn and Saunders rose.

"Please just ask for anything you need. Our schedule remains the same. Make sure your men get whatever they want to eat and plenty of rest."

Dunn grinned at the mention of food. "Thank you, Mr. President, the men will appreciate that. And so will I."

Roosevelt grinned.

Perkins turned the wheelchair around and the group of four left the room.

"I'd better go check on the body detail, Mac. Do you want to tag along?"

"Aye, may as well have something to do until I hear from the hospital."

"Aren't the phones off?"

"Oh, bloody hell. I'll go talk to Perkins and Thompson after."

The two men left the villa through the front door and turned left. When they reached the southeast corner, they found the body detail laying a German down. Dunn counted the dead Germans.

"Is this all of them, Rob?"

Goerdt nodded. "Yes, Sarge."

"I'd like you guys to check each one's pockets to see if you can find anything."

"Will do, Sarge."

Goerdt gathered his men together and they started the gruesome task.

"Twelve dead. I bet they had twenty or so all together," Dunn said to Saunders.

"Aye, sounds about right to me."

Dunn spotted Brooks' body placed far away from the Germans. He had been thoughtfully covered by a blanket from inside the villa. Walking over, he knelt and pulled back the blanket. Brooks' movie-star face looked serene, his eyes closed. Dunn felt a hand on his shoulder, but didn't look up. Instead he said a prayer for Brooks and his family back in Los Angeles. He covered Brooks and rose.

Saunders removed his hand from Dunn's shoulder.

Dunn looked around the villa's grounds which, for the most part, appeared unchanged in spite of the ferocious firefight. He looked at the window destroyed by the grenade. All of the glass was gone, some of it sparkling in the grass below. The wood frame was nearly completely gone, with wood chips everywhere, too. Hundreds of bullet-made pockmarks peppered the wall around the opening. He shook his head.

"If the German leader had brought twice as many men . . ."

"Aye."

"But he didn't." Dunn turned around to gaze out at the Mediterranean Sea, glittering in the distance.

"I'm sure he didn't know we would be here. He was expecting only the Secret Service and Churchill's bodyguards. He had faulty intelligence."

"Sounds about right."

"How did he not see us arrive? Wouldn't you have left someone to watch the target prior to the attack?"

"I would have, aye."

"So he made a major mistake. One that cost him over half of his men. He's gonna be mad as hell."

"What are you saying?"

"An attack of this magnitude had to have been ordered from the top."

"Hitler, you mean?"

"Yep. Or at least he approved it."

"I agree. What's your point?"

"Would you want to go home and tell the *Führer* you'd failed?"

"I would not."

"We'd better stay on alert until we can get out of here. I'm going up to the roof to relieve Jonesy."

"I'll go with you."

"No, Mac. You should eat and rest. Maybe find out how Steve, Al, and Chuck are doing a little later, after you fix up the phone situation with Perkins and Thompson."

"Right, okay. I'll let you know when I hear something."

"Everyone else can eat and rest. Let's start with four-hour shifts. Maybe I can get the villa staff to bring up some breakfast and water to the rooftop."

"Good idea."

Goerdt ran up to Dunn. "Sarge."

"Yeah?"

"Nothing in any of their pockets."

Dunn nodded. "Okay. Thanks for making sure."

"You're welcome."

Goerdt ran back to his men.

Dunn and Saunders separated with Saunders going to gather the Commandos and Rangers not assigned to the roof. Dunn found the butler, the head of the household staff, and explained what he needed. The butler nodded and said, "Of course, sir."

Dunn started to correct him, but changed his mind. In the man's eyes, he was a guest and entitled to 'sir.' He made his way to the roof and told Jonesy to head on downstairs for breakfast and some rest. Jonesy didn't argue. Checking in with each of the four Commandos, he told them breakfast was coming. They nodded gratefully.

The day passed slowly. It grew warm on the roof, but the breeze kept it comfortable.

At about noon, Martelli called Saunders from the hospital with good news—the phones had been switched back on. Barltrop and Higgins had made it through surgery and were resting comfortably. He himself had had the wood splinters dug out and his back treated and bandaged. Saunders passed on the good news to the men, and to Roosevelt and Churchill.

All of the German bodies had been taken to a mortuary in Cagliari. Corporal Brooks' and Agent Conner's bodies were taken in one deuce and a half, separate from the other one carrying the Germans, to the American airbase. The Secret Service agent was immediately placed aboard a C-47 to start his final journey home. Brooks would be sent to an American cemetery near Rome.

Chapter 31

Gertrude awoke with a start. Someone was shaking her, hard. She opened her eyes to find Louise, one of the instructors, leaning over her. She had her finger to her lips. She whispered, "Get dressed. Now!"

Gertrude rolled out of bed wearing blue pajamas. She quickly slipped out of them, snapped on a bra, and put on a pair of panties, dark pants, a top, and her boots. She automatically pulled the covers back over her single bed. She grabbed her jacket off a hook on the wall.

Louise beckoned for her to follow.

They left the four-person hut and were out in the cold night air, which helped shock Gertrude more alert.

"Where are we going?"

"The armory."

Louise took off running forcing Gertrude to do the same to keep up. Inside the armory, Louise asked, "Your pistol of choice?"

"Colt .45."

Louise unlocked the cabinet where the .45s were stored. She grabbed one, checked to make sure the chamber was empty and handed it to Gertrude, who also looked inside the chamber. Louise grabbed two magazines and gave them to Gertrude, who ensured they were full.

"Don't load it yet."

"Okay."

Gertrude dropped both magazines into her left jacket pocket.

"Go grab a holster over there." Louise pointed at a rack filled with leather .45 holsters.

Gertrude was already picking one. She buckled it on and holstered her weapon.

"Let's go."

They left and locked up the armory. Louise jogged ahead and Gertrude followed. They traveled about a hundred yards and stopped by the front door of a log house the trainees had been expressly forbidden to enter at any time. Being caught there meant immediate dismissal from the program. No one tried, although everyone wondered what was in there.

Rick was standing by the door.

"Hello, Peggy," he said, not smiling.

"Hi Rick," Gertrude answered, apprehensive.

Louise turned and ran back toward the huts without saying a word. Gertrude assumed she was going to wake up another victim.

"This is a combat shooting exercise. There's at least one Nazi soldier in there. Go in, find him, and kill him. I'll be right behind you to grade you."

"Okay, Rick."

"I should also say that shooting me is cause for immediate dismissal."

She stared at him briefly. "Uh, okay."

She noticed he hadn't instructed her to load the weapon. Clearly a test. She turned away and smiled to herself as she slipped a magazine in, and chambered a round. She tried the doorknob, only to find it locked. She stepped back and kicked it right next to the knob. The door burst open, banging against the interior wall.

She crouched and moved close to the door. She peered inside. Faint light made it possible for her to see a long hallway going straight ahead. She entered the log house and glided down the hallway. Rick followed from a distance of a few yards.

A large life-sized target, an armed German soldier aiming at her popped out into the hallway from an open doorway on her right. Her hair stood on end as she crouched and fired her double-tap. She knew she hit the target, but not where. It slid out of sight.

She forced herself to slow her breathing, which had grown rapid and shallow.

She continued down the hallway and found a set of stairs leading up. She looked at the top, but saw nothing. Climbing the stairs, she placed her feet near the right wall to hopefully reduce wood creaking. When she neared the top, she was able to see that at the top of the stairs, the landing U-turned left into a hallway. A railing guarded the stairs. She placed her back against the wall and went up the stairs slowly.

Rick stayed at the bottom of the steps.

Just as she was able to see over the top of the railing into a room, another German soldier target snapped into the doorway. She fired twice. She was able to see she'd hit it in the chest. It snapped back out of sight. She checked the hallway that went to her left and saw nothing. She turned to her right and found another open doorway by the landing. She leaned forward just enough to see inside the room.

A target popped into view by the window. She fired twice striking it in the head. She knelt and ejected her empty magazine. That magazine's seventh round was already chambered after firing the sixth. She slapped in the second magazine, but didn't pull back on the slide, to keep the chambered round in place, giving her eight shots left.

She left the room and continued along the hallway. She carefully entered the room where a target had popped up. Another one jumped at her from the window. She shot it and it disappeared. Four down, she thought. Would she run out of rounds?

She suddenly realized she was soaked with sweat and some was dangerously close to dripping into her eyes. She wiped it away with her left sleeve. Ready to advance, she carefully left the room and looked down the hallway. While she was inside the room, Rick had run up the stairs and stood with his back to the wall behind her.

The next room was about ten feet farther down the hallway. She positioned herself against the wall across from the railing over the stairwell. There was another room at the end of the hall. That doorway was to her left. She would have to clear the next room while being aware of the other. She slid along the wall until she reached the first open doorway. She peeked in.

A target popped out from behind a huge wooden wardrobe set on the far side of the room. She shot it and entered the room, checking it for others. It was clear. Five down. How many more? She could shoot two more with her four rounds left. What about those trainees who selected a revolver with only six rounds?

She shook her head and focused on her job. Exiting the room, she moved toward the last one on this floor.

Using the same technique, she slid along the hallway with her shoulder brushing along the wall. At the last doorway, she paused to take a calming breath.

She peered into the room. Her eyebrows flew up and she shot the soldier twice in the chest. He fell over backward, the cigarette in his hand falling onto the top of the desk he'd been sitting behind.

From a few feet behind her, she heard, "Well done, Peggy. You may stand down. Holster your weapon. Follow me. I want you to meet Hans."

Rick walked past her into the room. They walked around the desk and she could tell that her target had been a dummy dressed in a German uniform, including a helmet. He'd been unarmed.

"Good job of not letting the surprise of seeing a more lifelike target stop you from shooting. Also the same goes for the fact that he was unarmed."

"Thank you, Rick. How did I do on the others?"

"Very well. You hit each target in a fatal spot, either the face or the center of the chest. You really are quite an excellent shooter. Your reaction time was good. Your crouch and form were very good. Keep it up."

"Thank you."

Rick nodded. He bent over and picked up Hans and placed him back in the chair. He put the unlit cigarette back in his hand and the helmet on his head.

Gertrude looked closely at the dummy's face. It had blue eyes. Some detail to include.

"Head on back to your hut and get some shut eye. Say nothing to anyone. Be sure to return the weapon, but mark it so you can clean it sometime tomorrow."

"Yes, sir."

She left and jogged back to the armory. Mildred was there and she received the Colt and marked it for later cleaning. She said nothing to Gertrude. Nothing new.

After climbing back into her bed, Gertrude was asleep in seconds.

RONN MUNSTERMAN

Chapter 32

Villa Bellavista
17 December, 1022 Hours, Cagliari time, two days later

President Roosevelt and Prime Minister Churchill were seated side by side at a long table covered with papers and maps of Europe. Both were smoking their preferred tobacco source: Roosevelt his cigarette in a long black holder, Churchill his cigar. Smoke swirled around them like low lying clouds. They had spent hours over the previous two days drawing lines on the map of Europe showing where they'd like to see the Allies' front line by the end of January. That line was the Rhine River, about fifty miles east of the Allies' front line. They'd started working on the plan the day the German attack had been fought off.

The Rangers and Commandos had maintained a vigilant guard on the villa, day and night. Nothing else had happened. Commando Barltrop, and Rangers Higgins and Martelli were recovering well at the hospital. According to the last Roosevelt had been told, they would all be able to fly back to England when the conference concluded.

The soldiers who were off guard duty had pitched in to help the villa staff clean up and set to right the furniture that had been knocked over. Wood had been nailed over the broken and shattered windows. The front door had been repaired. Workmen from Cagliari had been arranged to come fix the other damage to the property.

Churchill had tried to entice FDR into paying for the damage to the villa, since he had more money in the treasury. FDR had politely told his friend no, a fifty-fifty split was more appropriate, especially since it had been Churchill's idea in the first place.

Someone knocked on the door once and a Signal Corps captain entered the room with a piece of paper in his hand. He stopped right after closing the door. He made eye contact with Roosevelt's aide, Jim Burns, who rose and walked over to him.

"An urgent message, sir," the captain said, holding out the paper. He was responsible for the SIGABA machine that traveled with the president. It was an encryption machine similar to the more famous Enigma machine. Dunn and Saunders had recovered a stolen machine from the Germans after breaching a castle in Austria. The U.S. Army had immediately changed all of the codes right after that.

Burns took the paper and as he read it, his mouth dropped open. He read it again and his jaw muscles clenched several times.

"You've authenticated the message?"

"Absolutely, sir. It's genuine."

Burns nodded, satisfied, but sickened.

He thanked the captain, who left. Turning around, he walked briskly straight to Roosevelt holding up the paper.

"I'm sorry, Mr. President, but I have bad news from General Eisenhower. At five-thirty hours yesterday morning the Germans launched an artillery barrage along an eighty-mile-wide line that lasted ninety minutes. Following that, they attacked through the Ardennes with armor and infantry. They're driving our units back."

"The Ardennes? Again?" Churchill shouted. "They surprised us just like 1940?"

"I'm afraid so, sir."

Roosevelt leaned over the map they'd worked on and argued about for so many grueling hours. He tapped a spot with his pencil. "Look here."

Churchill and the aides looked at the map where Roosevelt's pencil touched it.

"They're trying to split our forces apart. That's right along the seam between us."

"Yes, I see that," Churchill said, scowling.

Roosevelt glanced at his aide. "What else?"

"Casualties are high, and we've had whole units captured around Malmedy, sir. As you know, we're extremely thin on the ground there. On top of that the weather is terrible with thick cloud cover, so no help from the air."

Roosevelt dropped his pencil on the table. "Well, that makes all this work just wishful thinking." He waved a hand across the map and sighed deeply. He grabbed the map intending to crumple it into a ball, but thought better of it and let go.

"Gentlemen, we may as well prepare to leave. No point in staying here any longer."

Churchill waved his cigar. "May as well have lunch first."

"Yes. I am hungry." Roosevelt turned to Burns. "Please advise Mr. Perkins, as well as Sergeants Dunn and Saunders, and Detective Inspector Thompson that we'll be leaving right after lunch."

"Right away, Mr. President."

Burns left the room, closing the door behind him. He found Perkins and a couple of other agents standing outside the front door talking in the bright morning sunshine. They turned toward him as soon as the door opened.

"Mr. Burns," Perkins said.

"The president wanted me to tell you we're leaving right after lunch due to a change in plans."

"Very good. We'll get started on preparations."

Burns found Dunn on the roof, Saunders in the eating hall, and DI Thompson in a room meeting with his team of bodyguards. He passed on the president's message. By the time he returned to the meeting room, Roosevelt and Churchill were eating lunch at the same table they'd been working on.

"Mr. President, everyone is aware and starting preparations."

"Excellent, Jim. Go grab yourself something to eat and join us."

"Thank you, sir."

Dunn ran down to the top floor and into the wing where some of his men were in their rooms. "Rangers, out here."

Cross, Goerdt, and Jonesy came out of their rooms and joined him.

"I already told the guys on the roof, but we're getting ready to leave right after the president and everyone finishes lunch. If you're hungry, better get down there."

Dunn grinned as he had to step aside for the men so they wouldn't trample him on the way to food. First lesson in the army: never stand between a soldier and food. Or a beer.

He went to his room and started packing his gear. He double-checked his two .45 caliber weapons, the Thompson and the 1911 Colt to ensure they were unloaded. He had cleaned them both after the firefight, plus his Garand rifle, as had everyone else. Wrapping them in oilcloth first, he slipped them carefully into one of his bags.

He went downstairs and joined his men for a quick sandwich and some coffee.

Saunders and some of his men were finishing up their lunch. Saunders nodded to Dunn.

Cross and Jonesy were arguing the merits of the Boston Red Sox versus the Chicago White Sox, each a lifelong fan of their respective teams.

"My White Sox were the last one to be in the Series," Jonesy said.

"Yeah, but that was twenty-five years ago," complained Cross. "Plus, you lost to the Reds.

"Still more recent," Jonesy insisted.

"Our record is four and oh. That beats your two and one." Cross sat back, triumphant.

Jonesy held up his hands in surrender.

Cross got an evil grin on his face and tipped his head toward Dunn. Jonesy grinned back. He knew what was coming.

"So, Sarge, how about them Cubs? Aren't they two and three in the series? And didn't my Sox beat them in 1918?"

Dunn looked at his friend over his ham sandwich. He swallowed a bite. "Wait 'til next year. I know they'll go to the Series!"

Cross and Jonesy laughed.

"Isn't that the Cubbies fans' mantra?"

Dunn grinned. "No, it's true this time."

Cross shook his head. "Well, we'll see, I guess."

Perkins and DI Thompson entered the room. Spotting Dunn, they walked over and sat down next to the Ranger.

"We'll be ready to go in ten minutes, Sergeant Dunn," Perkins said.

Thompson nodded, seconding Perkins' remark.

"Okay, thanks. Want to review the convoy plan?" Dunn replied.

"Yes, I do," the lead agent replied.

Dunn waved at Saunders and when he'd gotten the Commando's attention, beckoned him over. Saunders got up, tapping Kirby on the shoulder. The two men walked around the table and dragged a couple of chairs close, and sat down.

"We're leaving in ten minutes. We should review the convoy plans," Dunn told the Commandos.

"Sure," Saunders said.

The group discussed everything for about five minutes. When they were finished, Dunn asked, "Anything we haven't thought of?"

Everyone shook their heads.

"Are the president and prime minister really okay with the plan?"

Perkins gave a wry smile. "He said whatever you want to do is fine with him."

"Mr. Churchill said much the same thing, Sergeant," Thompson added.

"Well, all right. Let's go, men," Dunn said, rising.

Thirty minutes earlier, the conversation about the plan with the president and prime minister had gotten off to a rocky start.

"Mr. President, Mr. Prime Minister, please do as we ask," Dunn pleaded, after a couple of minutes of discussion.

Roosevelt and Churchill glanced at each other.

"We simply can't have it said we stayed behind out of fear," Roosevelt said.

"Absolutely not, sir. Just think of it as making a prudent choice and leaving the battlefield temporarily."

Roosevelt knocked the ash off his cigarette in a nearby ashtray. "Have you ever left the battlefield? Temporarily?"

Dunn sighed, exasperated. "I'd have to say, no, sir. But that's different. I'm meant to be there. You're meant to lead from elsewhere. In this case, it means staying behind while we go see if we can flush out the bastards."

Roosevelt's lips twitched, as if suppressing a smile.

"I do believe he's got you there," Churchill said. He smiled, and chuckled as if enjoying Roosevelt's position. That it was his position also was beside the point.

Roosevelt nodded, and took a puff. He held the smoke briefly, and blew it out.

"Very well, Sergeant Dunn, I accede to your and Sergeant Saunders', Mr. Perkins', and I daresay, Detective Inspector Thompson's, wishes. We will remain behind until you're satisfied it's safe for us to 'lead' our way down the hill."

Dunn sighed again, this time in relief.

"Thank you, sir. And you, too, Mr. Prime Minister." Dunn had a thoughtful expression on his face.

"Uh oh," Roosevelt murmured.

"Sir, do you happen to have another cigarette holder?"

"Could be. Why?"

"I'd like to borrow it."

"Okay." Roosevelt turned to Burns, who nodded and walked away.

"Mr. Prime Minister, happen to have an extra cigar?"

Churchill's eyes twinkled as he reached inside his suit jacket. He pulled out a fresh cigar with a flourish.

Dunn took it and slipped it into his shirt pocket. "Thank you, sir."

Burns returned with an identical black cigarette holder, which he handed to Dunn.

Dunn slid that into the same shirt pocket.

"Thanks. Perhaps your hats, as well."

"As you wish, my boy," Roosevelt said.

"We'll leave a detail here with you."

"Thank you."

Dunn turned to leave, but Roosevelt held up a hand to stop him.

"May as well tell you why we're leaving early. It'll be in the *New York Times* tomorrow and the rest of the country's papers soon after."

"All right, sir."

"The Germans have attacked again through the Ardennes. We're scrambling to stave off the push."

"Oh, no. How bad?"

Roosevelt frowned. "It might be pretty bad."

"When we get back, I'll check with Colonel Kenton, see if there's anything our company can do to help."

Roosevelt nodded. Of course, Dunn would offer to help.

"Thank you. You're a terrific soldier."

"Thank you, sir."

Dunn asked Lindstrom and Goerdt to roll up the canvas sides on the deuce and a half trucks. While they were doing that, the Rangers boarded their truck and the Commandos theirs. Everyone had pulled their Thompson's out of their bags and loaded them, taking extra magazines, too. Dunn and Saunders met each other in front of the president's car.

"Who's driving for you?" Dunn asked because Barltrop, who'd driven to the villa, was out of commission.

"Dickinson."

Dunn nodded. "Shall we check on everyone?"

"Aye."

First, they stopped by the lead car, which Perkins was driving. Another agent sat in the front seat. Dunn put a hand on top of the car and leaned down next to the lead agent.

"All set, Mr. Perkins?"

"Yes."

"Okay, great. Remember, we'll be right behind you."

"Okay."

Dunn tapped the roof and walked past the truck Cross was driving to the car behind. Roosevelt's aide, Burns, was driving. One of the older Secret Service agents sat in Roosevelt's customary place in the back passenger seat, wearing Roosevelt's gray fedora. The cigarette holder dangled from his lips. Smoke swirled out the window.

Dunn leaned down to peer through the back window. "You all set, Mr. President?"

The presidential decoy gave Dunn a smile. "Yes."

Dunn patted Burns on the shoulder and moved on to the next car.

Saunders took the lead for this one. One of DI Thompson's bodyguard team was driving. The man in the back passenger seat was smoking Churchill's cigar, and wearing the PM's hat. He sat scrunched down to mimic Churchill's short stature.

"Are you ready, Mr. Prime Minister?"

"Too right, I am, Sergeant. Let's get this thing on the road!"

Dunn and Saunders walked past the second deuce and a half and visited the two cars behind it. The first car contained three Secret Service agents, and the second, two more.

The detail left at the villa was comprised of Perkins' second in command, Agent Adkins, and three other agents, plus four Churchill bodyguards, including DI Thompson.

Dunn turned to Saunders. "Better get going."

"Aye. We'll see if this works."

"Yep."

The two men jogged to their respective trucks and climbed in the passenger seat.

Dunn spoke into his walkie-talkie. He had given one to each driver. "Dunn to Perkins."

"Perkins here," came the immediate reply.

"Ready to roll, sir."

"Roger and out."

The lead car drove off and the rest of the convoy started moving.

Chapter 33

As soon as Perkins drove about twenty yards onto the road leading down the hill to Sinnai, he stopped, waiting, just before the road curved right to the southwest.

"Here we go, Dave," Dunn said.

Cross still had the monster truck in first gear, so when he took his foot off the pedal it slowed quickly. He eyed the right side of the road and steered the right tires as far over as they could go. When the truck was a yard behind the rear of Perkins' car, he stopped it. Dickinson guided his truck the other way, so its fat left tires were as far over as possible.

Burns drove his staff car between the trucks, right behind Perkins' car, nearly touching bumpers. His fenders were about five feet from each truck.

The next vehicle to position itself was the one carrying Churchill's decoy. The British bodyguard who was driving expertly threaded the gap between the trucks and stopped a foot behind Burns.

The two trailing cars pulled up so they were abreast of each other, right behind the prime minister's car.

"How's it looking, Dave?"

Cross turned his body and stuck his head out the window, looking backwards. He examined the position of each vehicle and nodded. Ducking back inside, he said, "Perfect arrangement."

"Good," Dunn said. He spoke into his radio, "Saunders, time to disembark."

"Roger."

Dunn watched the rearview mirror on his side of the truck as Saunders led a string of Commandos up the hill to the northwest. He checked his watch. He waited four minutes, long enough for Saunders and his men to get to their line of departure. It felt like an eternity. Into his radio, he said, "All drivers. When Mr. Perkins moves, we stay with him. It's all yours, Mr. Perkins."

Rather than replying over the radio, Perkins drove forward. All the vehicles moved in concert, perfectly choreographed, a rolling security box. With the decoys representing the President of the United States and the British Prime Minister smack in the center.

The convoy moved through the curve and headed down a long straight that was about a half mile long. Perkins reached the speed of ten miles an hour and held it steady there. The road was dry, and dust swirled up from the tires' passage, but not enough to trouble Dunn's view of the road ahead. Saunders and he had driven along the road earlier in the day, checking things. Being thorough. Dunn worried whether that had been enough. On the right side, the terrain went uphill, but on the left it sloped away from the road. Trees and shrubs, and yellow, and blue wildflowers dotted both sides.

Dunn raised his binoculars and surveyed the scene ahead. Nothing stood out. They were nearing the end of the straightaway. Fifty yards ahead, the road veered left at an angle for ten yards and then back to the right. The convoy would have to slow down to negotiate the turns. Several trees lined the right edge of the road at the point it turned left. His worry increased. After a few seconds, he could bear it no longer. He keyed his walkie-talkie.

"Dunn to Perkins. Slow down." Then he clicked his radio key three times.

Immediately the sound of four clicks came. He sighed in relief. Saunders was in place. Then came another two clicks. This was it! Saunders and he had guessed correctly. Some of the Germans were on the right side of the road at the left turn position. If it had been three clicks, Saunders would have been telling Dunn he was confident he had *all* the Germans in sight.

He keyed the radio again, "All vehicles stop. Some enemy troops are on our right at the turn ahead. Not all are accounted for. Dickinson, pull ahead and prepare to execute."

When Dunn and Saunders had met with the two squads, the American agents, and the British bodyguards, Dickinson had volunteered for this crucial, yet terribly dangerous role. No one had been surprised.

Dickinson looked across the cab of his truck toward Dunn, who was leaning forward to see past Cross. Dickinson raised a small salute. Dunn returned it.

Dunn watched Dickinson drive the truck past Perkins' staff car and take the center of the road. He was moving slowly, less than five miles an hour.

Saunders estimated he was forty yards from the Germans. He counted four, which meant there should be some unaccounted for. He swept his gaze across the terrain from straight ahead to the left at the convoy and the ground sloping away beyond. Still no sight of any other Germans. He watched Dickinson drive the deuce and a half forward at less than a double-time pace. He swallowed and his stomach churned.

Sturmbannführer Becker shifted slightly so he could see the vehicles better from his prone position seventy-five meters away. He turned his head to his left to his second in command, who had also survived the failed assault on the villa.

"Are you sure the men set it all up correctly?"

"Yes, sir. I checked it myself afterwards."

Becker nodded, but was still worried. This would be his last chance at redemption. Failure here . . . He may as well shoot himself.

"Get ready."

The second in command tightened his grip on a cord that led away toward the road. It was connected to a half dozen grenades.

Dickinson eyed the road and the terrain on the right. His front bumper was just passing a large colorful shrub, when his gaze shifted to a tree ten yards ahead. He didn't know what kind it was, but it was tall and the branches were filled with large green leaves. The trunk was at least two feet in diameter, the bark relatively smooth. An expert with explosives himself, he eyed the bottom of the trunk carefully. His eyes narrowed as he tried to make out what he saw there. Cut branches had been laid over something . . .

He had time to think, "Shite!"

The explosion was enormous.

His breath was sucked away and his head and chest felt as though they'd been hit by a massive hammer. He was barely able to shift his right foot over and step on the brake. The truck skidded a few feet only, thanks to its low speed, and the tires came to a stop.

The bottom of the tree trunk had been blown to the right, completely severed from the part in the ground. In nearly slow motion, the tree swayed to the left, like a drunken dancer, and tipped over. It crashed to the ground, blocking the entire width of the road with its thick trunk and tangled branches. An impassable object. A plume of dust lifted into the air.

He opened the driver's door and, without standing up, slid out of the seat and slithered to the ground as the empty truck began to roll forward, partly due to still being in first gear and partly to the downward slope of the road.

MP40s chattered from several places to the right. Metal slapping sounds came from the opposite side of the truck. Rather than attempting to fire back, he combat ran on a reciprocal heading away from the submachine guns. When he reached the left side of the road he dove into the underbrush there. Rising to his knees, he looked around.

The rest of the convoy was still about forty yards up the road, stopped. Dunn's squad had jumped down from their truck and were on the left side of it. Dickinson heard a sound to his right and looked that way. Motion gave away Germans just thirty yards from the convoy. They were crawling through the grass and shrubs toward the convoy. Ducking back down, he held his walkie-talkie to his lips and keyed it on.

"Dickinson to all. Several Germans thirty yards southwest of the convoy on the down side of the road."

Dunn answered. "Roger. Stay put. Stay low."

"Roger." Dickinson realized he might end up on the backside of a .45 caliber bullet fusillade. Staying down was fine with him.

The trailing two cars carrying the rest of the agents pulled up to the left of the decoys' cars as if protecting the president's and prime minister's cars. Everyone climbed out and took up positions on the right side of the cars, aiming over the roofs of the cars to the southwest.

Saunders and his men moved closer. They were on the Germans' left flank. Their shots would be difficult because of the tall grasses and shrubs that partly obscured their targets.

He raised his Thompson and aimed at the man on the farthest right. His men also sighted their targets, waiting for his command.

He gave it. "Fire!"

The Thompsons roared their deep powerful sounds.

The Germans reacted quickly, crawling forward and out of sight behind a small rise. Saunders thought all got away.

"Cease fire."

He directed Kirby to lead Myers and Talbot to the right, hoping for a pincer movement.

Dunn motioned to his men to go left and down into the shrubs on the south side of the road. When he reached a large shrub he knelt, waving his men into a kneeling battle line to his left, facing the direction of the Germans.

RONN MUNSTERMAN

Chapter 34

1,100 yards south of Villa Bellavista
17 December, 1155 Hours

Dunn sighted along his Thompson's barrel. In the distance he could hear Saunders' and the Germans' firefight. It seemed to be stationary. He knew Saunders would take care of it. He took a quick peek at the agents and bodyguards. They were still set up on the far side of their respective cars, aiming their .38s toward the same spot Dunn and his men were, having been warned by Dickinson.

Saunders had waited until Kirby led Talbot and Myers to their position far to the right, which was the Germans' new left flank. Kirby looked his way. Saunders raised a hand and dropped it like a car race starter. The three Commandos fired their Thompsons. The Germans, caught by surprise, tried to fire back, but in turning to face the new threat, exposed their upper bodies.

"Fire!" Saunders shouted. He pressed his trigger as did the four men with him, Alders, Bentley, Forster, and Holmes.

One German was hit, but the others disappeared from sight.

Saunders waved at Kirby to advance toward the road. He motioned to his men to follow him. He crept through the grass and shrubs toward Dickinson's truck, which had stopped rolling against the huge tree. The engine had died.

Becker told his second in command to give him his grenades. When the man handed them to him, he jammed the stick portion into his belt behind his back.

"Hold this position, no matter the cost," he ordered.

"Ja, Sturmbannführer."

Becker rose to a crouch and dashed through the grass behind a large shrub, past a tree, making it to the road on the side of the felled tree opposite the stalled truck. He ran around what used to be the crown of a beautiful tree and into the grass on the southwest side of the road. He looked northeast along the road. He could see the tops of some American helmets about fifty meters away not far from the road. He glanced left and spotted the rest of the convoy and the men standing guard with their pistols up. They were also about fifty meters away.

He moved quickly, but silently along the south side of the road. His focus alternated between the Americans in the grass and the men by the cars. He was surprised when motion to his right caught his eye. A shape moved and he recognized the British Brodie helmet. He fired a two-round burst from the waist, without bothering to aim. The shape went down.

He ducked himself to avoid being seen having given himself away with the sound of his weapon. He crawled to the left to get away from his last position.

Dunn heard the dual shot coming from somewhere down the road, but when he looked that way, he saw nothing. He thought there could be four or five Germans in front of him. He lifted his radio.

"Dunn to Perkins."

"Perkins here."

"Need your men to fire at that spot that's about twenty yards in front of me, so to your right."

"Roger."

Dunn put the radio back on his belt.

The Secret Service agents began firing their revolvers. Rather than just emptying the cylinder in a blind rush of trigger pulls, they fired two-round bursts with varying time between bursts. This meant that not all guns went silent at the same time to reload. Even though the distance to the targets was at the edge of the .38's effective range, it helped keep the Germans' heads down.

Dunn quickly got his men on the move and they advanced toward the targets.

Saunders just missed spotting the enemy leader go around the tree. He led his men down the road past the fallen tree and right back up the hill. They traveled about ten yards before turning right again. Saunders took a kneeling position and examined the terrain in front of him. He saw the Germans hunkered down prone. They were only twenty yards away. Two were aimed at the place he had just left. Two were aimed up the hill toward Kirby. He briefly considered attempting to get the enemy soldiers to surrender, but tossed that idea aside because these were no ordinary soldiers. No, they were SS. He'd dealt with them many times. He aimed his Thompson. His men did the same. He fired. They fired.

The Germans were torn to pieces by the .45 caliber slugs. Not a single shot had been fired in return.

Saunders told Alders and Holmes to go check on the Germans, while he and the others provided cover. The two Commandos stayed low and ran over to the jumble of bodies. They quickly checked for life. Finding none, they both placed a finger under their chins and drew it across their throats like a knife.

Saunders looked toward Kirby and waved. Kirby and his two men combat ran down the hill and joined the rest of the squad.

Gunfire from the direction of the convoy came their way. Saunders recognized it as the agents' weapons. They sounded like disciplined shooters.

Becker crawled along the roadside heading toward a position that would be perpendicular to the staff cars. As he passed by yet another shrub, he paused long enough to raise his head. He could see someone sitting in the back seat of one of the cars in the middle of the vehicles. His heart raced. That could be one of the countries' leader. At this point he didn't care which one. Just assassinating one would be good enough. He touched the grenades in his belt for comfort. He lowered himself and crawled closer. He no longer worried about taking a proof of death photograph.

Dickinson opened his eyes. He had no idea what had happened. One second there he was kneeling in the grass and the next, he woke up lying flat on his back. His ears rang and his head hurt like bloody hell. Groaning, he rolled over onto his side, which made his head feel worse. He lifted a hand and touched his head. When he drew it away to look at it, he was relieved to find no blood. He felt his head again and discovered a knot the size of a walnut just above his left ear. He looked around carefully, not wanting to move his head much. He found his helmet a few feet away. He slowly grabbed it and brought it closer, intending to put it back on. As he aligned the helmet's front, he spotted a shiny dent the width of his pinkie finger. It was about an inch long and was located . . . of course. At the spot that corresponded with his lump. He stared at the shiny dent for a time. He'd heard of this, of course, some bloke being saved by the thin steel covering his soft noggin, but he'd never actually seen it, let alone have it happen to *him*.

"Bloody hell. Bugger," he muttered softly.

He slowly put the helmet on, but it hurt too much when the interior touched his knot and he yanked it off.

"Shite."

The pistol fire finally had the desired effect, forcing the Germans to move. Dunn detected their motion ahead about twenty-five yards. They were moving to the southeast, perpendicularly away from the road. Dunn aimed his Thompson and shouted, "There!" He fired. The other men fired as well after checking Dunn's aim.

Perkins and his men changed their aim and began their two-shot bursts again.

A cry of pain came from somewhere in the grass. Then another.

Two Germans rose to a kneeling position and returned fire, but were wide of the mark.

Fierce Thompson .45 bullets cut them both down.

Saunders and his men ran through the grass toward the convoy. When they reached it, they saw Perkins and his men firing their revolvers at something moving in the grass across the road. Saunders spotted Dunn and his men firing at the same area. He heard the cries of pain. Two Germans foolishly rose up and fired back. They went down under blistering fire from two directions. All weapons went silent. Two Rangers, Jonesy and Goerdt, peeled off from Dunn's group and ran over carefully and checked the Germans. Jonesy turned toward Dunn and shook his head in an exaggerated way. Dunn waved his arms and looked at the convoy. Saunders waved. Dunn nodded. Everyone seemed to relax.

Becker heard the gunfight to his right. As well as the cries of pain, most likely his men. He raised his head to check his position. He was only ten meters from the nearest car, hiding behind a shrub. No one was even looking in his direction. He pulled the four grenades from the belt behind his back and laid them carefully on the ground in front of him.

RONN MUNSTERMAN

Chapter 35

1,100 yards south of Villa Bellavista
17 December, 1206 Hours

Dunn got his men together and they headed toward the convoy. Dickinson rose unsteadily to his feet about fifty yards away. He stumbled on the first step toward the convoy and almost went down.

"Hey, Bob, would you go help Dickinson? He may be hurt." Dunn pointed.

"Sure thing, Sarge," Schneider replied, breaking into a run.

Perkins and his men holstered their weapons. He walked around the front of his car about to say something to Saunders, who was standing nearby, facing him. His peripheral vision caught motion. Startled, he looked to the right. A German soldier, not ten yards away, rose to his knees and threw something. It tumbled through the air toward the center of the convoy, at the car carrying Roosevelt's decoy. It was going to go right over Perkins' head.

He eyed the stick and timed his jump like an outfielder at the wall. His right hand caught the explosive end of it. Not bothering to try and reposition it in his hand, he flung the grenade back in the direction it had come from.

It tumbled through the air again.

"Down!" he had time to shout.

The agents and Commandos hit the dirt.

His aim was off by about five yards and it exploded harmlessly inside a shrub which caught fire and blazed away.

Incredibly, the German stood up this time, and drew his hand back to throw another grenade.

A single shot sounded. The bullet struck the German in the chest. He let go of the grenade and it flew away backwards. He collapsed. The grenade exploded with a *crump*.

Perkins rose to his feet, his .38 Police Special smoking.

Dunn and his men ran toward the downed German, their weapons ready. Dunn got there first and found the man on his back. A bullet wound just below the heart pumped blood and more leaked from his lips. The man's eyes found Dunn's. He stared for a moment.

"Who are you?"

"Tom Dunn. U.S. Army Rangers."

The German nodded feebly. "I've . . . heard . . . of you."

"All good, I'm sure. Speer is especially fond of me. Are you the leader of this attack?"

A bloody grin. "I'm proud to say *Ja.*"

Dunn gave the dying man a disdainful look. "Not much of a leader who fails his mission."

The man frowned.

"Who sent you? Give me a name."

"Nein."

The German gasped. He stopped breathing, his sightless eyes still pointed at Dunn. There was no prayer for this one.

Dunn rifled through the man's trousers pockets and found a business card for Enzo Santoro with a Cagliari address and phone number. In an inside coat pocket, he also found architectural drawings of the villa. He slipped everything he'd found into his jacket pocket. He'd hand it all over to Military Intelligence at Barton Stacey. Obviously, this was someone they would be interested in talking to. He must have helped the SS unit somehow. Maybe they could use or roll up his network on Sardinia.

He rose and walked away.

Schneider and Dickinson had made their way to the convoy where Schneider helped the dazed man to the ground. He had a death grip on his helmet. Schneider checked him over thoroughly.

Saunders stepped close and knelt beside the injured man.

"Hey, Christopher."

Dickinson looked at his squad leader. "Hey, Sarge."

"You all right?"

"Ask the doctor." Dickinson smiled weakly.

"There's a possibility of a concussion, so we should watch him closely. If he gets sick to his stomach, we'll want to keep him awake, and to the hospital," Schneider said to Saunders, who nodded.

"I feel fine," Dickinson protested.

Schneider patted him on the shoulder gently. "I'm serious, Christopher."

"Yeah, okay."

Saunders plucked Dickinson's helmet from his hands and stared at the shiny dent. "Bloody hell, Christopher. You barely missed that one."

"Yeah." Dickinson lifted the helmet from Saunders' hand. "I think I'll be wearing that bugger until the war's over, don't you think?"

"I'd say that's a particularly splendid idea."

Dickinson nodded and hugged the helmet against his chest like a little boy with his stuffed animal.

"Be sure to show it to Chadwick when we get back."

"I sure will."

Dunn arrived with his men and they shook hands with the Commandos, Secret Service agents, and Churchill's detail. Dunn spotted Perkins standing off by himself staring out at nothing. He headed toward the agent. Perkins turned when he heard Dunn's footsteps on the road. Dunn offered his hand, and the agent shook it.

"Are you okay, Mr. Perkins?"

When the agent looked at Dunn, his eyes were steady, as had been his hand during the handshake.

"Yes, I'm fine."

Dunn tilted his head slightly. "Not your first, I take it?"

"No. I was a machine gunner during the first one."

"I see," Dunn said. What this man had seen and done would have been sobering for anyone.

"That was an incredible catch. Risky, too."

Perkins nodded, a faraway look in his eyes. "Yeah. I figured if I could just tip it and make it drop to the ground . . ."

"You'd have fallen on it."

When Perkins turned to look at Dunn, his eyes were calm, his expression determined. "Yes."

"You're a good man, sir. I'm honored to have fought by your side."

Perkins looked at Dunn for several seconds without saying anything. He nodded slowly. "The honor is all mine, Sergeant Dunn."

"Shall we go get the president and prime minister?"

"Yes. I'll get the cars ready. What do we do with the bodies?"

"I'll contact graves division at the airbase and tell them we have more German bodies here. They'll transport them to a mortuary in Cagliari."

"Oh, okay. Do you think that's all of them?"

"Yep. I'll check with Saunders to see how many he took out and see if it seems to add up, just to be sure. Still, we should reform the convoy for the ride down the hill, just to be on the safe side."

"Good idea. I agree. Be back shortly."

Dunn walked back to the convoy and bent down by Dickinson, who Schneider had refused to let get up.

"How you doing?"

"I feel okay, but your doc is stubborn as a mule."

Dunn laughed. "Yes, he is. He's so strict, you can't do anything fun with him around."

"And don't you forget that, Sarge!" Schneider said, his face stern.

"Yes, Doc," Dunn said.

While Perkins went back for the two world leaders, Dunn and Saunders coordinated using the lead truck and a length of rope to swing the fallen tree out of the way. Twenty minutes later, the convoy was back in formation and the real president and prime minister were seated in their respective cars. Dunn walked over to Roosevelt's window. "You ready to go, Mr. President?"

"Yes, I am, Sergeant Dunn. Thank you for a terrific job."

"It's my honor to serve, sir. Did anyone tell you what your Mr. Perkins did during the final bit of the attack?"

Roosevelt raised his eyebrows. "Why, no. What happened?"

Dunn told him the story of Perkins' potentially self-sacrificing move with the grenade.

"Oh, dear. That is simply incredible. When I get back, I'm going to look into getting him some kind of medal."

Dunn shook his head. "He won't want one, sir."

Roosevelt waved that comment aside. "Oh, that doesn't matter. You didn't want the Medal of Honor, did you? You wanted the squad to be recognized."

"You got me there, Mr. President," Dunn said, grinning.

Roosevelt grinned back and took a puff from his ever-present cigarette.

"See you at the airbase, sir."

"Yes, indeed."

The drive to the airbase was blessedly uneventful to everyone's relief. Dunn and Saunders went with Roosevelt, Churchill, and their protective details to the big C-54 on the runway. It would fly the leaders and their details to England. Roosevelt would spend the night in London before heading back to the States the next day. After handshakes all around, the two world leaders and their guardians boarded the plane. Dunn and Saunders walked back to the trucks where their squads were waiting.

Dickinson had ridden in one of the more comfortable staff cars with Schneider by his side to keep an eye on him.

Dunn leaned into the window by Schneider. "How's he doing?"

"He's fine. No concrete signs of concussion. Kept down a few sips of water. Travel is okay."

"Great."

Saunders was on Dickinson's side of the car. He opened the door and helped him get out. When the big redhead let go of Dickinson's arm, the Commando seemed quite under control.

The engines on the C-54 lit up and soon reached a steady pitch. Everyone stopped to watch it.

She rolled forward, picking up speed. Soon it was racing down the runway. The pilot rotated the aircraft and the nose lifted, a moment later she was in the air. When she was a couple of hundred feet off the ground, she banked right and soared northwest.

Eight silver Mustangs roared overhead to take protective positions around the president's and prime minister's plane. They were loaded with their underwing drop fuel tanks so they could escort the plane all the way to London.

"Ready to check on Steve?" Dunn asked.

"Aye."

Barltrop, Higgins, and Martelli had been released from the hospital and someone from the base administration section had helped out by picking them up. The men had been able to sit up on the drive to the airbase.

Dunn and Saunders walked over to their car.

"You guys holding up okay?" Dunn asked, peering inside. He thought Barltrop and Higgins looked quite pale.

"Yeah. Would like a lie down about now," Barltrop said faintly.

"Me, too," Higgins said.

"I'm okay to sit up, Sarge. I've got pretty thick bandages on my back," Martelli said.

Dunn nodded at him. "We'll get you guys situated as soon as possible."

Dunn stood and looked over his shoulder. A C-47 with its engines running was sitting where the C-54 had been parked. He patted the car's top.

"Let's get you closer to the plane."

He leaned over to talk to the driver. "Could you drive them over right by the C-47?"

The young corporal, a lanky man with unruly dark hair, glanced at him. "Absolutely, Sergeant Dunn."

"Thanks very much."

"I'm honored to help out. I read about you in the *Stars and Stripes*. You getting your Medal of Honor."

Dunn smiled and patted the man's shoulder. "What's your name?"

"Thompson. Allen Thompson."

"Where're you from, Allen?"

"Kansas City."

Dunn smiled. "Ever see the Monarchs?"

"Oh, yes. All the time."

"How about Satchel Paige?"

"Best pitcher ever." Thompson grinned wide at the memories. "Excellent."

With that, Thompson drove over to the C-47 and parked near the tail.

Dunn and Saunders eyed each other. Both were dirty and tired.

"Ready, lad?"

"Beyond ready, Mac."

They waved at the men who were waiting by the trucks not far away. The men formed a loose gaggle and headed toward the plane, carrying their travel bags. Not long after, everyone had boarded, with several men helping Barltrop and Higgins into the plane.

So that the two wounded men could lie down comfortably, Dunn put them opposite each other on the bench seats.

"Go ahead and lie down, fellas."

He took their soft travel bags, the ones without the weapons, and plumped them up for pillows. He helped them get comfortable. Using a couple of jackets as blankets, he covered each man from the neck to the waist.

"Okay?"

"Yes, Sarge," both wounded men replied.

Before Dunn even turned away to head forward, the two men had closed their eyes. He leaned into the cockpit and said, "We're all set, Lieutenant."

The pilot, who had turned to look over his shoulder, nodded. He increased the throttles.

Dunn found his seat next to Cross just as the plane began moving. He glanced over at his friend, whose eyes were closed.

"You okay, Tom?" Cross asked without opening his eyes.

Dunn sighed deeply. "Yes and no."

Cross understood, and simply nodded.

Dunn was thinking of the letter he'd be writing to twenty-one-year-old Sidney Brooks' parents when he got back to Barton

Stacey. The young man had completed exactly two missions with him. He tried not to, but images of the men he'd lost since May came to his mind. He counted them one by one, but remembered them as individuals, not numbers. Nine young men killed under his command. One forever scarred by the loss of a leg. An entire squad in terms of numbers. Ten families suffering for the remainder of their lives. *Damn it*, he thought.

When he'd passed on the news from Roosevelt about the Ardennes attack to the Rangers and Commandos, the men's shocked expressions said it all. Christmas was coming up in eight days. After the successful invasion of Normandy in June, everyone thought the war would be over by then. Fat chance. With the Germans opening a serious offensive, the outcome of which was unknown, it was bound to set back the war effort enormously.

With all the bad news in his head, he did what worked to keep himself sane. He thought of Pamela and their baby. He knew it was going to be a boy. Why that was he had no idea. Just a flash of knowledge that came out of nowhere. Pamela doubted him, of course, but he was certain. He thought of holding his son in his hands. Of smelling his hair. Of looking into his eyes. Blue of course, like his mom's.

With a contented sigh, he fell asleep.

Saunders looked toward the rear of the aircraft where Barltrop was sleeping. His best friend . . . his best man . . . had almost died. What would he do without him? What would Kathy have done? Maybe now they'd decide to hurry up and get married before it was truly too late. He felt guilty about Barltrop's getting wounded, and on a recent mission, Chadwick's, who also could have died. Life and death were sometimes in his hands. He made decisions that got men killed. But that was the job. He'd signed up for it. He'd accepted the responsibility. He had no choice but to bear it all.

He looked out the window across from him, between Alders and Holmes. The blue sky was gorgeous. He thought of his Sadie and, like Dunn, fell asleep knowing a spectacular woman loved him.

Chapter 36

The Farm, Area B-2, Catoctin Mountain Park
18 December, 0715 Hours, U.S. Eastern Standard Time,
the next morning

Although Gertrude was out in the cold, her excitement was keeping her warm. She and the other nine women—Rosemary's injury had turned out to be a slight sprain—were out at the demolitions range at the end of the field where the telephone poles and rail tracks were located.

Rick, along with Mildred, Louise, and the overall boss, David Walker, were helping the women attach an explosive device on each of the ten poles.

Gertrude set her timer so it would go off at 7:30, as Walker had just instructed everyone.

Using twine, Gertrude had tied the explosive block to the pole about six inches from the ground. She connected the timer's wires to the detonator's leads and pushed the detonator slowly and gently into the center of the grayish white plastic explosive. It was a six-ounce block, the one in the suitcase a few days ago that was the size of two cigarette packs laid end to end. She turned on the timer and checked to make sure it was working.

She withdrew her hands and rose. Stepping back, she raised her hand and said, "Done, sir!"

Rick looked her way and raised his hand. She retreated to a position about ten yards away, where she would wait until everyone else was ready. She didn't have to wait long, and soon all ten women were standing together, as well as the instructor cadre.

Rick checked his watch. "Ten minutes! Everyone back to the tables."

Everyone ran the entire distance and stood behind their tables. The instructors joined some of the women. On the tables were binoculars, enough for all to have one. Gertrude picked up hers and zeroed in on her pole, the far right one. She lowered the field glasses and waited.

Finally, Rick started the ten second countdown.

When he reached five, she lifted the glasses again, zooming in on the bottom of the pole.

The explosions went off within a split second of each other.

Gertrude's explosive snapped the pole off and it immediately started to topple over. The sound of the explosion was a sharp crack, a little disappointing she thought, expecting more of a booming sound. However, the telephone pole falling over and crashing to the ground was exciting enough. The poles all fell pretty much the same direction, toward the watchers due to everyone putting the charge in the same position.

Everyone cheered and several women hopped up and down in their glee at finally blowing up something.

"Well done, ladies," Rick said, beaming. "Anyone want to blow up some train tracks?"

A collective, "Yes!" went up.

"Okay. Grab your other suitcase and let's go."

Gertrude picked up her second case and headed toward the rail tracks.

She knelt by the end of the tracks on the far right. She opened her case and looked at the block of explosive. It was a little more than twice the size of the previous one. Almost a pound.

"Ooh," she said to herself.

She picked up the explosive block and placed it against the track where two rails were bolted together. She kneaded it into position under the top of the rail, covering the seam.

She leaned back and looked to her left. Rick was about ten yards away helping someone. "What time, sir?" she shouted.

He glanced at his watch. "We're setting this one for eight o'clock."

"Thanks!"

She carefully set the timer. Next she repeated the process of connecting the timer to the detonator, and slowly pushing the detonator into the explosive. She switched on the timer and the small second hand began its circular travel.

She stood, raised her arm again and shouted, "Done, sir!"

Rick raised his arm in reply without looking. He was beginning to recognize her gleeful shout.

A few minutes later, all were finished and heading back to the safety of the tables.

The time to detonation seemed to drag on for Gertrude. She found herself yawning quite a bit and stretching.

Rick started the countdown.

Gertrude raised her glasses and focused on her explosives.

This time, the sounds were a little deeper and she felt them in her chest. It was an exhilarating feeling. Plumes of dust shot skyward. She lowered her glasses and took in the sight of ten plumes of dirt. As the dirt settled, she raised her glasses again. The rails she had attacked were bent away from her and up, twisted like part of a pretzel. A crater that she thought might be several feet across ate into the rail bed.

"Wow! Holy cow!"

Some of the women glanced at her, smiling because they felt exactly the same way.

Rick walked out in front of the women.

"Well done, everyone. Let's go take a look at your work."

The women ran across the field. They oohed and ahhed at the railway tracks they'd destroyed. They chuckled at the snapped off telephone poles, admiring the way the wood had been sheared off near the ground, almost as if cut by a saw.

After a while, they began heading back toward the other end of the field. Ruby and Edna fell in with Gertrude.

"I'm loving this more and more each day," she told her friends.

"I don't know if I like shooting or explosives more," Edna said.

"Explosives," Ruby said. "My shooting is not as good as you two can do."

"You're passing, though," Gertrude said kindly.

"I am. I just need more work."

"Let me know if you want company on the range sometime," Gertrude said.

"Me, too," chimed in Edna.

"How's the language training going?" Edna asked Gertrude.

"Pretty well, I think, after eight straight days of it. My instructor is quite patient, but he's also demanding and precise. That actually helps me reach our goals for me. I can pretty much talk to someone a little bit without sounding like a complete fool."

She couldn't tell them which language she was learning, and they didn't tell her, either. That she was headed for the Philippines was exciting to her. The western Pacific just seemed so interesting. She'd read the newspapers, though, and knew she was going to a terribly dangerous location. She knew full well just how brutal the Japanese soldiers could be. Whether she lived or died would depend largely on herself. How well she learned what Rick and the others were trying to teach her could determine her fate. As could her reaction time to unexpected danger. She figured she'd be better off assuming there was danger everywhere around her, and to stay on guard at all times.

She'd also found a book on the Philippines in the small library. She read it at the library so no one would know where she was headed. It seemed to be a beautiful country with mountains and beaches. Manila was once a gorgeous city, but much of it had been reduced to rubble since the Japanese occupation. She thought about General Douglas MacArthur's promise to return that he'd made a couple of years ago. He'd kept his promise, wading ashore on October 20th, just a couple of months ago.

When the women returned to the camp, they washed up and headed back to the main classroom building.

Louise was the instructor for this class: advanced map reading.

She looked out at her ten charges and said, "I know that map reading is not as exciting as blowing up stuff . . ."

The women chortled.

"But it can save your life."
Gertrude nodded.
She was all for that idea.

RONN MUNSTERMAN

Chapter 37

Colonel Rupert Jenkins' office
Camp Barton Stacey
18 December, 1230 Hours, London time

Colonel Jenkins frowned, not an uncommon occurrence for him, but this time his face also bore signs of deep worry. His counterpart, Colonel Mark Kenton, looked much the same. The mission to protect the president and prime minister had been a success by any definition, especially the main one: President Franklin D. Roosevelt and Prime Minister Winston Churchill were still among the living. But it had been risky. And costly.

"Gentlemen," Jenkins said.

Jenkins didn't have a Christmas tree on his desk, but there was one by the entrance to the building, in the hall.

Typically, these meetings regarding joint operations between Jenkins' British Commandos and Kenton's U.S. Army Rangers took place in the American's office, but they'd recently agreed to alternate just to make things fair between them. Jenkins' office was also in a new administration building—the entire camp was new—and he had a map table similar to Kenton's. Although they wouldn't need it today.

Attending the meeting for the British were Jenkins, his aide Lieutenant Carleton Mallory, and Sergeant Major Saunders. For the Americans, Kenton had brought along his aide, First Lieutenant Fred Tanner, and Master Sergeant Dunn.

Both sergeants looked worse for wear with dark circles under their puffy eyes. Their flight had arrived at Hampstead the previous evening. Both men had escorted their wounded soldiers to the camp's hospital. They stayed to make sure the men, Steve Barltrop, Al Martelli, and Chuck Higgins, were checked in and made as comfortable as possible.

"Let's start with congratulations on a job well done," Jenkins said.

Dunn and Saunders nodded their thanks.

Jenkins leaned forward, clasping his hands together on the desk. He looked at Dunn. "I'm terribly sorry about Corporal Brooks."

"Thank you, Colonel."

"Tell me about your wounded men, please."

"Yes, sir. Sergeant Saunders and I just came from the hospital. Corporal Higgins was in a prone position and took a bullet in the right shoulder. It broke his collar bone, missed his lung, his kidney and lodged in his side. Surgery went very well and he'll make a full recovery. The broken collar bone will take six weeks to heal completely.

"Staff Sergeant Martelli received multiple wounds in his back from wood splinters after a potato masher went off just outside a broken-out window. He's recovering well, and should be back to duty in less than a week. Probably get out of the hospital in a few days if they're satisfied no infection has set in.

"Sergeant Cross got a nasty bullet graze on his upper arm, but he's doing okay."

"I'm relieved to hear the good news." Jenkins turned to Saunders. "And how is our Barltrop?"

Saunders shook his head. "It was a near thing, sir. Two rounds upper right chest, both missed the lung and exited cleanly. His surgery went well in Sardinia, too, and I'm quite grateful for their care of him."

Jenkins nodded. "Well, we are indeed grateful for your actions on Sardinia. You both took your squads in there with little information and provided excellent protection of the two most important leaders of the free world. You must never forget that." He glanced at Kenton to give the American a chance to say something.

"I echo what Colonel Jenkins said. You've done your respective countries a great service. An immeasurable service."

Kenton looked at Jenkins and cleared his throat.

Dunn nudged Saunders. When the Commando glanced over at him and mouthed, "What?" Dunn whispered, "Just wait."

Jenkins missed the two sergeants' little exchange because he was looking down at some papers on his desk. He picked up the first one and said, "Sergeant Saunders, I have here a letter of commendation from the Prime Minister himself. He wishes to award you the Distinguished Conduct Medal." He handed the letter across the desk.

Saunders took it, but didn't look at it. "I'd prefer not to, sir."

Jenkins frowned. "It's not a debatable matter, Sergeant Major."

"I'd rather see Barltrop get it, sir. He's the one who got shot."

"I understand your point. However, this is not something we can disappoint the Prime Minister with. If you'd read the letter, you'll see he's already sent the paperwork to the King."

Saunders looked down at the letter and read part of it. "Cor blimey, sir." He looked up quickly at Jenkins, who raised an eyebrow.

"Anything else to say, Sergeant Major?"

Saunders coughed. "Perhaps I should stop while I'm still ahead, sir."

"What a splendid, yet surprising choice, Sergeant Major."

Everyone laughed, Saunders the loudest.

Dunn patted his friend on the back. "Proud of you, Mac."

"Of course you are."

Dunn shook his head, laughing again. He turned back to Jenkins in time to see him pass a letter to Kenton.

Saunders saw it, too and chuckled lightly. "You'll get yours, too, mate," he whispered, but not low enough to keep everyone else from hearing it.

Jenkins' lip curled into a smile, and Kenton grinned.

Dunn closed his eyes briefly to get ready for it.

"So *my* letter is from President Roosevelt, Sergeant Dunn. You're to receive the Silver Star for your actions on Sardinia," Kenton said.

Dunn knew better than to argue the point and simply said, "Thank you, sir, I'm honored."

Kenton handed him the letter. Dunn read it quickly and set it in his lap.

"I'm glad things worked out okay. It was getting pretty dicey on the road to the airport," he said.

"Well, it's a good thing you decided to have the leaders stay behind in case there was an ambush. Which there was."

"Yes, sir. Any word on awards for the Secret Service and for their man who died? They all deserve something, getting thrown into firefights against the damn SS of all attackers."

"I've heard various medals are in the works for the agents."

"Okay. Sir, I'm trying to figure out why in the world they thought they could assassinate FDR and Churchill. They tried it last year in Tehran and it was botched up. This time, they obviously didn't know we'd be there, Saunders and me, that is."

"I agree. I think it came down to who had the better intelligence once again," Kenton said. "We knew they had already arrived, and we got you there posthaste. And like you said, they missed your arrival somehow, both in intelligence and on-the-ground observations."

"Well, that's true. Sergeant Saunders and I discussed this. If they'd had someone watching the villa all the time, they'd have spotted us, no question. If it had been us on the other side, that's what we would have done. And we could have called for additional support."

"But it was them not you or Saunders. I think that tells the story right there, Sergeant Dunn," Jenkins said.

Dunn shrugged. "Yes, sir." He looked at Kenton. "Any news on that German attack in the Ardennes? The president told us about it since it was going to be in the newspapers."

Kenton's expression turned dark. "The Germans caught us with our pants down. We were stretched way too thin along the front. As of this morning, they've pushed us back several miles at two points. One is east of Bastogne and the other farther north. I don't have much to tell you other than that."

"Damn, sir, it sounds bad."

Kenton nodded.

"Is there anything our unit can do to help out?"

Kenton shook his head immediately. "Nothing we can think of. That could change down the road, but for now, no. I believe the same goes for Colonel Jenkins' unit. Am I correct, Colonel?"

"Indeed you are. No plans yet."

"That being the case, we'll be working as usual," Kenton said. "I'd like to see your men take two days and go to London, or wherever they want. Just see Lieutenant Tanner for the passes."

"Certainly, sir. I know the men will appreciate it."

"The same goes for you and your men, Saunders," Jenkins said.

"Thank you, sir."

"That's all, gentlemen," Jenkins said, concluding the meeting.

Outside Jenkins' building Dunn and Saunders walked toward their vehicles, Dunn's jeep and Saunders' staff car. They stopped between the two vehicles.

"Sorry about Brooks. He seemed a good kid."

"Yeah. Yeah, he was."

Dunn looked skyward. It was overcast and the air was cold, made worse by a sharp northwest wind. He thought about lighting a Lucky Strike, but decided it wouldn't be worth the bother in the strong wind. He'd wait until he got in the covered jeep. For the moment he was content to stand with his friend.

"What are you going to do with your two days?" he asked Saunders.

"I think me and Sadie will go visit my parents in the East End. Maybe get the sisters over for lunch or dinner. You?"

"London sounds good. Maybe be a tourist for once. Pamela can show me the Tower of London or something equally terrifying."

Saunders laughed. "Be sure to watch your head."

"Ha ha," Dunn said. "When was the last beheading?"

"Oh, I don't know. Last week, maybe?"

"What!"

Saunders laughed at Dunn's expression and the Ranger punched him in the arm.

"Late seventeen hundreds, maybe. I do know there were almost a hundred over the centuries."

"Yikes."

"Aye."

"Maybe Buckingham Palace would be safer."

Saunders got an ornery look on his face. "Not necessarily."

"Oh, man, come on."

"Kidding."

"I knew that."

"Aye, sure you did. I'm glad we got back when we did last night."

"Why's that?"

"It was Sadie's twenty-second birthday. I managed to snag a card from a little shop downtown before I got home."

"Please wish her a belated Happy Birthday for Pamela and me."

"Will do."

Dunn offered his hand. "Good working with you again, Mac."

"Yeah, you, too," Saunders said, shaking hands.

The two dangerous men climbed into their vehicles and drove off in different directions.

Chapter 38

Hitler's office
The Chancellery
18 December, 1345 Hours, Berlin time

Adolf Hitler stood behind his enormous desk leaning on two hands placed flat on the surface. Little was on it usually, but today he had maps of the Ardennes Counteroffensive battlefield spread out. Only two days in, the attack was going well. His eyes darted right and left over the maps checking the current location of the front line. He eyed two distinct bulges pushing into the Allies' territory. One near Bastogne and the other farther north. He laughed out loud suddenly and clapped his hands. His eyes sparkled. Antwerp would be in his grasp soon. He would split the Americans from the English with an unbeatable wedge. Yes, things were looking up. His brilliancy stood out once more.

One of the five-meter-tall doors to his office opened and Martin Bormann, Hitler's efficient and controlling private secretary, stepped through, and stopped, waiting.

Hitler looked up at the sound, annoyed to have been interrupted enjoying the maps.

"What is it, Bormann?" he snapped.

"Mein Führer, Obergruppenführer Kaltenbrunner is here with a report for you."

Hitler thought for a moment, and smiled at Bormann, remembering the mission Kaltenbrunner was responsible for. He waved a hand. "Well, don't just stand there, Bormann, send him in."

"Ja, Mein Führer."

Hitler went back to gleefully examining the maps.

Bormann left the office and a moment later Kaltenbrunner marched in, his hat tucked into his left elbow. He went straight to one of the plush chairs in front of the *Führer's* desk and stood there.

Hitler sighed, as if sorry to have to stop looking at the maps. At his tremendous success. He looked at Kaltenbrunner, who immediately snapped a Nazi salute.

"Heil Hitler, Mein Führer."

Hitler half-heartedly returned the salute with a little hand flip, as if he couldn't be bothered. He sat down, but didn't invite the head of the *Reich* Main Security Office to sit. He directed his blue-eyed gaze on his subordinate, who was looking over Hitler's head.

"Your report."

Standing perfectly straight, Kaltenbrunner's imposing height couldn't help him one least little bit in the face of the much shorter *Führer*. He forced himself to meet Hitler's unwavering stare.

"Mein Führer, I have unwelcome news from Sardinia."

Hitler blinked slowly. He pointed at the chair behind Kaltenbrunner. "Perhaps you'd better sit down."

Kaltenbrunner sat, carefully straightening the crease in his trousers to reduce wrinkles.

Hitler's eyes flicked downward for a moment then back to Kaltenbrunner's face. *For someone with such an unfortunate face, he's quite vain,* he thought.

"We have lost contact with *Sturmbannführer* Becker. I sent another of our resources to the villa. There was clear evidence of a prolonged gun battle, but none of our men were anywhere to be found. Multiple unidentified bodies have been sent to a Cagliari mortuary. I believe it is Becker and his men. Additionally, there are reports that Roosevelt and Churchill were seen together in

London just this morning. I can only conclude that our mission failed."

Hitler steepled his fingers under his chin and continued staring at Kaltenbrunner. He dipped his chin slightly, which made him appear to be looking at you like a predator.

Kaltenbrunner, in spite of himself and his self-discipline, swallowed a sudden lump in his throat.

"Failed? Again? First in Tehran and now in Sardinia? Why do I even keep you around, eh?"

"I am at your service, *Mein Führer.*"

"But your service is failing, is it not?"

"I am deeply sorry."

Hitler suddenly and uncharacteristically smiled.

Kaltenbrunner was so taken aback, he thought for a split second he'd imagined it. He blinked his eyes a couple of times, but it was still there, a smile. Like in the past when Hitler could charm the skin right off a snake.

"Mein Führer?" he croaked.

Hitler jumped to his feet and waved his hands over the maps. "Come. Come, Ernst. Come look at our wonderful success in the Ardennes! I love the Ardennes. The English and Americans are so stupid. They didn't believe we could do it in 1940, and they didn't believe we could do it now. Our Skorzeny did a wonderous job of infiltrating the Americans' line and sowing confusion everywhere."

Kaltenbrunner rose to his feet, feeling unsteady, unsure of what was happening. He leaned over the desk.

"Look here." Hitler tapped a spot on the map with his forefinger. "And here." He tapped another. "We are crushing them! We'll be in Antwerp before long."

"Ja, I see, *Mein Führer. Wunderbar!"* No one could say he didn't know how to butter up someone.

"You have a new assignment, Ernst." Hitler was beaming. "All is forgiven, by the way. I no longer care about that Roosevelt or Churchill. Whether they live or die is of no consequence now. Not after this success!"

Kaltenbrunner sucked in a little air. *All is forgiven? Was he going to get out of this alive after all?*

"I await your instructions, *Mein Führer.*"

"I want you to take over all communications systems relative to the Ardennes Counteroffensive. That includes phone, telegraph, Enigma, and any other methods you can think of like hand delivery. You will start this effective immediately."

"Danke schön, Mein Führer."

Hitler nodded.

"Heil Hitler, Mein Führer," Kaltenbrunner said, shooting a Nazi salute to Hitler.

Hitler snapped off a much crisper salute in return.

Kaltenbrunner, still reeling from his good fortune, beat a hasty retreat from Hitler's gigantic office. He closed the massive door behind him quietly and marched down the wide marbled hall as fast as his nearly two-meter frame would let him.

Chapter 39

The Saunders' family flat
East End, London
19 December, 1148 Hours, the next day

Saunders and Sadie climbed out of a cab. He turned and paid the driver telling him to keep the change. They'd taken the mid-morning train from Andover to London, and the cab to his parent's flat, the home where he was raised. The building was located only four blocks from St. Mary-le-Bow, which made the family true Cockneys. Saunders, carrying their suitcase, led the way up the exterior steps and opened the door for Sadie. After she entered the ground floor foyer, he led her up the stairs to the flat. He knocked heavily on the door.

Almost immediately the door flew open and a woman in her late fifties with brown hair and blue eyes screamed. She rushed forward and hugged Malcolm so tight he thought he'd have trouble getting a breath.

"Hello, Mum," he gasped.

"Oh, Mac. Oh, Mac. I'm so happy to see you." She finally let go and leaned back to look him in the eyes. She was a good ten inches shorter, so she had to crane her neck. Her eyes were wet.

"I can't believe it's you."

Saunders nodded. "It's me, Mum."

She leaned around him so she could see Sadie. "Darling Sadie. Please. Come in and rest your feet. I imagine you're quite tired from the trip."

"Hi, Mrs. Saunders." Sadie stepped around Saunders and Mrs. Saunders pulled her into a gentle hug.

"Oh, dear. Please just call me Emily."

"Right. Okay, Emily."

"Welcome. Come through, you two. Don't just stand there. Lunch is ready."

The couple entered the flat directly into the living room, which faced the noisy street below. A sofa sat against the opposite wall and several soft chairs were spread out around the room facing the sofa. An undecorated Christmas tree stood, awaiting its adornments.

Emily closed the door behind them and looked Sadie over. "You're looking well, dear. Are you feeling all right?"

"I am, Mrs. . . . . Emily. I'm fine."

"Good. Good."

Saunders set down the suitcase by one of the chairs and looked at his mother. "Where's dad? In the kitchen?"

Emily smiled and tipped her head. "Where else? Probably trying to sneak a bit of the roast chicken's skin."

Saunders grinned. His dad was famous for stealing bits of seasoned crispy chicken skin when it first came out of the oven. He walked past the dining room and down a hallway toward the kitchen. When he was almost to the kitchen door, he shouted, "Put that chicken back!"

He stepped through and spotted his dad with his hand by his mouth and an almost-but-not-quite-guilty look on his face. Saunders laughed. "Caught you!"

Mr. Saunders, John, dropped his hand, chewing his prize quickly. He swallowed. "What? What'd I do?" He spread his hands and put on a look of pure innocence.

Saunders chuckled some more and in two long steps went over to his dad and wrapped his arms around him, patting his back. His dad patted him, too. They separated and looked each other over. John was simply an older version of Saunders. Wide shoulders, six-feet tall, two hundred pounds, bright red hair, all of it still there, and matching blue eyes. The only thing missing was a handlebar mustache.

"Good to see you, son. You're looking good."

"You, too, Dad. Day off today, huh?"

"Aye. Yesterday, I had the Cambridge and points north route. Up and back."

"Still loving the view from the engine?"

"Aye. Nothing like it in the world, son."

John snagged another piece of chicken skin and looked at Saunders, daring him to say something.

Saunders winked.

A commotion erupted in the living room as the door opened and shut again.

Sounds of laughter and giggling came from there.

"Ah. Your sisters have arrived."

"Really? How'd you know?" Saunders asked. He laughed.

He turned and made haste to the living room.

He found them all hugging each other and just enjoying the homecoming.

A tall red head, the only woman with that color hair, looked over her mum's shoulder.

She squealed in delight and ran around her mother. She ran full force into Saunders. He rocked back, but held firm.

"Red! You're here!"

"I am, Poppy."

They squeezed each other for a bit.

Poppy, otherwise known as Mary to the rest of the world, was the middle sister and four years older than Saunders. Only Saunders called her Poppy, after the flower. Likewise she was the only person who could get away with calling him Red.

While still in Poppy's embrace, he looked at his other sisters. Vicky, named for Queen Victoria, was the eldest at thirty-two. Annie, the youngest of the sisters, was twenty-eight, two years older than Saunders. Both women resembled their mother and had her brown hair and blue eyes. They ran over and joined in the hug of the baby brother, who towered over the two additions because they'd also inherited their mother's lack of height.

John came out of the kitchen, wiping his fingers on his trousers. Emily glanced at his hand and then his mouth. He shrugged. *What can I say?* He walked over and draped a massive arm over her shoulder, but gently. She leaned into him and sighed.

"Let's eat," Emily said. "I thought we'd decorate the tree afterwards. Is that all right?"

Everyone agreed that it was.

Emily and Vicky went to the kitchen and brought in the food and tea.

The family gathered around the dining room table and sat down. John said a prayer. Everyone dug in.

"How's Steve?" Emily asked part way through the scrumptious meal.

Saunders expression was pained. "It was a near thing. We stopped by to see him this morning before we left. He'll be okay, but recovery will take some time. He'll be out of action for a while."

"I'm sorry, Mac."

"Thanks, Mum." Saunders glanced at each of his sisters. "Have you heard from your husbands? Are they okay?"

All three of his brothers-in-law were serving in Italy.

Vicky answered first. "Jack's fine as of last week. Fighting is stalling due to the weather."

Jack was Colonel Jack Teasdale, who worked on the battalion staff of an infantry division located on the Gothic Line.

"Gilbert's in the same boat. Heard from him yesterday and he's fine."

Captain Gilbert Moore was a company commander, but in a different battalion.

"And the same is true of Royston. He said to tell everyone 'hi' next time I saw you."

Flight Lieutenant Royston Bennett flew a Spitfire.

Saunders felt relieved. He'd been worried they might not have heard from their husbands for a long time.

"I'm really glad to hear they're all okay."

His sisters nodded their thanks.

John looked over at his son. "We've been seeing news about something happening in the Ardennes again. Are we going to be able to stop it this time?"

Saunders nodded without hesitating. "Aye, we will. Our boys and the Americans are just too good. The Germans will never make it much farther."

"How do you know that? Do you know what the plans are?" Vicky asked.

"No, I don't have access to that level of planning. Not at all. But what I do know is the caliber and character of both the British and American soldiers. That's what'll see us through this, and on through the end of the war."

Vicky nodded. "We are going to win, right?"

"Aye, Vicky. We will win. That's all there is to it."

Saunders glanced at his dad.

John gave a crisp nod, then went about eating some more of his lunch.

Saunders turned to Sadie on his right. "All right?"

She laid her head against his shoulder. "Very all right, Mac."

Camp Barton Stacey Hospital
1412 Hours

Kathy Rosemond, Sadie Saunders' cousin and Steve Barltrop's steady girl, sat on a chair next to the wounded man's bed. She'd taken the train from London where she worked for the Royal Navy's Staff Department. Barltrop's bed under his upper body had been raised slightly. He was looking at her, never tiring of doing that particular thing. She was a vivacious redhead, although her hair was not as red as Saunders, being more of what people liked to call ginger.

The two had met at Sadie's wedding. Kathy had been the chief bridesmaid and Barltrop Saunders' best man. They'd hit it off right away at the reception with Barltrop surprising everyone with his swing dancing skills. In some ways, they were a mismatch, the kind that usually leads to a lifetime marriage lasting fifty or sixty years. Where he was hands-on, a natural-born mechanic, she was a performing arts lover, which included ballet, symphonic music, and opera. He learned to tolerate their visits to one or the other from that list when he made it to London and managed not to fall asleep during a performance.

She held his hand and returned his gaze.

"I love you, you silly bugger," she said. "Getting yourself shot. Not so lucky, eh?"

He gave her a weak smile. "I love you, too. No, not really so very lucky. Unless you consider that I survived rather than not."

"Yes, there is that." Her eyes filled with tears and some spilled down her left cheek.

He let go of her hand and used a forefinger to wipe the tears away.

"I'm sorry, I just can't seem to help it."

"Don't be sorry. I understand. I'm sorry to cause you pain, my darlin'."

"I guess this would be the 'worse' part, huh?"

Barltrop raised an eyebrow. "Uh, I guess so."

She grabbed his right hand with both of her hands and held tight. She stared intently into his blue eyes.

"Steve . . ." she faltered.

"Go ahead, please."

"This makes me believe even more we should get married as soon as possible."

"But I think we should wait until it's all over. I mean, look at me. It could have been it."

"Perhaps, but the thing is, it was not 'it' was it?"

"No."

"I want us to get married when you've been released from the hospital, Steve. Please, do this for me. So we . . ." she looked away briefly, then back. "So we can have at least some time together as man and wife."

"You really mean this, don't you?"

"More than anything ever."

He let go of her hand and said, "Help me out of bed."

"What? No, you're supposed to stay there and rest. I heard the nurse."

"She's not here, is she?"

She stood and helped him sit up and swing his legs off the bed. She backed up and grabbed one of his hands in each of hers. "Ready?"

Tired from just sitting up, he nodded.

She pulled and he rose to his feet. He stood there swaying slightly. She grasped his right upper arm to steady him.

"Help me down."

She frowned, puzzled. "What?"

"Help me down."

She helped him get down. Part way down she realized what he was doing.

He had made it to a one knee down kneeling position.

"Oh," she said, looking around the ward. They attracted the attention of some of the other patients. Some were getting out of bed to see better, smiling.

Barltrop took her hand in his and stared up at her.

"Kathy Rosemond, would you do me the honor of marrying me?"

"Yes! Yes, Steve Barltrop, I will marry you!"

She helped him to his feet and they hugged. Carefully.

Around the ward applause and whistles came from the other patients.

"Better get me back in bed. The nurse will be here any second."

They got him back in bed, and sure enough, the nurse entered the ward.

She looked around the room, but saw nothing untoward. She shook her head and left.

Barltrop and Kathy shared a laugh.

"So when?" he asked.

"Well, as soon as you're out of here."

"Why that could be next week! Can you plan a wedding in a week?"

"You forget I work for the Royal Navy! Plus, I'll have plenty of help. Sadie. Your mum. Mac's sisters. Sure, we can do it. I'm so excited!"

Barltrop grinned. Surprised, he felt excited, too. As if there suddenly was something important for him to do. A new road to travel.

"I better call Mac."

"Yes, darling, you better call your best man."

She leaned over the bed and gave him a long, deep kiss.

More applause and whistles.

The kiss continued.

RONN MUNSTERMAN

Chapter 40

Simpson's in the Strand Restaurant
London
19 December, 1730 Hours

Simpson's in the Strand opened in 1828. It grew to become one of the most famous and sought-after restaurants in London. Standing next to the equally famous Savoy Grill, it faced the Strand and was mere yards from the Waterloo Bridge and a half mile from Trafalgar Square.

The maître d' led Dunn and Pamela into the huge, opulent dining room. He stopped at a booth with high backs to provide privacy and smiled. Dunn helped Pamela slide into her seat, and he went around to the other side and slipped in.

They'd passed a beautiful Christmas tree on the way through the foyer. Other lovely decorations adorned each booth and table.

"What may we bring you to drink?"

Dunn wore his dress uniform. He'd gotten a haircut earlier and looked sharp. Pamela wore a yellow dress that was cut with a little more room around her tummy. Her blond hair was up and she wore a smidgeon of makeup and lipstick. They certainly looked well-dressed and refined enough for the restaurant.

Dunn grinned. "I'll have a pint, and my wife will have a Coke, if you have it."

"Certainly, sir." The maître d nodded, giving no negative reaction to having to serve a Coke in his fine-dining restaurant. He handed Pamela an already opened menu and did the same for Dunn. He walked away.

Pamela looked around the beautiful room. The ceiling had to be over fifteen feet high. Ornate inset rectangles painted a yellow close to her own dress and trimmed with white were in the ceiling. Four large chandeliers hung from white support beams. On the dark wood walls, pairs of brass lamps over each booth or table helped brighten the room.

The room was only half full, probably because they were having a relatively early dinner.

"This is just lovely, Tom."

"I hoped you'd like it."

"What's not to like?"

Dunn looked at the menu. "Huh. Listen to this: Sir Arthur Conan Doyle was a regular patron here, and he wrote two stories with Sherlock Holmes and Dr. Watson dining here, too. And get this: other famous patrons were Charles Dickens, George Bernard Shaw, and British Prime Minister Benjamin Disraeli. It opened as a chess club and coffee house. Some chess player named Howard Staunton, England's first world chess champion, came here to play."

"That's quite a history. Right up your old alley."

Dunn had been studying history until he'd enlisted.

"Yep."

A waiter, wearing a tuxedo like the maître d', suddenly appeared at their side with a tray holding Dunn's beer and Pamela's Coke—in its trademarked green bottle—and an empty glass. He set down her glass first, and poured the cold Coke into it, the foam stopping exactly at the top. He set down the bottle, which still had about a quarter left. He placed Dunn's dark ale in front of him.

"Have you decided?"

"Not just yet. This is our first time. Anything you'd recommend for us?"

"Certainly, sir. The roast is our specialty. Comes with potatoes and string beans."

Dunn glanced at Pamela, who nodded.

"That's what we'll both have, please."

"Certainly, sir. Thank you, sir."

He left them alone.

The table was wider than most and they had to stretch their arms across it to hold hands.

Dunn rubbed his thumb across the back of her hand, something he'd done since the beginning.

"I heard things weren't going well over in the Ardennes," Pamela said.

He shook his head. "No, it's not. They caught us flatfooted."

She looked away nervously, and back at him. "You're not going to have to go there, are you?"

"Oh, no, no. Don't worry. The colonel said it wasn't likely at all." He'd purposely left out the part where the colonel had said 'That could change down the road.'

She stared into his brown eyes for a moment. "Right. That's good, isn't it?"

He nodded, trying not to look guilty. He hated being untruthful with her. This damn war. He vowed right then and there, that after the war, he would always tell her the truth. Always.

He must have given something away for she said, "What is it?"

He recovered and said, "Just thinking about getting home to the States."

"I'm excited about that, too."

"I was thinking."

"Yes, I can see the smoke coming from your ears."

He grinned and shook his head. She'd gotten him with that again. When would he ever learn? He shook his head from side to side, not the 'no' shake but one where the top of the head tips left and right. "Can you hear my loose marbles, too?"

"Oh, you!"

"What would you say to traveling the country for our vacations? Maybe get a trailer to tow that we can sleep in."

"Oh, I'd love that. Kind of like camping?"

"Yep. I'd like to go west first, go through the Rockies, and on to California. See the Pacific Ocean."

"Sounds heavenly."

They chatted about other trips and eventually the waiter returned, rolling a silver-domed trolley. He stopped next to their table and opened the dome. The mouthwatering smell of roast burst out. The entire cut was lying on a pan heated from below by a can similar to the American Sterno. The waiter carved several slices precisely and laid them on the plates, which already had the potatoes and string beans laid out in a perfect presentation.

"Juice for your beef, Ma'am?"

"Yes, please."

He ladled a generous amount of the flavorful juice the roast was sitting in on her slices.

He looked at Dunn. "Sir?"

"Yes, please."

Another ladleful.

He glanced at Pamela's Coke glass, saw it was still nearly full, then checked Dunn's beer. Half gone.

"Another, sir?"

"Yes, please."

"Certainly, sir. I'll return with it straightaway."

"Okay, thanks."

He rolled the trolley away and Dunn and Pamela started on their meal.

The waiter returned quickly and set down another dark ale. He asked if they'd require anything else and Dunn said 'no.'

Halfway through, Dunn chewed a bite of roast and swallowed it. "I'm sure glad your dad is doing so well."

"Me, too. He's so happy just to be back at the farm."

"He's supposed to take it easy, right?"

"Oh, yes. That's hard on him. The neighbors have been coming over for the difficult chores."

"Of course. I so admire that. How's Winston doing?"

Winston was Pamela's collie, who'd been grazed in the head by a bullet. The shooter had been the woman teammate of the killer sent to destroy Dunn and his family. She was in jail awaiting trial. The killer was dead, by Dunn's own hands.

Pamela's face brightened. "He's doing well. Happy, and ornery as usual."

"Good."

"Are you still thinking about becoming a policeman?"

"Yeah. I am."

"I have one request."

Dunn raised an eyebrow. "What's that, dear?"

"I know there are things you are forbidden to tell me. The Secrets Act or whatever it is Americans call it. I understand that. I realize it's also to protect me that you keep things to yourself."

"Uh, okay."

"Please promise me that after the war, you'll always tell me the truth. You may as well, you know?"

"Why's that?" Dunn asked warily. Although, he seemed to know what she was going to say.

She giggled. "Tom Dunn. Really? It's quite simple actually. I can always tell when you're not being completely truthful."

"No, you can't."

"Oh, yes, I can. All the time."

Dunn shook his head, refusing to believe the point. "Prove it."

She grinned. "When you said the colonel said 'it wasn't likely at all' that you'd have to go to the Ardennes. You had something hidden behind your eyes. Tom, it's like a light bulb for me. I always see it."

Dunn's mouth dropped open. "Oh, boy, Pamela. I don't know what to say."

"It's okay. I told you I understand why you do it. I'm not mad at you or anything. I just want our future to be different."

"Well, I have a confession. Right then, when we were talking about the colonel? I made a vow to always, *always* tell you the truth."

She stared into his eyes. Her own misted over. "Thank you. I know you're telling me the truth and I appreciate that very much."

"No more secrets after?"

"No more secrets."

They finished their meal in loving silence, once in a while glancing at each other and smiling.

The waiter returned the moment Dunn set down his fork after the last bite.

"Dessert for you?"

Dunn groaned. He was stuffed. Pamela shook her head.

"I don't think so," Dunn managed to say, stifling a belch.

"We do have chocolate cream pie tonight, sir."

"You're kidding."

"Absolutely not, sir."

"I'll have some. With a glass of milk, maybe?"

The waiter nodded. "Ma'am?"

"No room, thank you."

Dunn slid out of his seat and stood up. He stretched a couple of times, then sat back down.

"What was that?" Pamela asked, mystified.

He grinned his schoolboy grin. "Making room for the pie."

She shook her head, but smiled. She glanced around the dining room and said, as if telling the world, "Yes, that's my husband."

Dunn chuckled.

When the pie and milk arrived, Dunn ate it in less than a minute and drank the entire glass of milk.

Pamela laughed.

"What?"

She pointed at his lip. "White mustache. Mac'll be jealous."

He dabbed it off with his cloth napkin. "Better?"

"Yes."

"Well, Mrs. Dunn, shall I take you home?"

They were staying at a hotel nearby. That was a version of their code for a lovemaking session.

"You think you're up to it, after that pie?"

"Ha. Funny. I might need a little time."

The waiter presented the check on a silver tray and left.

Dunn laid enough British money for it plus a generous tip on the tray.

He rose and helped Pamela stand.

She slipped her arm through his and they left the restaurant, after picking up her coat from the cloak room.

They walked quietly down the street, crossed the Waterloo Bridge, and entered their hotel.

Alone in the hallway outside their room, they kissed.

"I love you, Pamela."

"And I love you, Tom."

Dunn gently touched Pamela's belly. He bent over next to her tummy and whispered, "I love you, Tom, Junior."

Pamela shook her head at his stubbornness, but giggled, which of course deserved another kiss.

Author's Notes

"Yesterday, December 7, 1941—a date which will live in infamy—the United States of America was suddenly and deliberately attacked by naval and air forces of the Empire of Japan." These were the words that began Franklin D. Roosevelt's "Day of Infamy" speech, given to a joint session of Congress on December 8, 1941.

The concluding sentence was: "I ask that the Congress declare that since the unprovoked and dastardly attack by Japan on Sunday, December 7, 1941, a state of war has existed between the United States and the Japanese Empire." The speech lasted just over seven minutes. Just as mentioned in chapter one, the declaration of war was passed and signed by FDR within 3½ hours. It seemed fitting to start this December 1944 book on that date. Everything that happened from that date forward can be traced directly back to that attack.

The White House Rose Garden information is accurate. FDR was given the pocket watch by Eleanor on their wedding day. Charlie Bascomb and Betty Nichols are fictional characters. Here's FDR's Hoover Desk. My description of it is based on photos from an FDR museum virtual tour website (click the "Artifact" tab). The SIGSALY system of encrypted communications is real. It was also mentioned in Operation Devil's Fire. There really was a Ruth Ive to keep a rein on the talkative and sometimes careless Churchill. By the way, Churchill did delight in calling himself Former Naval Person with FDR.

Saunders' mission to Sweden to sink the cargo ships that have been supplying the German U-boats is based on this real 1942 British mission: Operation Postmaster. Dunn's mission to blow up the German's brand new super Radar station is fictional, although the Germans did use the Brenner Pass as the main highway to the front line in Italy. Radar controlled flak guns were real. The Scho-Ka-Kola chocolate tins that Rob Goerdt offered the unsuspecting checkpoint guards are real, too.

Ernst Kaltenbrunner was the head of the Reich Main Security Office. On September 30, 1946, the International Military Tribunal (IMT) at Nuremberg found Kaltenbrunner guilty of war crimes and crimes against humanity. On October 1, 1946, the IMT sentenced him to death. He was hanged on October 16, 1946. His ashes were scattered in a tributary to the Isar River along with the ashes of the other nine executed Nazis, and Hermann Göring's, who committed suicide the day before the hangings.

The main story line on Sardinia is based on the Operation Longjump plot in late 1943 to assassinate FDR, Churchill, and Stalin in Tehran, Iran. Not everyone believes the Germans were planning it, but you can read about and decide for yourself.

Tom Dunn's food group ketchup is based on me. I've mentioned this before, but in this book his action of checking to make sure the lid was on tight before shaking the bottle is based on a real story. Of me. It could have been really embarrassing but luck was on my side. In the early 90s, I served on the board of directors for the Missouri Chess Association, holding various roles including president. Before the days of easy online meetings, people from all over the state met at least three times a year in person. We were in St. Louis having a lunch meeting. I was seated on one end of the table, with everyone to my left. We were doing the self-introductions and the meal arrived. I had a hamburger and fries. The person talking was at the far end of the table. I grabbed the Heinz ketchup bottle and shook it vigorously, like Dunn. However, the lid was NOT screwed on tight and it went flying off the bottle and some ketchup ended up on the dark red (fortunate) carpet. I looked quickly at the guys at the table and not one had seen me do that because they were being attentive to the person speaking. So that's why I, and Dunn, check the lid on every bottle we are about to shake. (Yes, I quietly pointed it out to the server later.)

Gertrude's adventures continue at The Farm, the OSS training center located in the Catoctin Mountain Park, Maryland. By all accounts, it was a difficult place to be assigned. Check out the rope bridge the trainees cross with an explosion going off near them.

The villa on Sardinia is fictional, but the location is real. I picked a spot northeast of Cagliari that looks like the way I describe it, except there's no villa there. Too bad. Descriptions of the Secret Service agents come from this photo. All names are fictional. Churchill's bodyguard really was Detective Inspector Walter H. Thompson, who really did stop all those attacks he mentions to Dunn.

The Battle of the Bulge did start early on the morning of December 16, 1944. It really was looking bad. The Germans actually did send Lieutenant Colonel Otto Skorzeny, Kaltenbrunner's man, behind the American lines to disrupt traffic and communications. They were dressed as Americans, had Jeeps, and spoke English like any American. They were exceedingly effective. Skorzeny probably was the best Kommando the Germans had. He really did rescue Mussolini and the pilot of the small aircraft actually was terrified that the huge man's weight would kill them all on takeoff. The horrible Malmedy Massacre was one of several that the Germans perpetrated during the attack.

Like I often do, I had to draw a map for the attack and counterattack at the villa. I laid out exactly where each man or group of men was located, where they moved to, and what happened to them. I use engineering graph paper with ¼ inch squares so I have a handy scale.

Baseball has been and will continue to be a recurring source of conversation in the Sgt. Dunn books. The Cubs do go to the Series in 1945, as Dunn predicts while at the villa, but lose to the Detroit Tigers in seven.

Saunders' dad and the roast chicken skin is a direct nod to the dad in the movie The Christmas Story. Remember the Bumpes's hounds and the turkey? We finally meet Saunders' family and learn something about the sisters and their husbands who are all stationed in Italy.

Dunn and Pamela's dinner at Simpson's in the Strand Restaurant really does have the interesting history that Dunn reads to Pamela. I play and coach chess (scholastic students) so I enjoyed learning that Howard Staunton frequented Simpson's. There is a chess pieces style named for him.

The Allen Thompson character near the end of the book is named in memory of my high school friend who was murdered at the age of sixteen in his driveway on January 2, 1970. To my knowledge, the crime was never solved.

For book 13, I have Saunders' and Dunn's first mission and am researching for the main story line mission. My goal is to not let as much time elapse between books. For SS Assassins it was a matter of my making plans and god laughing, as they say.

Additionally, I'll be working on two new series this next year. If you guessed that Gertrude Dunn will have her own series "A Gertrude Dunn OSS Novel," you are correct. In this book, you learned where she's going to be assigned. A difficult and dangerous place. The other series will be called "A Nash Brothers Novel." Three brothers, three distinctly different assignments in the U.S. Navy: A PT boat commander (Peter – age 25), a submarine XO (Chuck – age 27), and a Naval officer at Pacific Fleet command in Pearl Harbor, Hawaii (John – age 31). I expect the story timeline to start around May to July, 1943, so it'll be about a year earlier than Dunn's novels.

RM
Iowa
September 2019

Please consider following me on my blog and or Twitter to get up-to-date info on what's happening with upcoming books.

www.ronnmunsterman.com
http://ronnonwriting.blogspot.com/
https://twitter.com/RonnMunsterman
@ronnmunsterman

The Sgt. Dunn Photo Gallery for each book is on my website.

About the Author

Ronn Munsterman is the author of the Sgt. Dunn novels. His lifelong fascination with World War II history led to the writing of the books.

He loves baseball, and as a native of Kansas City, Missouri, has rooted for the Royals since their beginning in 1969. He and his family jumped for joy when the 2015 Royals won the World Series. Other interests include reading, some more or less selective television watching, movies, listening to music, and playing and coaching chess.

Munsterman is a volunteer chess coach each school year for elementary- through high school-aged students, and also provides private lessons. He authored a book on teaching chess: *Chess Handbook for Parents and Coaches*.

He lives in Iowa with his wife, and enjoys spending time with the family.

Munsterman is currently busy at work on the next Sgt. Dunn novel.

RONN MUNSTERMAN

RONN MUNSTERMAN

Made in the USA
Monee, IL
06 December 2019

17975549R10173